THREADS OF THE PAST

STORIES OF PIONEER WOMEN AND THEIR QUILTS

LANIE TIFFENBACH

THREADS OF THE PAST: STORIES OF PIONEER WOMEN AND THEIR QUILTS
by Lanie Tiffenbach

Threads of the Past is a fictionalized account of actual historical events, real persons, and recorded facts of their lives. Some of the people portrayed, incidents, characterizations, and details of events are fictitious, as are dialogues, words, and emotions of the characters.

Published by Tiffenbach Publishing
1353 Shadow Mountain Drive
Highlands Ranch, CO 80126-2168

For information, contact: Lanie Tiffenbach at tiffenbach@gmail.com

Threads of the Past: Stories of Pioneer Women and Their Quilts

ISBN: 978-0-692-28185-7

Library of Congress Control Number: 2014915942

Edited by Helena Mariposa, www.EbookTransformation.com

Cover and Book Design by Nick Zelinger, www.NZGraphics.com

Cover Photos, Interior Photos and Illustrations from the collection of Lanie Tiffenbach

First Edition

Printed in the United States of America

1

SOPHIA'S STORY: UNTO A NEW LAND

This story is based on the life of my great-great-great-aunt, Albertina Stuewe Otto, born in 1815 in East Pomerania, Prussia, Germany. She and her family were our earliest known relatives to emigrate from Europe to America. Her husband, Christoph Otto, was the first of three Otto brothers to settle in Minnesota, the third being my great-great-grandfather. I have taken the liberty of changing the first name of Albertina Stuewe Otto to "Sophia," so as not to confuse her with my great-great-grandmother Albertina Minx Otto, whose story appears later in this book.

An ambrotype photograph of an unknown woman, circa 1858. This early photo process patented in 1854 produced a negative image on glass, with the back then blackened to create a positive image.

LETTERS FROM SOPHIA OTTO TO HER MOTHER IN GERMANY

October 6, 1857

Dearest Mother,

We are finally in America! This must indeed be the Promised Land for most surely we have passed through a kind of hell to arrive on its shores. God did not make us human beings for the seas. Our little ship the *Amalie*, out of Bremen, pitched and rolled on the mighty waves with nothing between us and the horizon on any side. When the storms or winds assaulted our ship, we felt we must surely perish beneath the waves, and oftentimes we were so ill that we almost desired it. Now that we have safely arrived, the question remains as to what lies before us—another hell or heaven or perhaps a bit of both?

When Christoph and I and our six children said our tearful farewells in our little village of Alt Belz in Pomerania, Germany, we had no idea how difficult the voyage ahead of us would be. We knew only that during this time of economic woes, Christoph was paid very little as a church sexton and teacher, and our children faced a bleak future. Henry could find no steady employment, only seasonal day labor, even though he is twenty-one and a reliable worker. I am proud of Frederick because even at fourteen years he was out there alongside Henry searching for any small job he could find. Although Augusta and Albertina are already nineteen and seventeen years, they have no marriage prospects other than young men as poor as ourselves. Of course, Hannah and Maria at nine and six are still children and not yet worried about such things.

When we heard glowing reports of prosperity and abundant farm-land in America, Christoph and I questioned whether those could be true. Being already in our forties, we feared that we were too old to undertake such a journey and did not want to risk our lives and that of our children for nothing. However, our Henry insisted that life was too hard and futile here and we must take risks in hopes of something better. And so Christoph and I bravely decided that for our children's sake we would seek a better life in this New World full of both danger and promise.

We immigrants were packed into the steerage or between-decks part of the ship, otherwise used for carrying cargo. This was roughly outfitted with double-deck wooden bunks set along both sides of the ship, with our trunks in the center corridor held in place by ropes. As the bunks were intended to hold four or five persons each, our family was allotted an upper and a lower bunk. We were given thin mattresses stuffed with straw but had to provide our own pillows and blankets. How cramped and uncomfortable it was to be squeezed four to a bunk, especially since we were forced to spend so much of our time there! Of course, the children squabbled and fretted constantly at being so confined. The privies were furnished with buckets to be emptied overboard and with small basins and salt water for washing. There was not a moment's privacy to be found anywhere, and the stench from the privies, unwashed bodies and seasickness often sent me scrambling above deck for clean air, with the children not far behind me.

Our meals were served in shifts in a common space with long tables and benches. The food consisted mostly of a thin gruel for breakfast and watery soup with potatoes, vegetables, and a meager amount of tough and stringy meat for other meals. We were disgusted to find weevils in the hard dry bread, and Maria retched the first time she bit into one. As you know, she has always had a sensitive stomach. Trying to gag down that foul bread for nourishment made us all reminisce about your light-as-air biscuits. As the food was sometimes nearly inedible, it was fortunate that we brought along dried fruit, hard cheeses and smoked sausages from home.

Open hatchways provided the only light, but during storms these had to be covered. It became dark as night below, and the air became dreadfully bad. Lice and fleas thrived in this wretched environment, and we spent much time picking these nasty vermin from our hair and persons. We were all stricken with the feared seasickness especially during storms, and at times we were barely able to leave our cramped beds or keep food down for days at a time. We are so relieved to have our feet once again firmly planted on solid ground, although we are still feeling a bit wobbly from being so tossed about for three weeks in that little ship.

We entered our new country at the Castle Garden Immigration Center at the tip of this island where New York is located. There our information was checked against the ship passenger lists, and we were given a quick examination by a doctor. Clerks from transportation companies laid before us maps, explained the routes, schedules, and prices, and helped us to determine how best to proceed to our destination. We were assured that the money changers, food sellers, and boarding house operators seeking customers there had to comply with strict rules of fairness. We were quite thankful to be welcomed so kindly, as we had fears of being preyed upon, robbed or cheated of what little we had.

How very big, noisy, and dirty this city of New York is! I would not have believed that there are so many people in all the world as seem to be in this one place. You cannot imagine how people live packed so tightly together and how large their buildings are, crowding out the sky. It is quite frightening and overwhelming for us, having lived only in our small rural village.

We must now journey on across this vast land to a place called Wisconsin. We have the address there of a man who has written to his family back home that rich farmland is available for the taking by anyone willing to work. It is every man's dream and ambition to be his own master and to plant and harvest and subdue the earth, as God commanded the first man Adam to do. Christoph and I have always dreamed of owning land to support our family and to leave as an inheritance for them. We plan to travel by train as far as we are able. How I already miss you!

Your loving daughter,
Sophia

November 15, 1857

Dear Mother,

You must be very concerned for us, but I have not had opportunity to pen a letter before this time. We are all suffering with homesickness and often compare this confusing New World to our dear motherland. I wish you had come with us as we urged you to, but I realize how very difficult the long journey would have been at your age. I do so miss you and the rest of the family!

We took a number of trains from New York to another large city called Chicago, which is as far west as the trains go at present. We endured many long hours of riding on hard benches with only short stops at stations along the way to stretch our legs and buy food. At night the conductors passed out thin blankets to share, and we slept as best we could sitting up, jammed together, leaning against each other with the heads of the little ones in our laps. We have traveled for days and nights and have only traveled halfway across this broad country. I realize now how very far from home we have come and how there is no turning back—ever.

As our money has been depleted by our long journey, for the present we will stay here in Chicago. God has been with us, for Christoph has already found a position as a teacher in an area where many Germans have settled. We have rented lodging in a nearby tenement house, where a great number of people are crammed into small rooms on four levels. As we have only a kitchen and two tiny bedrooms with a bed in each, one for us and one for the four girls, the boys must sleep on pallets on the kitchen floor. The streets here are narrow, crowded, noisy and filthy with rubbish. How we miss our familiar little cottage and fresh air!

Yet there is a certain promise in the air, as everyone is intent on hard work and improving their station in life. Henry and Freddy have found jobs in a factory, and Augusta and Albertina are working as maids in a wealthy household. Hannah and Maria attend the school where Christoph teaches, and I do everything needed to care for our family. We are all pulling together to save enough money to travel on to Wisconsin in a year or two and buy a farm. Please write to us at this address as we so long to hear news from home.

Much love,
Sophia

January 26, 1858

Dearest Mother,

I was ever so happy to receive your letter with news of the family and village. I have read it over and over, and I carry it with me in my apron pocket in order to feel you close to me.

We are living in a cold climate where the winter days are short and dreary, and the dark winter nights seem endless. The fierce winds blow the snow sideways across huge Lake Michigan in blinding, howling blizzards. When it snowed back home, the fields looked as white and clean as freshly laundered bed sheets, but here in the city the snow is quickly trampled, strewn with garbage and dirty from the black soot belching out of the factory smokestacks.

While we are preparing for our further move to Wisconsin, I am determined to replenish our worn clothes, which after our long travels are looking rather shabby. Christoph needs new shirts for his teaching job and the girls have nearly outgrown or outworn their dresses. Yesterday my neighbor took me to a large dry goods store nearby, and the selection of fabrics was beyond belief. The beautiful cotton prints and calicoes are available in such rich colors—Prussian blues, double pinks, greens, madder reds, and browns and black. It was difficult to choose my favorites, but I bought as much as I was able with the little money I had in my pocket. I can hardly wait to begin sewing. You know how much I love it!

Your devoted daughter,
Sophia

April 1, 1858

Dear Mother,

God in heaven be praised! I have some wonderful news to send you. Even though it is late in my life, we will be blessed with a new babe. The family is quite excited, particularly since this child will be born an American.

I find myself sometimes feeling poorly and having to spend time confined to bed. I feel guilty that I am not able to do for my family as I ought during those times, but the girls have been wonderful, urging me to rest while they do my chores. We had given away all the baby clothes when we left Germany, thinking that our family was complete, and so I will soon need to knit and sew new clothing and diapers for the babe.

We have made some good friends among our new neighbors. Johanna Jahnke is from Germany but has lived in this country for ten years. She has taught me much about American quilts, which vary from fine bedcovers with tiny pieces in the shapes of flowers or figures sewn onto a background all the way down to simple coverings made of homespun scraps salvaged from worn clothing and pieced together for warmth. Whether held together with fine stitches or roughly tied with string, all the quilts here have three layers in common —a top, a filling or batting, and a backing.

This neighbor Johanna makes the most amazing patchwork quilts, and she has been instructing me on how it is done. How fortunate I am to have such a fine new friend and willing teacher. I truly am enjoying learning this new handiwork. Small pieces of various fabrics are cut out with the use of paper templates and sewn together by hand into blocks. The blocks are then assembled to make the quilt top. The quilt itself is assembled using the pieced part as the top layer, a cotton or wool filling in the middle, and a large piece of backing fabric for the bottom layer. It is then stitched together with needle and thread through the three layers or instead tied at regular intervals with knitting yarn or string. Either a long narrow strip of fabric is used to enclose the raw edges or else the backing is turned over the edges to the front and stitched down.

Quilt-making will be a fine way for me to use up my leftover scraps, make something for our home, and also help pass the time in a pleasant way when I need to rest. I am most eager to begin my first quilt, which will be a simple four-patch design. I do wish you were here to sew with me as we have so often sewn together in the past.

With the arrival of spring, our family is feeling confined living in such a large city, and we long for the fresh air and the quiet of the countryside. There is scarcely a tree for shade or a green blade of grass here to rest one's eyes on. We are still determined to buy a farm, but with only meager savings and myself being in a family way, Christoph and I do not feel that we can make this move at this time. However, we will continue to study on how best to obtain the farm that is our fondest hope and dream.

Your loving daughter,
Sophia

May 28, 1858

Dear Mother,

Your recent letter was comforting in our homesickness and enjoyed by the whole family. I believe I have read it so often I know it by heart!

I am feeling better but still spend a great deal of time resting and sewing clothing for the family and the expected babe. I especially enjoy piecing my quilt blocks whenever I can steal a spare moment between chores. I will be almost forty-three years when I go to childbed, and I pray that both the babe and I come safely through the birthing. I know I will long for you to be with me through that ordeal, as your comforting presence helped ease the pain and anxiety when my other children were born.

We had planned to settle in Wisconsin but have recently heard most of the good farming land there has already been taken. However, friends we met on the boat have written that abundant farmland is available further west in Minnesota. They tell us the area has rich soil and a climate much like our home in northern Germany. Christoph brought a newspaper home with a headline announcing that Minnesota has been admitted as the thirty-second state of the United States. He read the article out to us, which told that Minnesota had only been established as a territory for ten years. It was frightening to learn the native population may still outnumber the white settlers in the state. I questioned the wisdom of choosing such a raw and dangerous place to settle. Nevertheless, Christoph and Henry had already determined that Minnesota offers the best chance of securing the farm of which we all dream.

We have sent Henry and Freddy ahead to Minnesota to survey the conditions and have entrusted them with our hard-earned savings to purchase farmland. I cannot travel now, being in a delicate condition, and we will need the money that Christoph and the older girls earn in order to provision a farm. As there is no railroad to Minnesota at present, our sons joined a wagon train that left last week. Some of our savings went to buy a team of oxen and a wagon, plus provisions and food for their journey. They were eager to leave on their grand adventure and stake a claim before all the good land is taken by others.

We fervently pray that our sons will be successful in purchasing a farm and God will keep them safe, for we have heard tales of wild savages and untamed wilderness out on the frontiers of this country. Our neighbor Johanna's brother settled there recently, and he has written that the natives are a very primitive people that move about living off the land. They are said to torture and mutilate their enemies in dreadful ways and that they even cut off their scalps as trophies.

How it broke my heart to send away my boys, who are but twenty-two and fifteen, and how fearful I am for their safety. However, I have learned that being a mother means knowing when to hold on and when to let go. They are grown men and I must cut them loose from my apron strings, as hard as that may prove for me. I can only imagine now how bereft you must have felt when we left Germany forever.

After the great distance we have come, I truly do realize that I shall not see you again this side of heaven.

I dearly miss you,

Sophia

October 15, 1858

Dear Mother,

I announce with great joy that our daughter has been born and she is a healthy and well-formed babe. We christened her Bertha Magdalena Louisa Otto, but we are finding that her third name Louisa suits her best. The childbirth was as difficult as I feared at my advanced age, and I so longed for your aid and comfort. I am still feeling weak and sickly but fortunately have my four daughters to help me. They are all wonderful "little mothers" to the new babe, and she can barely utter a cry before one picks her up.

A tintype photograph from the Civil War era shows an unknown couple with their baby, whose movement during the long exposure time caused blurring. Invented in 1856, the tintype photo process created a direct positive image on a thin sheet of iron that had been blackened.

I spend some time each day quilting on my four-patch quilt, which will soon be finished. What satisfaction and joy it has given me to create something both beautiful and useful, and I can hardly wait to display it on our bed. I know pride is a sin, but I cannot help feeling just a little proud of my work! Hannah at ten years has become a good little seamstress and has made a small four-patch quilt for baby Louisa. Maria at seven is already learning to sew, and she is making a little strippy quilt for her rag doll. Thanks to the excellent sewing skills they learned at home, Augusta and Albertina have been hired as seamstresses in a dress shop. They will earn better wages and will even be allowed to bring fabric scraps home.

We were most relieved to receive word from Henry and Freddy in Minnesota that they arrived safely and are employed on a farm near the town of New Ulm. They are happy to be working outdoors instead of in the dark, dirty and noisy factories of Chicago and feel quite at home because most settlers living there are also from Germany. They have started to scout for land to purchase but plan to earn more money first in hopes of buying the best land available. Henry has written somewhat of the wild natives called Indians who live in those parts, but I expect he has been careful not to distress us with frightful tales. We miss our sons ever so much, pray earnestly for their safety, and look forward to our family being reunited soon.

Your loving daughter,
Sophia

September 2, 1859

Dearest Mother,

Praise the Lord! Henry and Freddy have purchased a farm for $650 in Nicollet County, Minnesota, near New Ulm. We can barely contain our excitement at this great news and wish we could join them at once. They tell us that the soil is rich, and there is a nice stream and some woods on the property. They have begun clearing the land and will build a log home for us as soon as they can fell enough trees and enlist some men to help. When winter arrives they plan to find jobs in New Ulm at a brewery or flour mill to earn additional money for supplies and equipment with which to begin farming next spring.

During the past summer while looking for land, Henry and Freddy met a number of settlers who, like us, were Evangelical Lutherans from Germany and were organizing a church. Henry was proud to be a founding member of this Immanuel Lutheran Church, but Freddy was disappointed that at sixteen he was too young to sign the charter. The members gather informally for worship as they do not yet have a pastor. We are thrilled that these early settlers brought their childhood faith and their Bibles along with them, so we will have a church to attend when we move to that harsh wilderness.

In honor of our new home that will be constructed from logs, I am excited to be starting a quilt with a "log cabin" pattern. These quilts have become quite popular of late and are of a simple and pleasing design. To construct a block, strips of fabric representing logs are sewn in rows around a central square, which represents the hearth as the center of the home. An actual log cabin is constructed in much the same way around a stone chimney with one log placed on top of another. Two of the round sides of each log are cut off with an ax to flatten them, and the ends are notched so the logs can be set together at the corners. The boys tell us that the winters are very cold there, so the girls and I are busy making some simple warm quilts before we move to Minnesota.

With love,
Sophia

December 20, 1859

Dear Mother,

I send Christmas blessings to you and the rest of the family. This will be a somewhat sad season for us as the boys are in Minnesota and we are still in Chicago. We have baked the Christmas stollen breads and the anise cookies just as we did at home, and have told Louisa, Maria and Hannah the stories of the Baby Jesus and Father Christmas. Our sweet Louisa is more than a year old and is already walking and speaking a few words. I warn the older children not to spoil her so with treats and hugs, as children need discipline as well as love.

It has taken longer than we imagined for us to be able to move to our own farm, but we are ever closer to our goal. Christoph and I have determined that I will journey with the three younger girls to Minnesota this spring. I can help our boys with cooking, laundry, furnishing the house and planting a garden, so they can concentrate on doing the all-important farming work. Christoph will remain in Chicago to earn additional funds to buy the needed livestock and supplies for our farm. Albertina and Augusta have chosen to stay and keep house for their father and continue earning money also. It saddens me that our family will be divided, but within a year we should all be together in our new home. We are making plans for the long journey I must take in the spring with the little ones.

My log cabin quilt top is progressing ever so nicely. I hope to finish piecing it before I leave for Minnesota, as there will be much hard work to set up a household. For the light halves of the blocks I used a variety of pink fabric scraps left over from making the girls' dresses, and for the dark halves I used brown scraps from making shirts for Christoph and the boys. The girls and I spent some happy hours together rearranging the log cabin blocks to create different overall designs. We finally settled on a layout where a large star appears in the center of the quilt, representing the stars in the flag that our new country flies, and I am calling it "Log Cabin Star". I am thrilled at how well the many different fabrics blend together and how the quilt top is becoming so pleasing to the eye.

I hope you are keeping well this winter and I send my greetings for the New Year.

Blessings at Christmas,

Sophia

LOG CABIN STAR QUILT: Designed, pieced in pinks and browns, and machine quilted by Lanie Tiffenbach.

May 30, 1860

Dearest Mother,

God has protected us on our journey, and I have arrived safely in Minnesota with Hannah, Maria and Louisa. The railways now go as far as St. Paul so we spent several days on the trains. We then took a steamboat down the Minnesota River to the town of St. Peter, where the boys met us at the steamboat landing with the oxen and wagon to take us to the farm. How good it felt to embrace them after two long years spent apart and to see that they are safe and well! Freddy has grown from a boy to a man and is now insisting that everyone call him Frederick, as he thinks the name of Freddy is too childish for him.

Once I saw it with my own eyes, I could scarcely fathom that such a large beautiful piece of God's good earth could be ours. There are woods on our land and a small stream from which we get our water. You would not believe how rich the soil is here. When a field is plowed, it is as black as coal. What wonderful crops we should be able to grow! We can see for miles across the flat open prairie, with our nearest neighbors being a mile away. After the noise, filth and crowded living conditions of Chicago, I am constantly amazed at the silence, clean air, vast open spaces and huge dome of the sky here in Minnesota.

The boys had help from neighbors in building our sturdy cabin of thick logs, though there is still much work needed to furnish it. It is composed of one large room with a stone fireplace for cooking and heating the home, as well as a loft for sleeping. The girls and I are working at chinking the cracks between the logs with mud and clay to keep out the wind and rain. My lovely four-patch quilt on the bed has brightened our home. How I wish I could show you our wonderful farm and our new log cabin!

A photo postcard from about 1910 shows a typical log cabin built during the 1860s in this area. The Ottos' log cabin would have been very similar to the main part of this house, with the addition being of later construction.

I cannot fully express the pleasure I derive from piecing my quilt blocks after the work is done at the end of each day. We have a great deal to accomplish right now, so I will have to wait until winter before I begin to quilt my Log Cabin Star. Because our cabin is small, the boys have promised to rig up a quilting frame that can be suspended from the ceiling and pulled up out of the way when not in use.

It was a very difficult task to break the virgin prairie sod with its tall grass and long roots. Henry and Frederick helped a neighbor seed his crop and in return were able to borrow his plow to pull behind our oxen to break the sod. They sowed the grain by hand, then smoothed the ground by having the oxen pull a drag with wooden teeth to break up the lumps of soil and cover the seeds. Henry remarked, "It works about as well as dragging a cat by its tail!"

My clever Frederick is always bartering for items we need. Recently he brought home five fat hens and a rooster. What a treat it is to have fresh eggs again! We are letting three of the hens sit on their eggs and the baby chicks should hatch soon. Later this summer the boys plan to build a log stable for the milk cow, oxen, pigs, and chickens. The neighbors here have the custom of helping one another in what they call "barn raisings." The men gather to build the house or barn, and their wives come along to cook and enjoy the company of others, while the children have a great time frolicking together. In the evenings, there is singing and dancing if someone can be found to play a fiddle or harmonica. It is lonely on the farm, and I am so looking forward to getting to know my new neighbors and making women friends. How I miss you, our family and friends and life in a village.

Sending love,
Sophia

July 10, 1860

Dear Mother,

My dear girls Augusta and Albertina, who are working as seamstresses in Chicago, have sent me a great supply of fabric and scraps.

First I'll make new dresses for Hannah, Maria and Louisa, as they are growing so quickly. I have devised a pattern for a quilt using the smallest scraps, and there is a stripe fabric that will look wonderful as sashing and borders for it. This sewing and piecework will keep my hands busy until such time as Christoph and our daughters can finally join us in Minnesota.

I keep much busier here and have learned many new skills, as there is no one else to do the work. The boys bring me fish from the river and deer, squirrels or rabbits that they have hunted. I have learned to cut up and preserve the meat, as well as to prepare tasty meals with whatever supplies we have on hand. The cow must be milked each morning and evening and some of the cream skimmed from the milk and churned into butter. I bake my own bread twice a week, along with an occasional pie. Next week a neighbor woman is coming over to teach me how to make lye from ashes. With the lye and animal fats that I have saved from cooking we will then make soap. It must be cooked over a fire outdoors in a big iron pot as it is quite messy and especially smelly! The lye soap will do a good job of getting the laundry clean along with the hard work of scrubbing it on a washboard.

Sometimes I look around me and have the strange feeling that I have been plucked from the warmth of my childhood home and set down in the stark reality of someone else's life. It is really quite lonely out on the frontier. In the village at home we had a butcher and a baker and shops where we could readily buy or barter what we needed. Here we have to make everything ourselves, and all we buy are staples such as flour, sugar and salt. But in spite of the hardships, we are quite proud and pleased with what has been accomplished in a short time.

God bless you,
Sophia

August 3, 1860

Dearest Mother,

This is truly a promised land of milk and honey! The soil is fertile and the rains are generous. Our large garden is flourishing and we are enjoying fresh vegetables. The fields that the boys plowed and planted in wheat and corn are ripening. They have just completed harvesting the oats, which was done by cutting the grain stalks with a hand sickle, binding them into bundles, stacking them to dry, hauling them onto a platform, and threshing the grain with a flail. It was much hard work, and the girls and I also helped as we were able. There are now oats in our new barn to feed our livestock, as well as hay that was cut and dried earlier. We will shortly begin the wheat harvest, but meanwhile the girls and I are preserving vegetables from the garden for next winter. Hannah at nine is already a great help to me with the cooking, laundry and gardening, and Maria at six helps with smaller chores such as washing dishes and caring for little Louisa.

You asked about the natives who live in this wilderness. They are called Indians in general, with the local tribe known as Sioux. They have dark ruddy skin and long braided black hair, dress in animal skins decorated with beads and feathers, and are quite fierce-looking and fearsome to behold. They make their living by hunting game, fishing, and gathering fruits, berries, nuts and roots. We understand that the Sioux sold their hunting grounds to the government in 1851 and were confined to a reservation along the Minnesota River, with the promise of money and goods to be paid to them each year. Recently the government took back half of their reservation land, which seems to us a most unfair way of treating them.

Missionaries have been here for years, trying to transform these heathen savages into civilized Christian farmers, but with limited success. We hear that the natives will on occasion come into the homes of settlers and steal whatever they like, but on the whole they are said to be friendly. They have given us no trouble thus far. Henry says they had been living on this land for many generations before we came, and so we ought not begrudge them a share of its abundance. In fact, he had shot a deer by the river yesterday and was skinning it when two Indians appeared. They indicated with signs that they were hungry and so Henry took only what we could eat while it was fresh and allowed them the rest of the deer. He believes that as these people were once considered to be fierce warriors, it is far better to have them for friends than enemies!

Your loving daughter,

Sophia

A trade card from 1893 depicts American Indians, with an advertisement for Arbuckle Bros. Coffee on the reverse. These colorful advertising cards were distributed by businesses to potential customers from about 1875 through the early 1900s.

December 15, 1860

Dear Mother,

I hope you are in good health and enjoying the holiday time. I remember fondly the Christmases of my childhood, where you always managed to find something special for each of us children and prepared what seemed to us a feast, no matter how dire our circumstances. Christmas is almost upon us, but it will be a bleak time for our family this year.

Henry and Frederick had worked so hard to get fields plowed and crops planted this spring. I think you would be proud of what good farmers they have become. Our crops had gotten off to a great start, and the rains were plentiful all summer. The oats harvest had already been completed, with the wheat ready to be harvested next. I had begun to put up some fruits and vegetables from our garden with the help of my girls.

We were all feeling very thankful for such a good beginning on our new farm, when one afternoon the sky suddenly turned dark. Hordes of blackbirds descended on us from above like a terrible nightmare and proceeded to demolish our crops in the fields and our gardens. How those ugly birds frightened little Louisa! The truth be told, Mother, the sheer numbers of them frightened me also, as they seemed to be a plague sent to us.

The boys stood guard, shooting off the musket and flapping sheets to scare the birds off, while the girls and I collected what vegetables we could salvage from the garden, but we could do nothing about the crops in the fields. We had spent days trying various methods to drive those black devils away, when to our relief government agents came around and furnished us with poisons. They also offered a bounty of forty cents per one hundred birds, but there were just too many of them for it to be of much help.

As a result of this calamity, we ended up with only a little wheat to have ground into flour this winter, but, as I told the children, we are better off than most. Christoph and the older girls are still working in Chicago and regularly send money, so we will be able to purchase what we need and also buy seed for next year's planting. Others are not so fortunate and have given up and moved back east where things are more civilized. We praise God that we all remain healthy and pray that better times are ahead.

With winter approaching and only a few close neighbors, we have commenced to get lonesome out here on the frontier. Our family is still separated, and I do so miss Christoph and the older girls. However, I can now spend hours each day contentedly quilting my Log Cabin Star quilt, and I will have it completed soon. I do so wish you could see how handsome it is!

Last month our country elected its sixteenth President, a tall lanky man named Abraham Lincoln. He comes from humble beginnings and was born in a log cabin much like the one we live in. We find this surprising, since in Europe most countries have been ruled by kings, queens or emperors for hundreds of years. How wonderful that an ordinary man can rise to the highest level because he is a good and respected leader, rather than one who attains the position based solely on his ancestors. Despite the many hardships, we are proud to live in a country such as this.

With love,
Sophia

July 15, 1861

Dear Mother,

Hallelujah! Our family is finally reunited! Christoph, Augusta and Albertina traveled safely from Chicago to Minnesota late in May after Christoph finished the school term. We are a bit crowded now in our snug cabin but have hung a quilt down the center of the loft to separate the boys' side from the girls' side. Christoph and I have our bed in the back corner of the kitchen. We plan to build an addition onto the cabin later this summer, so we can have a separate bedroom, the boys can take our bed in the kitchen, and the girls can enjoy the privacy of the loft.

Only two weeks after their return, Christoph's brother Gottlieb Otto, his wife Henrietta, and their three boys arrived from Germany in response to our urgings. Their greatest dream is for their sons to someday be landowning farmers, a feat that would have been nearly impossible in Germany, as they were quite poor and land is expensive there. They can scarcely believe that in only a few short years we have acquired this wonderful farm. Henrietta and I were always fond of each other and have greatly been enjoying exchanging stories about family and friends.

Sadly, our new country is now at war, the North against the South. President Lincoln was no sooner in office than some of the Southern states tried to secede from the Union and insurrection began. One of the reasons we left Germany was so our boys would not get drafted into the mighty Prussian army to fight their wars. Now we find this country at war, but it seems a great distance off and with God's grace those of us living out here in the wilderness will not be involved in it.

Your devoted daughter,
Sophia

October 30, 1861

Dear Mother,

Your recent letter with news of the village and family was quickly devoured. I am happy to hear that you are enjoying a year with good weather and good crops.

There is as yet no school established nearby, so Christoph has been instructing Hannah and Maria in the evenings while the older girls and I quilt. Being a teacher, Christoph owns a few books and slates and, of course, the Bible is in itself a fount of knowledge. I am amazed at his patience and gentleness when teaching the girls. He has even taught three-year-old Louisa a few of her letters and numbers.

As soon as we finish the warm quilts we are making for the coming winter, we plan to start piecing quilts for the older girls' dowries. Augusta and Albertina are now young ladies of twenty-three and twenty-one years, and they seem to be attracting much attention from the young men in our church and community. I hope they each find a man as worthy as my Christoph. They are such good girls and work so hard without complaining, but I wish they had more opportunity to see other young people. Our social life centers around our church, with baptisms, marriages, and funerals followed by a meal and gathering. In the summer we have picnics with everyone contributing food, and in the winters occasionally we have a dance when someone can provide music with a fiddle. The Nicollet community will be holding a harvest festival once the field work is done, and my girls are excited to attend and meet other young people. The boys pretend not to care, but they both have an eye for the girls! Last Sunday after church when we met our newest neighbors, the Blank family with a comely young daughter, I noticed that Henry (usually so well spoken) stammered and blushed like a girl!

Our crops this year have been good, and we feel quite rich to have sufficient food put up to feed our family over the coming winter. With the help of a neighbor, Christoph and the boys have dug a well near the house, so we no longer have to carry water from the stream for washing, cooking and bathing. It was such a wearisome job carrying two heavy buckets back and forth some distance several times a day, especially in foul weather.

We did have a surprise early blizzard with strong winds during the night last week. As we had not yet re-chinked the cracks between the logs in preparation for winter, we awoke in the morning to find a light blanket of snow covering the quilts on our beds!

I was sadly mistaken in believing that our country's War Between the States would not affect those of us on the frontier. Minnesota was the first state to volunteer a regiment when President Lincoln called for troops in April, as our Governor Ramsey happened to be in Washington. Under different circumstances our boys, at ages twenty-five and eighteen, would be eager to join up, as young men are always ready for adventure no matter the risk. Why do men think war honorable and noble, while women see only the loss or mutilation of their men and boys?

After all the trials we have gone through to provide a future for our children, I could not bear to lose my precious sons to a war that has nothing to do with us. Christoph and I have convinced Henry and Frederick that we could not possibly manage the farm without them. Thankfully, they do realize their duty and responsibility to our family and have promised they will not leave. My heart aches for all the parents who are losing their sons in this bloody conflict.

Love,
Sophia

The young woman in the first photo is dressed much like Augusta and Albertina Otto would have been during the Civil War era. The tax revenue stamp on the reverse dates it to 1866. The second photo illustrates that children's fashions imitated that of adults. The dresses are typical for the time with a slightly high waist, full sleeves, checked or plaid fabrics and a gathered skirt over a hoop. These small carte de visite photographs, patented in France in 1854, were the first photos to have negatives so copies could be made.

October 28, 1862

Dearest Mother,

A most dreadful thing has happened here, which is being called the Great Sioux Uprising. I want to assure you that we are safe now, but we barely escaped this tragic event with our lives. I will try to describe what we have pieced together from our own experiences, the experiences of others, and newspaper reports of the events.

The local Indian tribes had sold their land to the government, but dishonest agents and traders swindled most of their payments. There was unrest this summer as the government was preoccupied with its Civil War and was late in sending the annual shipment of money and goods. To make things worse, we all suffered a severe drought this summer. We have heard that the starving Indians petitioned the local trading post operator for food on credit, but he cruelly remarked, "If they are hungry, let them eat grass." (He was one of the first whites later killed by the Indians, and his body was found with grass shoved down his throat.)

When four young Indian braves murdered five people in Meeker County, their leaders knew that revenge would be swift and harsh. They debated whether the time was right to try to reclaim their lands and independence. Chief Little Crow had worked hard to promote peace, and he argued that his people could not win a war against the whites. However, the other leaders insisted they would rather die honorably in battle than starve to death. "Little Crow is not a coward," he consented. "He will die with you." Unfortunately the frontier was poorly defended as thousands of young men from Minnesota had been shipped off to fight in the Civil War.

On the morning of Monday, August 18th, the Sioux set out on a murderous rampage. They first targeted the homes and stores of the traders, and then fanned out across the prairie ferociously attacking the towns and homes of white settlers, massacring men, women and children, and plundering and burning their houses and barns.

Early that afternoon a neighbor came riding up to our farm wild-eyed and frantic, shouting that we must flee for our very lives! Henry and Frederick grabbed our rifle, muzzleloader, and our two horses and immediately enlisted in the Nicollet Guards, a group of armed citizen-soldiers hastily being formed under the leadership of Captain A. M. Bean. I was greatly torn between knowing we had to defend ourselves and having my sons put in harm's way, but they seized their duty without a second thought and rode off before I could protest.

Mother, those boys took a piece of me with them, and I did not know if I would be able to stand it if anything happened to them. As I watched them disappear into the horizon, I had to bite my lips to keep from screaming out to them.

We were then in fear that the Indians might attack us at any moment. With great speed Christoph hitched the oxen to the wagon while the girls and I swiftly gathered some provisions and quilts, and we started out for New Ulm. Oh, how very slowly those oxen plodded! Along the way we met others traveling in that direction, and terrible fear gripped our hearts as wild tales of mayhem and murder were told to us.

At last arriving safely in New Ulm we were directed to brick buildings in the center of town, where barricades were hastily being built. There were only forty-two armed men for the defense of the town, and so the sixteen men of the Nicollet Guards, including Henry and Frederick, were a much-welcomed addition to their little militia. Christoph was assigned to the "reserves" which consisted of men who were armed only with pitchforks, hoes and other crude weapons in case the Indians should breach the defenses, which was a horrifying thought. The five girls and I were sent to basement shelters where frightened women and crying children were cowering. I tried to calm my girls who were all openly weeping and wailing in terror, but inside my head I was screaming too.

The first attack was made on New Ulm by about a hundred savages led by Chief Little Crow the following afternoon, while others continued to wreak havoc in the countryside. I had been gathering supplies from a nearby building with some other women, when the Indians, decorated in war paint and feathers and uttering bone-chilling shrieks, charged wildly from all directions out of the woods and ravines around the town. We froze in shock and terror, before we were able to gather our wits and race for our lives across the street and down the steep stairs into our shelter. The natives took possession of some of the outlying buildings to use as cover while aiming their arrows and rifles at our troops. Our men, stationed behind barricades, on rooftops, and in the windows of downtown buildings, returned their fire.

Oh, Mother, you can't imagine how frightened we all were that afternoon as the Indians repeatedly withdrew out of range only to regroup and commence another charge. Throughout the attack the girls and I huddled in the dark damp basement with the other terrified women and children, wondering if our loved ones fighting above or those of us weeping and praying below would survive the conflict. To our great relief, after several hours God heard our fervent pleas for aid, and the skies opened with torrential rains, lightning strikes and great thunder, forcing the Indians to withdraw.

For the next three days we were all on edge anticipating another battle. We had no way of knowing that the Indians were busy gathering forces and attacking Fort Ridgely, where many settlers had also fled for protection. We were desperately hoping that Gottlieb, Henrietta and their sons had found safety there, as they had not come to New Ulm. During this time hundreds of additional refugees streamed into New Ulm, many wounded and bearing dreadful tales of violation or captivity of women, murder, mutilation and scalping. Small parties were sent out to search for missing settlers and bury the dead, sometimes becoming victims themselves. About three hundred men from the nearby towns of St. Peter, Le Sueur and Mankato arrived to aid in our defense, but they were still woefully short of firearms and ammunition.

The second attack on New Ulm came on Saturday morning, August 23rd, by a huge force of warriors about double the number of our defenders. The savages surrounded the town and terrified us with their war paint, bright feathers and fast horses. All the while, they were emitting high yipping sounds to unsteady our nerves. Then with a hair-raising yell they descended upon us like the wind and opened fire.

The Indians attacked over and over again throughout the day and set most of the town's buildings afire, so we were in almost as much fear of the flames reaching us as the Indians. Between attacks we women were kept busy finding food and water for everyone and caring for the wounded and dying, as well as our terrified children.

Only later did we learn a young woman was put in charge of a powder keg and fuse. She had orders to blow up our building and everyone in it for a quick death should the Indians get past our brave defenders, rather than deliver the women and children into the hands of the cruel savages to be violated, enslaved or killed. What a difficult decision that must have been for our men to make!

Although the outcome of the battle often hung in the balance, our brave defenders managed to prevail. How greatly relieved and thankful we were at nightfall when the Sioux finally retreated into the woods. By then only twenty out of two hundred buildings were left standing, and the rest of New Ulm was burned to the ground. When we emerged from our underground shelters and looked around us at the dead and wounded and the destruction of the town, we could scarcely believe we were still alive! Most of the women and even some of the men collapsed in tears of relief and gratitude, although by then most of the children had run out of hysteria and tears and were in a dull stupor.

Supplies of food and ammunition were running dangerously low. With two thousand people crowded into a few buildings, an outbreak of disease was feared. With no sighting of the Indians on Sunday, it was decided that the town would be evacuated on Monday. The wounded, children and elderly were loaded into wagons, with the rest of us marching on foot the thirty miles to Mankato. It was a frightening journey, not knowing if the Indians would attack our band, but we arrived safely and were sheltered there until peace was restored. During this time we were greatly relieved to learn that Henrietta and Gottlieb's family had found refuge at Fort Ridgely, and that they were safe and had later been removed to St. Peter.

It was some weeks before the hostile Indians were finally either captured or driven west into the Dakota Territory by federal troops, and it was deemed safe to return to our homes. The loss of friends and neighbors in this warfare greatly saddened us, and on our return journey we saw many burned homes, barns and fields. As you can imagine, we were in terrible dread that our home and crops and everything we owned had been destroyed also, but praise God, our farm was passed by in the uprising. There was no time to waste, as we needed to turn our attention to the much-delayed harvest of wheat and corn before winter began.

Thousands of frightened settlers have since abandoned their farms and homes and returned to more populated areas. Although the girls and I are very fearful, Christoph and the boys have decided that this is where we have cast our lot and this is where we will stay. They believe that with so many leaving we would not be able to find a buyer for our farm, and all of our money, hopes, and dreams are invested here.

It will take a long while for the families that remain to recover from this time fraught with danger, terror and privation. We still find ourselves startling at every noise and lying awake at night with fearful hearts, with the children screaming in terror from their bad dreams. Only God knows what lies ahead and only time will tell whether we made the right choice when we came to this New World. We can only hope that someday when we look back the good will outweigh the bad.

God blessings,
Sophia

November 29, 1862

Dear Mother,

I hope my last letter did not frighten you, but I know you must be wondering after our health and safety. Even though it is too early to have received a reply, I did want to reassure you that we are well.

The newspapers report that between five to eight hundred white settlers and soldiers were killed in the recent Sioux Uprising, nearly three hundred women and children were taken captive by the Indians, and there was massive destruction of homes and property. It is further reported that this is the greatest massacre of whites by Indians in this country's history.

Because of the recent losses suffered at the hands of the savages, Henry is determined that he must do his part for our new homeland. Christoph has preached forgiveness, telling him the government tricked the Indians into selling their land to make room for white settlers like ourselves. We have profited while they were starving and desperate. I begged Henry not to join up and tried to impress on him that his first duty was to his family. I simply cannot bear the thought of Henry fighting against those wild Indians and possibly being killed or, even worse, tortured and mutilated by them.

However, despite our tearful pleas, on October 31st Henry rode to St. Peter and enlisted in the Union Army as a private in the First Regiment, Company E, Minnesota Cavalry, also known as the Mounted Rangers. This is a volunteer regiment organized for frontier duty against the Indians with a term of enlistment of one year. I know you will understand how very fearful I am for my son after the dreadful happenings of this past summer. But however much we resisted Henry's enlistment, we do have to accept that he is a man and must choose his own path in life.

This photo of an unknown Union Army cavalry soldier with his horse was taken during the Civil War.

The Army supplied his uniform, but as soon as Henry told us he had enlisted, the girls and I spent some busy days sewing shirts, knitting socks, and making a simple warm quilt of dark fabric for use as a bedroll. Our one consolation is that Henry is garrisoned at nearby Fort Ridgely to help keep the peace on the prairie and may be able to come home on occasion. We prefer that to his being sent to the South where he would have to fight against boys of his own kind, and we might not have a letter from him for months. We had thought that this war would not touch our family, but how wrong we were! Please keep our dear Henry in your prayers.

After the sorrows and suffering of the past months, I find it soothing to sit and sew when there is a quiet moment. I am piecing a new quilt with nine-patch blocks, which are just nine squares sewn together. When we went to New Ulm last week to sell butter and eggs and obtain supplies, I purchased some lovely fabrics at a bargain price. The owner was closing his store because he did not feel safe and wished to return east as quickly as possible. I am eager to sew some new dresses for the girls and hope to have fabric left over for my quilting as well.

Hoping you are well,
Sophia

February 28, 1863

Dearest Mother,

I have some joyful news to share with you after all our recent trials and tribulations. Henry is to be wed to Wilhelmina Blank, a lovely German girl of twenty-two years. Henry has been sweet on her ever since her family settled on a neighboring farm two years ago. He asked her father for her hand when he was on leave at Christmas, and they plan to marry in April if Henry can get a weekend pass to return home. When he completes his one-year enlistment in the Army, we will help the young couple purchase a farm of their own.

Some of the young men from this area, who first enlisted in the Union Army and were sent to fight in the South, have been killed or have returned home maimed. We are ever so grateful that thus far Henry's regiment has done nothing more than training exercises and maintaining the peace between the settlers and the Indians who remain.

Wilhelmina is eager to learn to make quilts for her upcoming marriage, and her mother has asked if the girls and I would come over for a few hours each Sunday afternoon to help them sew. How I have missed the company of other women, and how fast time goes when we can visit while we stitch!

Our little Immanuel Lutheran congregation, numbering about twenty-five families, has moved a building to a site on the Nicollet and Courtland Township line. As our members come from both townships, it seemed most fair to situate the church centrally. We have called a pastor, who will also establish a school and serve as its teacher. I am proud to say that Christoph and our Frederick have been elected as trustees of the church, mainly because Christoph was a teacher and a church sexton in Germany and as such was responsible for the property of the church. Hannah and Maria will be fifteen and thirteen years old when school starts and are thus past the eighth grade level, and Louisa will be under five and still too young to attend.

We had a huge blinding blizzard last week with strong winds that continued for four days. The snow is now piled in high drifts all around our little cabin, in some places up to the roof. The men went out only to tend to the livestock, and they needed to tie a clothesline between the house and the barn so as not to lose their way in the raging storm. We had to melt buckets of snow for the livestock to drink, as we could not let them out of the barn for fear they would become lost and freeze to death.

The girls and I began quilting my nine-patch quilt during the storm. The work goes quite quickly with myself and the three oldest girls quilting from all four sides of the quilt frame, while Maria keeps needles threaded for us and Louisa plays on the floor underneath the quilt with fabric scraps. We are all agreed that this special quilt will be a lovely wedding gift for Henry and Wilhelmina.

Your devoted daughter,
Sophia

This striking tintype photograph of an unidentified young couple has a tax revenue stamp on the back that dates it to 1864. The hairstyles and dress are typical for the Civil War era. Often the cheeks (occasionally clothing or jewelry) were hand-tinted to enhance these photos.

October 30, 1863

Dear Mother,

Your letter with recent news was most welcomed, but I am afraid I have nothing but sorrowful news to send you. We were so happy this spring when Henry was married, but now only sadness and grief fill our hearts. The Lord giveth and the Lord taketh away. (Blessed be the name of the Lord!) He has taken your grandson Henry to be with him in heaven.

This past June Henry's regiment of Mounted Rangers under the command of Colonel Samuel McPhail was employed in the Sibley Expedition, a punitive operation against the Sioux Indians in Minnesota and the Dakota Territory. Many of the privates that joined up had belonged to the citizen militia that participated in the defense of the settlers during the Sioux Uprising or else had family killed at that time, and thus they were eager for revenge. The expedition led by General Henry Sibley marched west across the dusty plains that were stricken by drought for several years. The troops engaged in a number of hard-fought battles with the Indians in the Dakota Territory during the month of July. When we later saw Henry, he told us he was quite sickened when after the first battle some of the cavalry "played Indian" and took scalps until General Sibley forbade it.

Because of the drought and resulting low water level in the Missouri River, steamboats could not provide the needed rations, supplies and troops to continue the campaign, and so the expedition was forced to begin the return march in August. Water was oftentimes scarce and the men had to drink what could be found, even if it was brackish, alkaline or foul tasting. As a result, some of the men, including Henry, had fallen ill by the time they reached Minnesota.

The Mounted Rangers set up camp west of Fort Ridgely and were resupplied, and on September 7th they marched south to the Iowa line to search out and destroy any hostile Indians. Henry was too ill to participate, and on September 11th he was removed from the camp to the post hospital at Fort Ridgely. When we received word of this, we immediately made the trip to visit him, and the post surgeon informed us that Henry was suffering from typhoid fever. We were advised he was receiving the best of care, and we fully expected him to recover. Thus, it was a terrible shock when he died there on September 30th, having lived only twenty-seven years on this earth.

We are all quite prostrate with grief. I do so pity Wilhelmina as she is a widow after only five months of marriage, almost all of that time spent apart. After their wedding they had only a few days together on two occasions when Henry could get a short leave from the Army. As Henry had only about six weeks remaining in his military service, we were all anticipating having him home soon. Henry's captain consoled us by sharing with us that he died an honorable death for a noble cause, but I expect that is what they always tell the families of soldiers, and it is not of much comfort.

It seems that almost every mother loses at least one child or more as babes. When I myself had suffered the deaths of two of my young children back in Germany, I did not know if I could bear the unbearable, but life did somehow go on. Is it harder to lose a babe at your breast, an innocent young child, or a son or daughter fully grown? I do not know the answer. I know only that our hearts are very heavy, and the sorrow of losing a child of any age is devastating. I cannot write more now. Pray for our family and for the soul of our dear departed Henry.

Sending love,
Sophia

May 16, 1864

Dearest Mother,

We all miss Henry terribly as he had been our "guide" in this foreign land. It was his idea for our family to come to America, and he did the planning for our journey. Later he and Frederick went on ahead to Minnesota to purchase land and build a house while we stayed in Chicago. Henry was always wise beyond his years and everyone trusted him. He felt a terrible responsibility for choosing this place after so many suffered at the hands of the Indians. I fear that he died in an attempt to avenge their deaths and make this a safe place to live.

I have heard that the Good Lord never sends more suffering than a body can stand, but at times I feel myself sliding down into a pit of despair. I fear my soul will be consumed by grief, and my mind will leave this world and go into a world of its own. But if I were to allow that to happen, who would then care for my family? Somehow I manage to put one foot in front of the other and persevere. I do thank you for your words of comfort and wisdom, dear Mother. Even as old as I am, how I wish I could feel your loving arms around me once more!

With love,
Sophia

August 6, 1865

Dear Mother,

The Good Lord has blessed us over this past year by providing husbands for our two older daughters. Augusta was married in May to Ernst Wicherski, and Albertina will be married in December to Julius Schwandt. Both girls have worked ever so hard for the past eight years to help buy our farm and support our family. I am so pleased that they have found good Christian men to marry and can now start families of their own. Ernst is a shoemaker in New Ulm, and Julius has been working for Christoph to earn money so he can buy a nearby farm of his own. I also rejoice that I will have my daughters close by so we can visit often. I have sorely missed the village life in Germany, as here the farms are so spread out that quite often one only sees the neighbors in church on Sundays.

Over the past several years the girls and I spent many happy hours together making quilts for Augusta's and Albertina's wedding trunks. While stitching the quilts the girls loved to reminisce about the dresses, shirts or pinafores that were made from each of the fabrics. Quilt-making has been such a joy in my life, as it allows me to use my imagination to design and produce something of beauty in between the tedious and routine chores of each day. Hannah and Maria, who are now seventeen and fourteen, are becoming excellent quilters and are eager to start piecing quilts for their own dowries. Louisa at age six is practicing her stitches by sewing on scraps and making clothes and quilts for her little rag doll.

Some women are quite unhappy and upset when they find they have fallen with a "change of life babe", but our Louisa has been such a joy and blessing to all of us. She is everyone's pet but remains sweet and unspoiled by the attention she receives. It may seem selfish of me, but it is also a great comfort to know that we will have a child at home to help care for us in those later years after our older children are grown and out on their own.

The young girl in this photograph would have been about Louisa's age at the time of the Civil War. Fashions for little girls of this era often featured plaids and wide necklines.

Against our wishes and tears, our only remaining son Frederick enlisted in January as a private in the Union Army, Company F, First Minnesota Heavy Artillery, and began training at nearby Fort Ridgely. After losing Henry in the Indian Wars, I could scarcely bear it when Frederick joined up. But I thank God that this dreadful Civil War ended a few months later, before he could be sent off to fight in the South. Frederick anticipates that he will be discharged from the Army shortly, and by the grace of God he should soon be safely home. Tragically President Lincoln was assassinated in April, just when the war was finally ending. Our whole nation is in mourning, not just for him, but for all the young men from the North and the South who died so young and so needlessly.

Your loving daughter,
Sophia

May 17, 1866

Dearest Mother,

I am now a grandmother and you are a great-grandmother! Augusta was safely delivered of a fine son last week. We were quite worried for her, as at twenty-eight she is late to have her first babe. Our son-in-law Ernst sent someone to fetch us in the wee hours, and we woke a neighbor woman who has acted as midwife for others. Poor Ernst could not bear to hear his wife's cries of pain, and he suddenly remembered an urgent chore to be done outside and took Christoph with him. I told Augusta what you had told me during my first birthing—that like Eve, we must bear our children in sorrow, but once you hold your child in your arms, you know it was worth any amount of pain. How wise you were, Mother!

This tintype photo of a young boy from the 1860s illustrates that both boys and girls wore dresses as infants and toddlers. After being trained a boy was "breeched" and dressed in short pants.

After the birth Augusta and Ernst informed us that the babe is to be called Henry after our dear son who died two years ago. It brought tears of joy to my eyes and even Christoph had to turn away to blow his nose, and you know how stoic he is. Last winter Christoph fashioned a beautiful wooden cradle, and I sewed a lovely little quilt to fit it. A neighbor woman told me it was foolish to spend so much time and effort on something that will be much used and often washed, but I told her this first grandchild is very special. I was rather proud that I was able to piece the top using my smallest fabric scraps, as you had taught me never to waste anything.

In other good news, Henry's young widow Wilhelmina remarried about a year ago and already has a babe. Strangely, the man she married has a very similar name to our deceased son's name, being called Henry Ott. We see them regularly at church and social functions, and we are pleased that Wilhelmina is once again happy.

As soon as the crops are planted this spring, Christoph and Frederick will begin building a two-story wooden frame house for us. There is a sawmill at West Newton where logs can be sawed into boards. Our little log cabin has served us well, but I am looking forward to having a bigger house with more bedrooms, a sitting room or parlor, and most especially a larger kitchen!

Much love,
Sophia

July 21, 1867

Dear Mother,

I am pleased to tell you that with the help of many of our neighbors and friends, Christoph and Frederick constructed a lovely frame house for us last summer. I have been much occupied with the furnishing of this new home. It is wonderful to have more space for our family and also to be able to buy a few nicer pieces of furniture and household items for it.

Last November we were blessed with the happy occasion of Frederick's marriage to Paulina Netzke, a fine German neighbor girl. As Frederick is our only surviving son and is doing much of the farming work, Christoph transferred the title of the farm to him for the token amount of $300. Frederick also began homesteading forty acres of nearby land, to which he will receive full title in five years. This summer the men are busy constructing a home for the young couple on that property, but they are living in our old log cabin until it is completed.

Sadly, our Immanuel Lutheran Church has split between the members residing in Courtland Township and the members residing in Nicollet Township, over a matter of distance and convenience, not of doctrine or practice. A Courtland faction desired to move the church westward into their township, while those of us living to the east in Nicollet Township felt this move would unduly lengthen our travel to church. Those of us in Nicollet Township have now organized a new congregation, abandoning the use of the church on the township line and locating more centrally to Nicollet Village.

This has resulted in some good news for our family. Our church has decided to start a school of its own and has hired Christoph as its first teacher. He is honored and excited to return to his teaching profession. The church cannot yet afford to build a schoolhouse, and so Christoph will be teaching children from first to eighth grade in our own home. Louisa is ever so excited for school to begin. The house will be crowded, but you know how I have always loved little children. When my morning chores are finished, I hope to be of help with the younger ones.

Sending my love,
Sophia

October 22, 1868

Dearest Mother,

Can you believe our sweet Hannah is to be married? We are all so excited for her. In December she will wed Christian Stolt, who owns a neighboring farm and is a veteran of the Civil War, having served with the Illinois Cavalry for three years. He was wounded in battle, being shot through the right lung, but has since made a good recovery. Although Hannah is only nineteen years to Christian's twenty-six years, she is very determined and mature for her age and eager to begin this new stage of her life.

We are piecing a special wedding quilt of Hannah's own choosing and hope to have it quilted before her wedding. Augusta and Albertina each have two children, and Frederick's wife Paulina just birthed her first babe. Needless to say, I have been kept busy making cradle quilts. We thank God that he kept these mothers and babes safe through their ordeals and that all are thriving. We are greatly blessed to be grandparents, and I wish that you too could hold these sweet little ones in your arms!

With my love,
Sophia

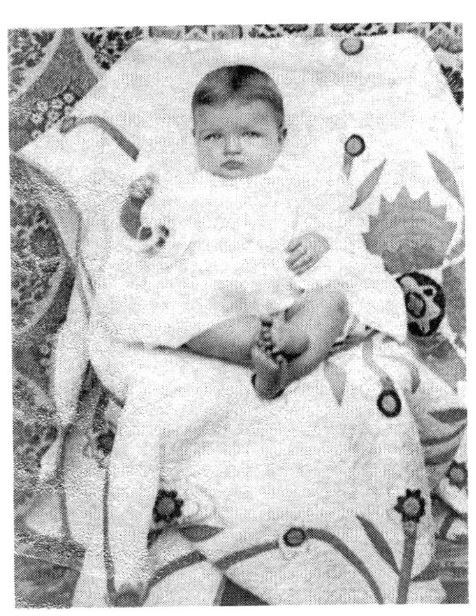

In this photo from about 1865 a baby is seated on a beautiful Whig Rose quilt, usually made in red, green and cheddar on a white background. This applique quilt pattern was inspired by a political party and was very popular in the 1850s and 1860s.

August 21, 1869

Dear Mother,

Last February a constitution was adopted, formally organizing our new church in Nicollet as Trinity Evangelical Lutheran Church. I am proud to say that the first signer of the constitution was Christoph, as he was the leader of the thirty founding members. As a former church sexton and the current teacher in our church school, he was the most educated and knew the workings of a church. Next year a church building and parsonage will be erected and a pastor can then finally be called to lead us.

I cannot believe it is almost twelve years since we left Germany! There have been so many changes and new experiences, as well as trials and losses, that it seems we have lived an entire lifetime in those twelve years. While it has been more difficult than we ever imagined, yet our Christian faith carried us through and kept us strong and resilient like this land we have grown to love. The hardest part has always been the separation from you and the family. You have been much in my thoughts and prayers of late. God bless and keep you until we meet again in heaven.

Your loving daughter,
Sophia

April 15, 1870

To My Dear Sister Anna,

We were deeply saddened to receive your letter telling us that our beloved Mother has gone to join our Maker. Yet it is a great comfort to know that she has been reunited in heaven with our long-departed Father, our dear son Henry, and the two sweet babes we lost back in Germany.

With the recent births of two more grand-babes and with two more "in the oven," we are reminded that the cycle of life goes on. I am greatly enjoying being a grandmother and I am kept busy sewing cradle quilts for all the new babes. I find that my greatest joys in life are the simple pleasures of home, children and grandchildren.

I have missed Mother and you and the rest of the family greatly over the years. It was heartbreaking to leave our home in Germany, knowing that we would never see any of you again in this lifetime, but we truly believe that we made the right decision. Our children have thrived and prospered with the opportunities that they would not have had in the Old Country. We endured much change and adversity, and it was not without hardship and sacrifice, but we praise God that He has so greatly blessed our life in America.

Your loving sister,
Sophia

An elderly woman's creased and wrinkled face and sad expression testify to her hard life in this photograph from about 1870.

2

HENRIETTA'S STORY: LAND IS EVERYTHING!

This story is based on the life of my great-great-great-aunt, Henrietta Wehrmeister Otto, born in 1822 in East Pomerania, Prussia, Germany. Her family was the second Otto family to emigrate to America. Henrietta's husband, Gottlieb Otto, was a brother to Christoph Otto, whose wife Sophia told their family's story in the first chapter of this book. I have taken artistic license in having Henrietta's family live in a sod house, which was common at that time on the open prairie especially in the case of homesteaders. It is not documented where her family fled for protection during the Sioux conflict, but I have chosen to portray them at Fort Ridgely.

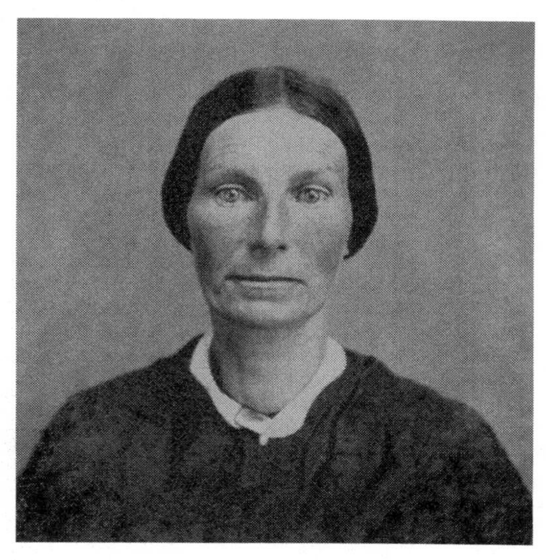

Tintype "gem" photographs (about one inch square), such as this one of an unknown woman from about 1870, were very popular at the time because they were quite inexpensive.

LETTERS FROM HENRIETTA OTTO TO HER SISTER IN GERMANY

May 23, 1861

Dear Sister Dorothea,

What a long and dreadful voyage we have had! We departed our motherland of Germany and our beloved village of Kratzig forever amidst many tears and doubts. Our family took the train overland to Bremen, and from thence we sailed across the endless ocean on the steamship *Atlanta*, arriving in New York just two days past. The iron belly of the ship was so packed with people and their belongings that we scarcely had room to move about, and the food was of dubious origin and poorly prepared. There was much seasickness, dysentery, weeping and misery on our world-crossing journey.

A week out we were caught in a terrible storm at sea. As our little ship rose and fell on the huge waves like a bucking horse, creaking and groaning, we feared it would either be smashed to bits or else sink into the deep like an iron casket with us inside. Everyone took to their beds, as most were sick, and it was impossible to stay upright with the tossing of the ship. There was loud weeping, screaming and praying, but God did indeed hear our cries and after two long days and nights the seas finally calmed. The three weeks spent on the ocean felt like the longest weeks of my life! I could never face another crossing such as we have just endured. I truly realize now what a momentous decision we have made and how our mother country is forever lost to us. When I think that I will never see my family and friends again, my feelings quite overwhelm me.

I fervently hope that the letters sent by Gottlieb's brother Christoph, who emigrated to America in 1857 with his family, hold to be true. He urged us to come to this young and prosperous America and described the jobs available, the money to be earned, and most importantly, the cheap and plentiful land to be found. As difficult as it was to leave our families and home, Gottlieb and I knew that we must take this great leap of faith for the sake of our sons, so they might escape the poverty and hopelessness of our lives. If we were to journey to the New World, it could not be put off any longer. Gottlieb is already forty-seven years, I am thirty-nine, and our three sons Carl, Henry and August are ages fifteen, twelve and ten and in a few short years will be grown.

This photograph of three young siblings was taken in Germany around 1865. In old photos it is difficult to determine whether an infant is a boy or a girl, as both were dressed alike.

We are at a boardinghouse in New York for a few days while Gottlieb plans our travel to this Minnesota where Christoph and Sophia live. What a blessing it is to finally bathe properly before setting off again, as we had only small basins and salt water for bathing on the ship. This city is so crowded and confusing, with everyone speaking in different languages. It is a huge maze of row upon row of tall gray buildings, divided by narrow dirty passageways of streets, with noisy throngs of people everywhere speaking in a babble of languages. We will be glad when we are in Minnesota, where there are farms and villages and other German-speaking people. I will write once we have come to the end of our next journey, across this big new country that we will now call home.

I miss you already,
Henrietta

August 1, 1861

Dear Dorothea,

I finally have time to pen a letter to you, as you must be wondering how we are faring in this new country of ours. Now that you have our address, please write soon with the news from home. I often long for family and friends left behind and wonder what has happened in our village since we left.

After many days of travel by train, steamboat, and wagon, we arrived at Christoph and Sophia's farm in Nicollet County, Minnesota. They have a wonderful large farm with fine crops in the fields and gardens and a snug log cabin and barn. We stayed with them for a short time while Gottlieb looked for work in the area. As you know, Gottlieb did not earn much in Germany working for a nobleman's family weaving baskets and knitting stockings. It was a lowly and poorly paying job, especially in such a time of economic woes, overpopulation and crop failures. We had barely enough money to pay for our travels to reach this far place, and we will now need to work for a time to save money to purchase land, build a house and barn, and buy all the livestock and supplies needed to begin farming on our own.

It was crowded staying with Christoph, Sophia, and their children, but we were much worn down by our long journey and happy to have a place to lay down our heads, even if it was only a pallet on the floor. Sophia confided in me that living on a farm instead of in a village is oftentimes very lonely, and she was so enjoying our company. As Sophia and I had formed a close bond as soon as we became sisters-in-law,

I was much cheered to know that I had at least one good friend in this land of strangers.

By God's grace, Gottlieb was soon hired by a German farmer, a Peter Schmidt with a large farm near the Minnesota River in Nicollet County. He and his wife are older and require help to manage their farm, as their children are now grown and off on their own. Their family had first lived in a tiny cabin until they could build a larger house, and they have allowed us the use of their old cabin. How thankful we are just to have work and a roof over our heads!

At fifteen years of age Carl can almost do the work of a man and has been hired on as well. Henry and August are often given smaller chores to do. Clara Schmidt and I get on well together, and it is wonderful to have another woman close at hand. She has been very kind to me and gives us milk, eggs and produce from her garden. In return I am helping her with her household chores and with the gardening and chickens. You will laugh to hear that I have even learned to milk a cow.

Your loving sister,
Henrietta

October 30, 1861

Dear Dorothea,

What a wonderful country this America is! The soil is fertile and the crops have been abundant. Gottlieb and the boys worked long hours during the harvest season to bring in the hay, grain and corn, and I helped Clara Schmidt harvest and preserve the fruits and vegetables from her large garden and orchard. Peter Schmidt paid good wages to Gottlieb for his and the boys' labor, and Clara shared her bounty with me in exchange for my help. Their kindness in helping us make a start in this new land has been such a blessing to us, and they treat our boys like their own grandchildren. We are so happy to have both food and money put by to get us through the coming winter, and we are saving every penny possible in order to buy a farm in a few years. Meanwhile, we are all learning much about farming that will help us successfully acquire and manage our own farm.

In our agrarian society, land is everything. If you own land you can grow food and raise animals, and your family will never go hungry. Sons most often follow the occupation of their father, or they work with and later inherit their father's farm or business. I do not have to tell you that with Gottlieb having a low-paying job, our sons would not have had a bright future had we remained in Germany. As you well know, even families that do own land find that they cannot break it into pieces for all their sons, for within a few generations the bits of land would be too small to support a family.

You will recall the hardships of growing up in our own large poor family where our father did not own land and worked only as a day laborer. Do you remember the times when he could not find work and there was little food to put on the table? The only reason we did not starve was due to the generosity of kinfolk and friends, who had little more than we did but were willing to share their meager sustenance. Is it any wonder that I live in terror of poverty? When my sons were born, I vowed that they would never go hungry and that I would do everything in my power to help them obtain land. By the grace of God, they could all be landowning farmers in this new country someday, a status they could hardly have reached in Germany.

The newspapers tell of a bloody Civil War between the Northern and the Southern states of our newly adopted country. It seems that the main issue is slavery, which thankfully does not exist where we live, although some say that the war is about preventing the Southern states from splitting away from the rest of the country. Since we brought our boys all this way to avoid the compulsory military service in the mighty Prussian Army, we are most grateful that this Civil War does not look like it will come this far west. I want to raise my boys to be

God-fearing men, not trained to kill others. Although the Union Army has been recruiting soldiers from Minnesota, there is no requirement to serve. Our oldest, Carl, has just turned sixteen and thankfully is not old enough to enlist. And, God willing, this conflict should be settled soon.

Sending my love,
Henrietta

December 30, 1861

Dear Dorothea,

Thank you for your recent letter and good wishes for the Christmas season. We were invited to Christoph and Sophia's home for Christmas dinner, where we feasted on wild turkey hunted by their sons. After dinner Sophia showed me the beautiful quilts that she has been making. They are amazing, each with the top constructed of small pieces of colorful fabrics arranged to make an attractive pattern, a thin cotton or wool batting in the center, muslin on the back, and tiny hand stitching to hold all the layers together. Sophia has promised to teach me to quilt, and I am ever so excited to learn how to create something so lovely. It will also give us an opportunity to spend more time together and renew our friendship.

You expressed curiosity about the natives of this country. They are called Indians, belonging to the Sioux tribe, and are quite wild looking, going about almost naked in warm seasons. They are fearsome to behold but at the same time have a certain grace and nobility about them. The government purchased all their land in this area and removed them to small reservations west of here. However, the natives sometimes return and camp in the woods nearby to hunt, trap and fish. Gottlieb says we cannot forbid them, as their lands and livelihoods have been taken away. We have heard that the government in Washington is so involved with the War Between the States that it has been lax in keeping its promises to the Indians of money and goods. I thank you for your concern, but please do not fret for our safety. We have been assured that the tribes hereabouts are friendly, and they have thus far given us no reason to fear them.

Wishing you a blessed New Year,

Henrietta

May 20, 1862

Dear Dorothea,

Oh, Sister, you would not believe what a fright I have had! One recent fine spring day I was alone in the house with the door propped open to provide fresh air and light. Suddenly a shadow fell across me and I felt my scalp prickle. I turned with my heart beating like a drum to see two young Indian men standing in the doorway. They had skin the color of copper, eyes as black as night, high cheekbones, long black braided hair, and clothes made of animal skins decorated with beads. They indicated with sign language that they were hungry, and with my hands shaking, I quickly gave them some meat and potatoes left over from our noon meal. After they had eaten, they poked around our cabin, grabbed a loaf of bread from the cupboard and departed. I had to sit down, as I was shaking like a leaf and weeping with relief at still being alive.

The two natives have since returned several times, and I always give them meat or bread or whatever I have at hand. I am most afraid of them, but Gottlieb says I must not show my fear and try to win their favor so they do not harm us. After all, we are living on land that was originally theirs and so we owe them some of our bounty. Yesterday these two men again visited our cabin, as they must have been camped nearby and smelled my bread baking. I was forced to part with several loaves, and so I will need to bake again tomorrow.

Henry and August, at thirteen and eleven years, have no fear and are most curious about the Indians. The young men seem to enjoy the children and try to speak to them in sign language. Our boys examined the bows and arrows of the Indians, and we were given a demonstration of their skills with these weapons. I must say after that display I would not want to make enemies of these people.

My sister-in-law Sophia and her family are coming for dinner on Sunday, after which she is to begin my quilting lessons. I am so looking forward to exchanging news of family and friends with her and learning this new skill and pastime.

Much love,
Henrietta

June 2, 1862

Dear Sister,

When Gottlieb returned from a trip to New Ulm yesterday, he brought the most amazing news. The newspapers report that on May 20th President Lincoln signed a new law called The Homestead Act. Apparently, a head of household can file a claim on up to 160 acres of federal land, build a house, cultivate the land, and live on it for five years. This is known as "homesteading." Then for a small filing fee, he can obtain the title to the land free and clear. It is almost too good to be true, but if so, we are much closer to having a farm of our own. We will still need to save money to buy the building materials, livestock, tools, seeds and supplies required to operate a farm, but just imagine how much sooner this can be accomplished if we do not need to buy the land itself. What a wonderful country this is and what hopes we have for the future!

Sophia is teaching me to quilt, and we are having great fun designing patterns, choosing fabrics, and stitching while we talk about old times and new. Not only is it enjoyable, but also economical as I can use the fabric scraps left over from my dresses and aprons and from Gottlieb's and the boys' shirts. If necessary I could buy a few pieces to add to what I have, but it would be far too costly to purchase the yardage needed. My boys are growing like weeds, and it seems that I am forever sewing or altering shirts and pants for them. It makes me proud to see them growing so strong and healthy from working outdoors. I am grateful too that I am able to put plenty of good food on the table to fill their growing appetites.

Your loving sister,
Henrietta

October 8, 1862

Dearest Dorothea,

We have had the most terrifying experience of our lives! Mid-morning on August 18th the two Indian men who had visited us and enjoyed my bread came racing up on their ponies. With excited gestures, they let us know that we were in great danger of being attacked by others of their kind. They urged us to leave speedily and pointed us in the direction of nearby Fort Ridgely. Carl immediately mounted one of the horses in order to ride off to raise the alarm to our neighbors. I begged him to come with us instead, but Gottlieb urged him to go, saying we had been warned and so we needed to warn others in turn. Most were stacking grain in their fields and had to be persuaded that the danger was grave enough to leave everything and flee.

While Gottlieb and Peter Schmidt quickly hitched the other horses to the wagon, Clara Schmidt and I gathered up some food, quilts and a few precious belongings in great haste. The boys let the livestock out of their fences and chased them into the woods, where they would not be as easily killed or stolen. With our hearts quaking in fear, we set out in the wagon as fast as our horses could go. We were greatly relieved when Carl on horseback finally caught up with us.

When we reached the safety of Fort Ridgely, we were surprised to find it defended by only twenty-nine soldiers. Captain John Marsh had left with forty-six men to quell an Indian uprising at the trading post, and another fifty soldiers were out on patrol. The fort was poorly situated for defense with wooded ravines on three sides. The various stone and wood buildings were spread out on an exposed plateau with no stockade for protection. We wondered if it could be successfully defended and worried how safe we would be there, but there was no alternative. All day terrified and wounded settlers poured into the fort in a steady stream, with fearsome stories of men shot and scalped, women violated and dragged into captivity, children mutilated or stolen away, and homes and barns and grain fields set afire. Gottlieb and I tried to keep the boys calm, but we were in great terror ourselves of losing our lives in a most dreadful manner.

A vintage postcard from approximately the turn of the century shows a drawing of Fort Ridgely as it looked at the time of the Sioux Uprising.

By evening about two hundred refugees were huddled with us in the large two-story stone barracks. A few survivors of Captain Marsh's company returned with news of having been ambushed and most of the men killed. A soldier was sent on the fastest horse to Fort Snelling in St. Paul to request reinforcements with utmost dispatch. We often thought of Sophia, Christoph, and their family. We fervently prayed that they had also received a timely warning and had found refuge at nearby New Ulm. I don't believe any of us slept a wink that night for fear of the Indians attacking under cover of darkness. Many a bargain was made with God that night, if only he would spare our lives and save us from a fearsome death.

The following day the soldiers out on patrol returned, a group of Union Army recruits arrived from St. Peter, and additional settlers found their way to the fort. We remained in constant fear that the Indians would come charging out of the woods at any instant. It was not until later that we learned they had been busy attacking New Ulm that day. Fortunately for us, the soldiers, green recruits, and able-bodied civilians at the fort had a day's time to practice drills, position the six pieces of artillery, and care for the wounded and dying victims. Gottlieb, like many of the settlers, does not own a gun but he and the boys did all they could to assist in building barricades, standing watch and carrying supplies. I worked in the hot kitchens helping to prepare meals for the multitude from the supplies in the storehouses. We spent another sleepless night in fear of attack, with those around us worrying, weeping and praying that the Lord would protect and save us.

On Wednesday, August 20th, about four hundred Sioux warriors led by Chief Little Crow commenced a furious assault on Fort Ridgely, swarming out of the ravines whooping and shooting, and striking great fear into our hearts. The cannon fire quickly broke up their charge, but they continued with constant attacks from all sides. Gottlieb and Carl assisted in carrying ammunition and supplies to the soldiers and keeping watch on all sides. I had to insist that the two younger boys stay with me for safety, although they desperately wanted to be of help and appear brave. We huddled with the other terrified women, children and wounded in the stone barracks while the fighting went on around us, all the while wondering what great horrors would befall us if the Indians managed to take the fort.

Once during a lull when I was carrying water to the men upstairs in our building, I caught sight through a window of the mounted savages, riding as if they were extensions of their horses, dressed in animal skins, feathers, and beads and with their faces painted like demons. In addition to firing arrows and rifles, they were howling like banshees. I had never been so frightened in all my life and stood as if frozen to the spot! Thankfully, God heard our fervent prayers and cries. At sundown the heavens opened with rain, and the Indians finally left off their siege for the day.

We were all greatly relieved when the Indians did not resume their attack on Thursday, but there was much work to be done. Our defenses and barricades had to be strengthened and strategies planned. Food had to be provided for three hundred fifty souls and the many wounded needed care. Small arms ammunition was running low, and so some of the cannon balls were melted down and made up into cartridges. But the greatest worry was that the requested reinforcements from Fort Snelling had not yet arrived. Could our small band of soldiers and civilians hold the fort against a better-planned attack by a greater number of Indians? There was much weeping, praying and misery among the refugees as we readied ourselves for another attack.

On Friday morning, August 22nd, the Indians began arriving in large numbers and encircled the fort just out of reach of our guns, making no effort to conceal themselves. The soldiers estimated there were eight hundred braves or about twice the number as in the previous battle. It was frightening to note that they seemed so sure of victory that their women brought along empty wagons to fill with spoils of war. The Indians began the attack by charging furiously from all sides with demonic yells and a hail of arrows and bullets. The soldiers returned gunfire and cannon fire and the savages retreated into the trees. The assault continued all day from all directions, with the Indians seizing possession of some of the outbuildings. Our men had to shell the buildings and set them on fire to drive out the Indians.

It was a most dreadful day with the wild shrieks of the Indians, the cries of the wounded and dying, the roars of the cannon, the cracks of the rifles, and the smoke of the burning buildings. We all knew full well that if the fort were taken it meant certain death or far worse for all within it. Thank God, the superior firepower of the cannons enabled our brave men to hold back the Sioux, until they finally withdrew in defeat at dusk. How exhausted everyone was, but how thankful we were that our lives had once more been spared!

Two German advertising trade cards from the late 1800s depict Sioux Indians dressed for war on the fronts, with advertisements for Liebig's meat extract on the reverse sides.

The next morning we tracked the Sioux heading towards New Ulm by the columns of smoke as they set fire to farms along the way. We fully expected them to return and attack the fort again, and we were kept on edge and in constant fear for the next several days and nights. Finally, to our great relief, on Wednesday, August 27th, an advance guard from Fort Snelling rode in, and two days later Colonel Sibley arrived with the rest of his troops. We welcomed them with tears of happiness running down our faces, delirious with relief after having been delivered from certain death. The following day troops escorted us to St. Peter, where we remained until peace could be restored to the frontier. For another month the rebellious Indians continued to attack settlers and engage in hostilities until Colonel Sibley's troops finally defeated them on September 23rd in a decisive battle in Yellow Medicine County.

When we were finally allowed to return to our homes some six weeks after the uprising began, we were most fearful of what we would find. Would our houses be looted or destroyed, our crops burned in the fields, our livestock killed or stolen? Praise the Lord, our cabin and the Schmidts' house were still standing, but what a mess we found. The Indians had taken with them every scrap of food and had gone through our belongings and strewn much of it around. The men have rounded up the livestock that escaped into the woods, although we are still missing a pig and a few chickens. Clara Schmidt and I have cleaned our belongings and put our houses to right again. We praise God and consider ourselves most blessed that we did not lose much in the way of goods, but even more so that we were saved from an unspeakable death and still have our scalps attached to our heads!

It is reported in the newspapers that many hundreds of white settlers were killed in this conflict, now being called the Great Sioux Uprising. How thankful we are for the two Indian men who returned our kindness by warning us to flee. Gottlieb and I asked ourselves often during those frightening days and nights whether we did the right thing by bringing our family to this raw new country fraught with its unknown perils. Although we have been assured that the hostile Indians were all rounded up and removed from the area, it will be a long time before we sleep well and do not startle at every unexpected noise. Praise God that He was with us and protected us through this dreadful calamity!

Sending my love,
Henrietta

January 6, 1863

Dear Sister,

I last wrote of the frightful Indian Uprising and how we were spared by the grace of God. I am sorry to have frightened you so, but I assure you that we are no longer in any danger. While I would not mind returning to Germany (except for the dreadful ocean crossing), Gottlieb and the boys firmly believe in this land of opportunity. We have survived the worst possible disaster and believe things can only get better.

When we discussed our experience in the uprising with our boys, Gottlieb cautioned that we must not judge the Indians too harshly but leave that up to God. Even with the terrible brutalities and destruction that these savages wrought upon our people, we must also consider that our government had taken away their hunting grounds and broken its promises of food, money and supplies. We had a harsh winter last year, followed by a terrible drought this past summer, and having been restricted to small reservations the Indians were unable to find enough food for their families. We wonder how we, as civilized people, would react if we had everything stripped from us and our own children were starving.

Over four hundred Indians were eventually arrested by the militia and imprisoned for their parts in the uprising. On November 9th they were carried in wagons through New Ulm on their way to Mankato to be tried for their crimes. Gottlieb went to see if the two Indians who had saved our lives were among them, thinking that he could speak out on their behalf and have them pardoned. However, we had never learned their names, and he was unable to identify them among the many that looked so alike. Gottlieb was horrified when angry mobs attacked the prisoners chained in the wagons, throwing stones and attempting to lynch the Indians on the spot.

Only a few days later, three hundred Sioux were swiftly sentenced to death by a military court in Mankato, although most were subsequently pardoned by President Lincoln. However, thirty-eight of them deemed to be the most ferocious were hanged in a public spectacle on December 26th in Mankato. We are told this is the largest mass execution in the history of this country. I hope and pray we can now put this tragic time behind us, move on with our lives and focus on the future.

On a more mundane level, I have finished piecing the blocks together for my first quilt top and am quite excited to quilt it. I purchased some inexpensive pink gingham check fabric for the backing. Gottlieb has devised a simple quilting frame for me that basically consists of two strips of wood a little longer than the width of the quilt and two other shorter pieces. The ends of the quilt are wrapped around the longer strips of wood and rolled up tightly, leaving a nice firm space for me to stitch. The other two strips hold the first two strips apart, and four ladder-back chairs are used to support the quilt frame. I hope to complete the hand quilting over the rest of the long lonely winter still ahead of us.

With love,
Henrietta

October 20, 1863

Dear Dorothea,

I have written about our terrible Civil War, pitting the North against the South and sometimes, we understand, brother against brother. The Union Army enlisted many of our young men, first to fight against the South, and then after the Sioux Uprising, to fight against the Indians in the Dakota territories. Many of the young men hereabouts were anxious for revenge for the atrocities committed by the Indians and eagerly joined the Army. Our nephew Henry was one of them, but tragically he died at Fort Ridgely last month from typhoid fever. His family is heartbroken, as they all looked to Henry for guidance in this new country. I do not know how I would bear such a great loss, as my family is my whole life.

As you recall, Gottlieb has a gruff manner about him, and he is very strict with the boys, wanting them to grow up to be tough enough to withstand the trials of life. Our oldest son, Carl, turned eighteen yesterday and broached the idea of joining the Army to avenge his cousin Henry's death. Gottlieb was very harsh with him, saying there has been far too much killing and death, and he would under no circumstances allow him to enlist. He reminded him that one reason for leaving Germany was that we did not want our sons serving in the military. To soften Gottlieb's words, I stressed to Carl just how much we have depended on his help and hard work to get settled and save money to buy our own land. I told him how close we are to realizing our dream and that the whole reason for the dream is that he and his brothers will someday be landowners and have a promising future for their families.

Although our sons are grown almost to men, they still need a firm hand to guide them from time to time. I think Carl felt honor-bound to raise the subject of enlisting, but was secretly relieved when Gottlieb forbid it. Carl made a show of reluctantly agreeing, but we feel he understands that he is needed here. Besides, he is a gentle soul and has a great love of the land and all living things. He has the makings of a good farmer but would be a poor soldier.

Oh, Sister, when we came to this New World, I did not know how hard I would have to work! Since I do not have any daughters to help me with the housework, I often have to enlist one or both of my younger boys to help. As the oldest, Carl works alongside Gottlieb and is thus excused from helping with housework. But, at fourteen and twelve years, Henry and August are a tremendous help to me, especially on laundry day when there are many buckets of water to tote from the well and much firewood to bring in to keep the stove hot. Then there is scrubbing the clothes on the washboard, boiling the whites in the large kettle, rinsing them in fresh water, wringing them out, and pegging them on the line to dry. It is much hard physical work, takes up most of a day each week, and leaves me exhausted.

This colorful trade card for Lavine Soap from the late 1800s illustrates that before modern times doing laundry involved a lot of hard work.

The boys are also in charge of feeding the chickens and collecting the eggs, as they would rather do outside chores than housework. This job falls to most farm women, but I loathe those hens with their beady eyes and sharp beaks that peck my hands when I reach under them for their eggs. However, I do love to cook a good fried chicken dinner of the hens when they have stopped laying eggs!

Now that the harvest season is over, I am so enjoying finally having some spare time to work on my quilting again. I have missed that during the past months when I worked until I was totally exhausted and then fell into bed, only to rise early and begin all over again.

Your loving sister,

Henrietta

January 4, 1864

Dear Dorothea,

Would you believe that we are already landowners? No, we have not yet saved enough money to start a farm of our own, but Gottlieb has purchased twenty acres of densely wooded land along Nicollet Creek. Most farmers find it necessary to own a woods lot since there are few trees on the open prairie. Whenever Gottlieb and the boys have time to spare they will cut firewood for cooking and heating our home, and it will also be a place to fish and hunt and trap animals for food or pelts. Later they plan to cut down trees to be milled for lumber with which to build our house when we eventually are able to have our own farm.

I am staring out the window at the bleak and barren fields under a pewter-gray sky and thinking how lonesome it is here. In Germany we lived in little villages with the farmers' fields surrounding the village, but here everyone has their home situated on their own land, often some distance from any neighbor. How fortunate my sister-in-law Sophia is with all her girls, and how I wish I had even one daughter to talk with of ordinary things and share the family stories while we do our household chores. Gottlieb and my boys just do not have any interest in such talk. Why is it that men don't seem to have the same need to express their feelings and connect with others that we women do?

It helps me get through the winter to have my quilting to look forward to in the evening when I have finished the never-ending drudgery of cooking, cleaning, laundry and chores. I also love to do my piecework on quiet Sunday afternoons when the boys walk to neighboring farms to play games with other boys. I am glad that they have made friends and have occasion for some fun in their lives. Gottlieb is a good Christian man, but I sometimes think he is too harsh with the boys and expects too much of them. During these quiet times Gottlieb likes to read the Bible and often naps in the midst of his reading. If I mention it, he claims he was only resting his eyes for a moment, but he works so hard during the week that I do not begrudge him an afternoon nap on the Lord's day.

I am piecing a new quilt with rows of uneven nine-patch blocks set on point and with shirting fabrics for the background. Nine-patch blocks are just nine squares sewn together, but for this quilt they are uneven, that is, not all the same size. It should be a handsome quilt, as I have saved some scraps of browns, blues, pinks, reds and greens that look lovely together. When we went to New Ulm last week to have wheat ground into flour at the gristmill, I bought some yards of a beautiful black print fabric, which I plan to use for sashings, borders and backing. I can scarcely wait to see what it will look like when it is finished. I find it so rewarding to create something of both comfort and beauty out of little but scraps.

With love,
Henrietta

June 8, 1865

Dear Dorothea,

We are overjoyed! Our biggest dream has been realized. Yesterday Gottlieb filed homestead papers in New Ulm on eighty acres of land in Nicollet County, very near both the town of Nicollet and his brother Christoph's farm. I am most excited that Sophia and I will be neighbors and able to see each other much more often. If we live on this homestead for five years and make the necessary improvements, the farm will be given—yes, given—to us for only a few years of work. And so, Dorothea, every minute of the next five years of our lives will be invested in this chosen piece of earth, along with a lot of muscle, sweat and hope!

Since it is already June, Gottlieb and the boys will need to get the fields cleared and plowed so that some crops can be planted immediately. Some of our new neighbors have pledged to help as soon as they can spare time from their own farms. Next they will need to dig a well and an outhouse must be built. Then we will have to acquire a team of horses, a cow to supply milk and butter, and a pig or two to provide meat in the winter, in addition to the small flock of chickens that we already have to lay eggs and also serve as an occasional meal. The animals can be kept outside in the summer, but we will need to build a shelter for them before winter sets in. If we allowed ourselves the time to think about it, this amount of work would be daunting.

Unfortunately, there will not be time to build a house for us just yet, as the priority is to get the farm started. After many discussions, it has been decided that as soon as the crops are planted, the neighbors will help us build a sod house. We will live in it for a year or two until Gottlieb and the boys are able to construct a proper wooden frame house. We are told that a team of men can build a "soddie" in a few days with little more than strips of sod cut from the virgin prairie grassland.

Needless to say, I am not happy that we will have to live in a house made almost entirely of dirt, and I am very worried how I will be able to maintain some cleanliness! However, others have assured us that if constructed properly a sod house can be quite snug and warm in the winter and pleasantly cool in the summer.

The past winter was long and lonesome, but I found sufficient time for my quilting. I completed piecing my uneven nine-patch quilt, added an attractive outside border of "flying geese" blocks and quilted it. I am pleased to say that it turned out to be quite a beauty, and I do wish I could show it to you. I am naming my quilt "Fly Away Home," both because of the flying geese border and because my thoughts often flew back to happy memories of my former home while working on it. I do worry that there will be more work with having our own farm, and I will not find time to quilt in the future.

Much love,
Henrietta

FLY AWAY HOME QUILT: Designed and pieced by Lanie Tiffenbach using Civil War reproduction fabrics. Long-arm machine quilted by Karen Niemi.

July 30, 1865

Dear Sister,

I am writing to you from my new home—a house made almost entirely of sod and completed in just three days' time. It was most interesting and amazing to watch it being built. One morning, near the end of June, a dozen of our neighbors showed up, along with a man who owns a sod-breaking plow. They cut the thickly-rooted prairie grass into strips of sod, each about eighteen inches wide and four inches deep. The strips were then cut into bricks of a uniform size about two feet long. An area was cleared and staked out and the sod bricks stacked up for the walls, alternating the placement so the cracks did not line up. Wooden frames were set in place for a door and three windows. The roof was built with cedar ridge-poles and timbers and then covered with a layer of clay and more sod on top of that.

Vintage postcards from the early 1900s show the exterior of a pioneer sod house in Holdrege, Nebraska, and the interior of a sod house from the House of Yesterday Museum in Hastings, Nebraska.

The windows and metal hinges for the door were purchased. We plastered the inside walls with a mixture of sand, clay, and lime which dried to a clean-looking cream color. So far we have only a dirt floor, but it is hard packed and smooth. Gottlieb nailed a muslin sheet to the ceiling beams to keep any dirt from sifting down on us. I hung a calico curtain on a wire stretched from one wall to the other to divide the kitchen from our bedroom area. The boys have cots in the kitchen that also serve as benches during the day.

You know how fastidious I am about keeping a clean house. I feared my new home would be no better than a dirt dugout which we have heard some settlers first live in, being little more than a cave dug into a hillside. As much as I had dreaded living in a "soddie," I am amazed that it really is quite comfortable. At sixteen feet by twenty feet, it is larger than the log cabin where we lived.

With our belongings installed in it, the house is beginning to feel like home. I think you would be very surprised to see how nice it looks. My lovely quilt on the bed adds a touch of color and cheer. The thick walls provide deep windowsills inside for my flowerpots, and I have grass and wildflowers growing on my roof!

I am most pleased to tell you that the Civil War between the states finally ended in April past. It is said that the North won the war, but a generation of young men from both sides died in the fighting. So I do not think that anyone but death won. How my heart goes out to all those mothers and fathers who lost their sons, some no more than mere boys. And how grateful I am that our sons were not involved and that they are growing into fine upstanding young men.

I hope you and your family are well. Please write to us in care of the post office at Nicollet Town, Nicollet County, Minnesota, as we long to hear news from home.

With love,
Henrietta

June 15, 1866

Dear Dorothea,

We are so pleased that a church has already been organized in what often seems to be nothing but a wilderness. As we are isolated on our farms, the church serves as the center of our social life. I do so look forward to visiting with Sophia and other neighbors and friends on Sunday mornings or special occasions.

Oh, Sister, you could not imagine the backbreaking work needed to build a farm from scratch! I grow a large quantity of vegetables in my garden, and for winter I store them in a root cellar or cook and preserve them in stone crocks and jars. I prepare whatever game the men hunt such as deer, rabbits, ducks and geese, supplemented by our own pigs and chickens. Then I churn butter and bake six loaves of bread about every four days, and sometimes cakes or pies. When weather permits, I do as many chores as possible outdoors because our soddie is fairly dark inside.

Gottlieb and the boys have put in long hours every day over the past year plowing and planting, tilling and harvesting, acquiring and caring for livestock, and putting up outbuildings and fences. Carl and Henry are strong boys and hard workers, although August, being the youngest at fifteen, is not yet fully grown, is more frail and more of a dreamer. Even so, Gottlieb does not believe in coddling him and insists that he do his share and try to keep up with his older brothers. Sometimes I requisition his help around the house in order to give him a break from the more difficult farm work. We have never worked so hard in all our lives, but we know that it is worth it when we look around us and see that this is truly our very own clod of God's earth.

God bless you,
Henrietta

March 15, 1867

Dear Sister,

I sit and pen this letter to you by the failing fire in this primitive house. The thick walls retain the heat and keep out the cold, but with only three small windows, it always seems dark and dreary. During rainy seasons or when the snow is melting, the moisture seeps through the ceiling and mud drips on the floor or the bed. I had to put my lovely quilts in a trunk so they do not get ruined from constant washing. I am tired of continually squashing insects and spiders that crawl through the walls and ceiling.

Our little farm is surrounded by the vast emptiness of the prairies still covered in snow, and the sky is perpetually an iron gray. It has been a long bitter winter, and sometimes I think I may go quite mad from lonesomeness. When we have storms or the roads are bad, I can go for weeks without leaving home or seeing anyone outside of my husband and sons. I confess that I sometimes carry on a conversation with myself, speaking my own part and another's too. You would think me crazy if you heard me, but it helps to keep my sanity. I am thankful to have my quilting to occupy my hands during the worst of times. It is satisfying to see a pattern emerge from the scraps and how the various colors work together to form the whole.

However, we are all quite proud of how well we have established our farm in less than two years. Gottlieb and the boys cleared land, planted and harvested crops, built a barn, chicken coop, granary and outhouse, planted fruit trees and a windbreak of trees around the farm, and built fences to contain the animals, all in addition to the daily chores. It has turned out to be more difficult than we ever expected, and although this land is free by way of homesteading, it is not without great cost of time, work, tears and sweat.

Our sons are now twenty-one, eighteen and sixteen years old, have grown strong and muscular from hard work, and are handsome with their new men's bodies and deep voices. They do tuck away a considerable amount of food, and it is a never-ending task to prepare enough to put on the table at each meal. But it does my heart proud to watch them eat and to know that we can provide for them from our own land and from the labors of our own hands.

I have saved the best news for last. Gottlieb and the boys will begin building a proper wooden frame house for us as soon as the crops are planted this spring. They go out to our woods lot whenever they have spare time, even in the winter when the weather is suitable. They chop down trees to be taken to the sawmill to be milled for lumber for our new house and cut up smaller branches and dead trees for firewood. Other family members and neighbors will help with the building as much as they can between their own work, and our new home should be finished by fall. How I look forward to once again living in a real house!

Sending my love,
Henrietta

July 15, 1869

Dear Dorothea,

Your recent letter with news of family and friends greatly cheered me. I am sorry to have been remiss in writing. There are always so many chores waiting to be done, and by evening I am too tired to put pen to paper. As I had hoped, we did get our new house built two years ago. It is a lovely house with a sitting room off the kitchen and our bedroom beyond that. There are two rooms upstairs, a large bedroom that the boys share, and a smaller room for storage. It took me some time to finish the inside, make or buy the necessary furnishings, sew curtains for the windows, and plant flowers in front. I know that it is a sin to be prideful, but I do admit that after living in a sod house, I am ever so appreciative of my fine new home!

Our oldest son, Carl, was married in March to a young woman

named Emelia Ziemer, whose family had come from Germany a few years ago. They joined our church, and soon Carl sought her out after church every Sunday and later began to court her. When they married Gottlieb helped them purchase a farm near Courtland in return for all the work that Carl had done to help establish our farm. A large part of my dream has been realized with our oldest son now having land of his own!

When Carl and Emelia announced their intention to marry, I started piecing a wedding quilt for them. I had only six months to complete it, so I used every spare moment that I had to work on it. When the top was ready to be quilted, Sophia and some of the women from our church came for a "quilting frolic." They arrived as soon as their morning chores were completed, and each contributed some food for our noon meal. When we set up the quilt frame in my sitting room and placed chairs around on all sides, we scarcely could move around it. We spent the entire day with our fingers flying through the stitches, and what fun we had talking and laughing! It is a great blessing to have women friends with whom to share experiences, opinions, joys, and sorrows.

With love,
Henrietta

June 8, 1870

Dear Sister,

This is a most joyous day for us! Gottlieb went to the land office in New Ulm today to "prove up" our homestead, as it is exactly five years to the very day since his original homestead application. He paid a four-dollar fee to file for the final title to our square bit of earth. We recall how we arrived in this New World with hope and little else, and we remember, too, how scarce and expensive good farmland was in Germany. We can hardly fathom that this large and fertile farm is truly ours, just in return for living and working on it. What an amazing gift! We are already putting aside money for more land so that our two younger sons can also have farms of their own when the time comes for them to marry.

Before proving up, Gottlieb traveled to the courthouse in St. Peter last month and filed the second paper in the naturalization process, fulfilling the residency requirement. We are now official citizens of the United States of America. How we have been blessed in this country and how proud we are to be called Americans!

This tintype portrait, circa 1870, shows a baby in a very long christening dress seated on what appears to be a quilt with a wide white border.

I am also greatly pleased to announce that Gottlieb and I are grandparents, as Carl and Emelia had a babe in December. I was able to assist Emelia in her labor, which fortunately was an easy one, and Matilda is now a fat and happy child. After having had only sons, it is such a joy for me to have a girl in the family, and Gottlieb, in spite of his gruff ways, is quite besotted with this little granddaughter. Of course, as soon as I found out that Emelia was with child, I started piecing a little quilt. But a babe's quilt does not take as long as a wedding quilt, and so it was done with plenty of time to spare.

Your loving sister,
Henrietta

July 9, 1872

Dear Dorothea,

We are indeed now "bauers" or landowning farmers. The Homestead Patent Title for our eighty-acre farm was issued to Gottlieb on June 5, 1871. What a happy day that was, as our greatest dream has been fully realized!

Our little family is growing quickly. Carl and Emilia had a second daughter last October. Our middle son, Henry, was married in March to Friedricka Dallman, a neighbor girl whose family belongs to our church. I sometimes think my sons attended church willingly because it was practically the only place they could meet young women. Friedricka is a lovely well-mannered young woman, and I am happy to note that she is already carrying a child.

As he did when Carl married, Gottlieb gave Henry a fine sum of money to help him purchase a small farm nearby in Nicollet Township. So we now have two landowning sons, in addition to our own farm, and it is wonderful to have all our family close by. As you can guess, I have been kept busy in the past year sewing both wedding and cradle quilts.

Sending love,
Henrietta

August 1, 1875

Dear Dorothea,

A terrible curse has befallen us! We were invaded by locusts like one of the Biblical plagues right out of the Old Testament. We had heard of the terrible destruction wrought by these insects the last two summers in Iowa, but this summer they arrived here also. They flew in swarms of such size that they almost darkened the sun. When they landed in a field they stripped it clean of all vegetation so that it looked like it had been plowed. I had tried to save my nice tomato plants by spreading a sheet over them, but when I woke the next morning I found my sheet as well as my tomato vines gone! The hungry pests devoured our crops in the fields, my garden, and all the fruit and leaves on the trees. We are devastated by the loss, but fortunately have had ten years of good crops and have enough money put by to see us through this trial. We pray that next year will be better and that these dreaded locusts do not return.

Our youngest son, August, was wed last year to Paulina Hopp, who like our other two daughters-in-law, had come with her family from Germany and settled nearby at Nicollet. She is clever, outgoing, and a good match for our quiet August. The happy young couple had a fine girl babe born this May. We had planned to assist August in buying a farm of his own, as we did with our two older sons when they married. Unfortunately, because of the loss of our crops to the grasshoppers, we will need to put that off for another year or two. Meanwhile, they are living with us and helping with our farm. Thankfully, Paulina is a delightful and hardworking woman, and I truly feel like I have gained the daughter I never had. And, of course, we are so much enjoying having a babe in the house again.

In other news, Gottlieb's youngest brother Carl, his wife Albertina, and four of their children joined us in our new homeland this past spring. Their oldest son had come over a few years previous and has been working for Gottlieb's brother Christoph. We are most pleased to have more family nearby, and I am especially enjoying the company of my sister-in-law once more. So, you see, we have been given both blessings and loss, but isn't that what life is made of?

Your loving sister,
Henrietta

August 28, 1877

Dear Dorothea,

I am sorry not to have answered your letter sooner, but we have had some hard times the last two years. I wrote of our devastating grasshopper ravage in 1875, and I am sad to say that 1876 was just as bad. Again the disgusting creatures with their dreadful chewing noises destroyed our crops and gardens. The government paid a bounty of one dollar per bushel of dead grasshoppers, and farmers tried many imaginative ways to kill and collect the pests. Nothing worked very well, and after two years of losses there were many farmers who admitted defeat and left to try their luck elsewhere. But we had invested so much of our time, toil, and sweat in this farm that we felt we had no choice but to stay and hope for better times.

When the grasshopper eggs laid down in the soil last year began to hatch this spring, our governor designated a special day of prayer to beg God's mercy. He did indeed hear our fervent prayers and sent a heavy sleet and snowstorm a few days later that destroyed the grasshopper eggs and again sent a torrent of rain in June that killed many of the grasshoppers themselves. The few remaining pests formed a swarm, rose up into the air, and flew out of sight on July 1st. We pray that by the grace of God this scourge has passed from us, never to return.

Now that Gottlieb and I are getting on in years, being ages sixty-three and fifty-five, we do not think we can manage this farm by ourselves. We decided that August should have our homestead farm, and last week Gottlieb deeded the farm to August for the nominal sum of $200. We will continue to live here with August and Paulina and their babe. It is a joy to have another woman in the household after raising a crop of boys, and what a blessing the little one is! Paulina and I are busy stitching a warm cradle quilt for the next babe, expected to arrive in the winter.

Much love,
Henrietta

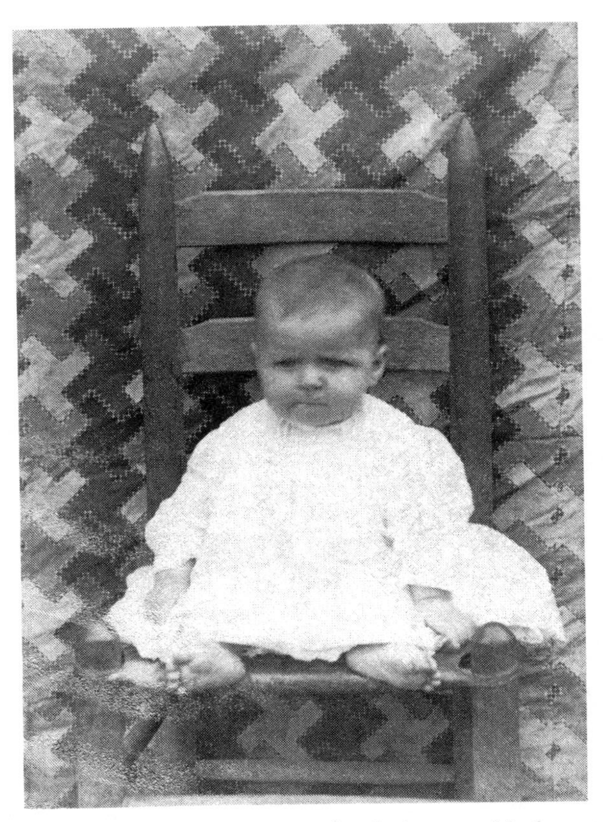

This circa 1875 photograph shows a barefoot baby seated before an interesting quilt. Quilts were often used in early photographs to provide a pleasing background.

July 30, 1881

Dear Dorothea,

I thoroughly enjoyed your recent letter describing the news of the village. I regret that I have grown lax in my letter writing, as there always seems to be something more pressing to do.

This past March our son August decided to relocate to Eden Township in Brown County. That area is said to have some of the richest soil anywhere, and there was a farm available at a good price. In addition to our homestead, August had increased his holdings in Nicollet County to 130 acres, which he sold to purchase the new farm of 160 acres. Even though it was August's decision to make and it seemed like a wise move, still Gottlieb and I were sorrowful to leave behind the farm that had been our greatest dream and in which we had invested sixteen years of our lives.

We have moved along with August and Paulina and their three little ones under the age of six, and they have assured us that we are welcome to make our home with them for as long as we live. I love Paulina as if she were my very own daughter, and I do whatever I am able to help her with the children and house. She was always such a dutiful daughter-in-law while she was living in my home, and in return I try to respect that the tables have turned and I am now living in her home. How fortunate we are to have children who will gladly care for us in our old age!

Last month Immanuel Lutheran Church was founded in this recently settled Eden Township. Among the thirteen men who signed the charter were Gottlieb, our son August, Gottlieb's brother Carl, and Carl's two older sons. I am proud to say that our son August generously donated a corner of his new farm for the church building and cemetery. Of course, this means that we will not have far to travel when we go to church. To God be all the glory, this is already the third church that members of our Otto family have helped establish in this new land.

In 1878 our middle son, Henry, and his wife sold their small farm in Nicollet County and acquired a large farm in Lynn Township,

McLeod County. Unfortunately, this is about fifty miles from where we live, which makes it difficult to see them and their five children very often. Our oldest son, Carl, and his wife, Emelia, already have seven children, and they have also acquired additional land in Nicollet County. All three of our sons have prospered and now have sufficient land of their own so that they and their children will never be poor or go hungry. Thanks be to God, my life's greatest hope and dream has been accomplished.

God's blessings on your family too,

Henrietta

Three unknown gentlemen who appear to be brothers are pictured in this tintype portrait from around 1880.

September 4, 1886

Dear Dorothea,

Please forgive my lapse in writing, as we have had much sorrow in our lives the past few years. Our oldest son Carl and his wife Emelia lost a three-year-old daughter in 1884 to that frightening plague called "black diphtheria," which has visited our area nearly every summer for the past five years. It causes a dark membrane to grow in the windpipe and strangles the children so afflicted.

With a daughter born later, Carl and Emelia now have eight children, and yet another is growing in Emelia's very fertile belly. Our middle son, Henry, and his wife Friedricka have had their eighth child, the oldest being thirteen years. Our sons were ever so competitive, and I sometimes wonder if they are competing to see which one can have the largest family.

As you know, we live with August and his family. After earlier birthing three healthy children, Ida, Hedwig, and Herman, three years ago Paulina had difficulty holding on to the latest one until his time could come. Tiny little Wilhelm lived but one day, but was mourned greatly in proportion to his short life.

In 1885 Paulina birthed a healthy son named Martin, but tragically he died in a diphtheria epidemic at a little over three months of age. We did not have the doctor out, as we know from the experience of others that there is nothing to be done for it. The child will either live or die according to the will of God. It was a hard death, both for the babe and for those of us helplessly watching him struggle to breathe.

It had been difficult for August and Paulina when they lost the first babe born too soon, but to lose a healthy babe was almost more than they could endure. They collapsed into each other's arms and wept bitter tears when he breathed his last. Gottlieb and I tried to console the older children, and he then took them to the barn to help with chores while I washed and prepared the babe for burial.

The tombstone of Martin Otto, son of August and Paulina Otto, who died on July 29,1885, at three months and ten days old, features an angel kneeling in front of a little grave.

Our sorrow finally eased this January when Paulina was delivered of healthy twin boys, Robert and Paul. The whole family was overjoyed, as we felt those two little angels had been sent to replace the two boy babes that had been earlier lost. Our happiness ended two months later when the "strangling angel" of diphtheria struck again and carried off both within days. How that double loss affected us all! We could not even hold a funeral to mourn their short lives, as public gatherings were cancelled during the epidemic. Paulina just lay in her bed for days and cried from pure heartbreak, while August grew quiet and spent a great deal of time alone in the barn grieving. Despite my own sorrow, I went through the motions and took care of the other children and the house as best I could. After some days, Paulina finally rose up from her bed saying, "Both my breast milk and my faith in God have run dry." I tried to console her, "This sorrow too will pass. God is not through with you yet, as you are still young and He most surely has more babes waiting for you in heaven." I pray that my words do come true for her.

Much love,
Henrietta

This heartbreaking photo of twin babies sharing a small casket dates to about 1900.

December 31, 1892

Dear Sister,

Our family had a sad Christmas this year. As you know, August and Paulina had previously lost four infant boys. Paulina had about given up hope of having any more children, but they subsequently were blessed to have another son, Albert, now a plump and active two-year-old. How treasured he was by all of us, and how joyful we were when yet another son joined them last summer. However, tragedy struck again as their latest babe George died of influenza on Christmas Eve at six months. We are once again devastated by the large hole this tiny one's departure leaves in our lives. Poor Paulina has once more slipped into a deep depression, but I remind her that she is still of childbearing age and could have more children. It makes me weep to visit the cemetery and see the row of headstones on those five little graves.

Our oldest son, Carl, and his wife Emelia lost another daughter to influenza in 1889, although they were blessed with another son that same year, leaving them with nine living children. Our middle son, Henry, and his wife Friedricka now have ten children, and they are so thankful to have all of them surviving. So you see we must remember to rejoice in the many grandchildren that we have been given and not just mourn our losses.

We do, however, wish that we could see Carl's and Henry's children more often and know them as well as we do August's children. It involves a long journey for us to visit them or for them to visit us, and so we do not see them nearly as often as we would like. Since August and Paulina can manage the farm by themselves for a time, Gottlieb and I try to spend several weeks at their homes following the birth of each new babe, in order to help with the other children, the cooking and chores. As the babes keep on coming, we rejoice in these opportunities to remain connected with our other two sons and their families.

I have continued with my quilting in the evenings or sometimes in the daytime when I need to sit and rest a spell, as I am getting on in age. I have tried my best to make a small quilt for each new grand-babe, and there have been times when I had trouble even keeping up with those!

Love,
Henrietta

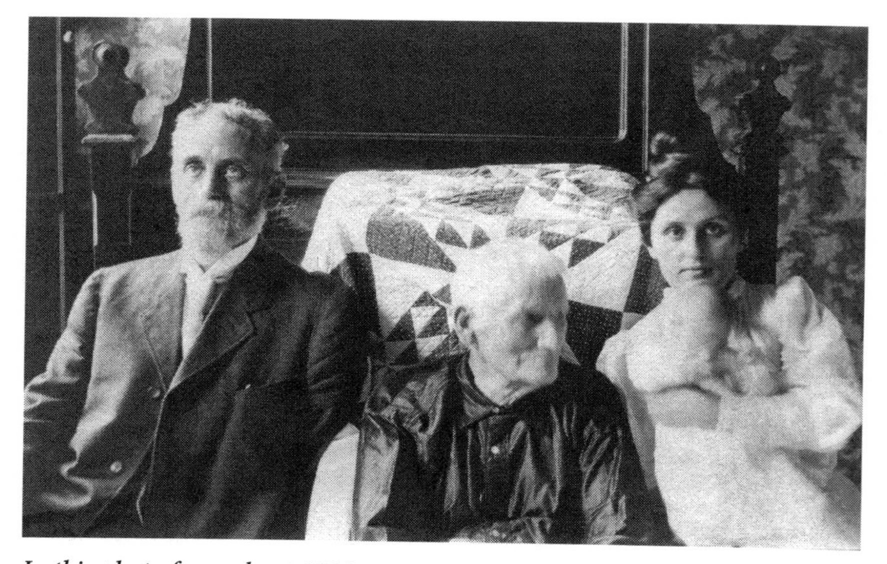

In this photo from about 1900 a woman is posed with her grandparents and baby (whose movement caused blurring). The "Birds in the Air" quilt proudly displayed on the bed behind them may have been made by the grandmother.

June 24, 1896

Dear Dorothea,

After putting my dear husband into the ground two weeks ago, I feel like an old woman, bearing the weight of widowhood. Gottlieb died at eighty-one years from the complications of old age. As we were married in Germany in 1844, we had over fifty years together, and it seems strange to wake in the morning and not find him next to me. But Gottlieb was through with the pain and suffering of this life and was ready to meet his Maker. I know that one day soon I will join him, both in my narrow coffin in our little Eden cemetery and also in heaven.

For now, I am thankful to be able to live with August and Paulina and their five children so that I am not so lonesome. Of course, I depend on them greatly, but I do what I can to earn my keep and not be a burden on them. Paulina was fortunate at the age of forty-six to give birth to another son in January, who is most likely my last grandchild. He is all the more cherished and treasured by August and Paulina for having lost five babes, and I believe their spirits are finally recovered and their faith in God restored.

Even though God saw fit to give me only three children, I have been greatly rewarded with many grandchildren. Carl had eleven children, with nine surviving; Henry had twelve children and lost but one; and August had ten children but with the loss of five infants has only five surviving. This means that I have twenty-five living grandchildren ranging in age from twenty-seven years to one month old. Even more than the all-important land that we have been able to acquire for our sons, I feel that these grandchildren are my most important blessing and legacy.

God be with you,
Henrietta

Large families were common about the turn of the century when this intriguing photo was taken of an unknown family with twelve children. With a high mortality rate, having many children ensured that at least some of them would survive to adulthood.

August 21, 1900

Dear Sister,

Forgive me for not writing for so long. Everything becomes more difficult as one becomes older. In recent years my eyesight has begun to fail me, and my joints and bones hurt all the time. I can barely write or do my quilting. As you know, I am an old woman of seventy-eight years, and you are not far behind me!

Gottlieb and I once made a brave journey with our young sons to a frontier area fraught with unknown dangers. Our dream was for them never to know hunger or want and that they might someday own land with which to support themselves and their families. Through the grace of Almighty God, all three of our sons are landowning farmers, and I understand that they are all considered to be wealthy men and leaders in their communities. Although I have missed you and the rest of our family, we have been greatly blessed beyond what we could have asked for or even imagined in our fondest dreams when we made that momentous decision to come to America those many years ago.

God be with you and bless you too,
Henrietta

June 6, 1905

Dear Aunt Dorothea,

I regret to inform you that my mother, Henrietta Wehrmeister Otto, passed away on May 20th of this year. She had slipped and fallen on the ice this spring, which resulted in a broken hip, and she had been confined to her bed since that time. Although my wife Paulina tenderly gave her the best of care, she never recovered from that injury. She was eighty-two years of age, but was still possessed of a good sound mind. All of our family will miss her greatly.

As I was only ten years old when we left Germany, I do not remember much of life there. Now, as an adult, I cannot imagine how difficult it was for my parents to leave everyone and everything behind to start over in a new country. Their only hope and dream was that their sons would have a better life and a better future because of it. My parents were possessed of great courage and were true pioneers. God bless their souls!

Your loving nephew,
August Otto

3

LOUISA'S STORY: A DIARY OF BLESSINGS AND LOSSES

This story is based on the life of Louisa Otto, the youngest daughter of my great-great-great-aunt, Albertina Stuewe Otto (also known as Sophia Otto in this book). I felt that the story of Sophia's family was not finished, and so Louisa picks up where her mother left off in Chapter 1. Louisa tells a coming-of-age story, which includes her surprising marriage. She shares her lifelong struggle to keep her faith alive as she cycles between extreme sorrows and great joys.

The young girl in this tintype photograph, circa 1870, has a lovely "Mona Lisa" smile.

DIARY OF LOUISA OTTO

October 1, 1870

Dear Diary,

I received this notebook for my twelfth birthday today, and I will use it to record my thoughts and feelings about the important events of my life. My name is Bertha Magdalena Louisa Otto, but everyone calls me Louisa. I was born on October 1, 1858, in Chicago, just one year after my family arrived in America. When I was two years old, we moved here to Nicollet County, Minnesota. My parents are Christoph and Sophia Otto. Besides being a farmer my father is the teacher for our church's school, but because there is as yet no schoolhouse, he teaches the children in our home.

I have four sisters, Augusta, Albertina, Hannah and Maria, and one brother, Frederick, all older than myself and all married except for Maria. I had another older brother Henry who died seven years ago in the Indian Wars. My earliest memory is of the Great Sioux Uprising that occurred when I was almost four years old. I remember hiding in a dark basement with many weeping women and terrified children, imagining that the frightful savages would burst in and kill us all. Upon returning to our farm after the uprising to find our house and barns still standing and our crops untouched, my family began weeping with relief. It was the first time I had seen my parents cry, and I could not have been more amazed if the trees had suddenly started to talk!

January 1, 1871

Dear Diary,

I am excited that Mother has promised to teach me to quilt this winter. It makes me feel quite grown up. When I was little and my mother and sisters were quilting, I loved to play with fabric scraps and pretend I was making quilts too. When I was six I stitched together little strips to make a quilt for my rag doll. After that I learned to hem towels and handkerchiefs and do mending, and now I am able to sew seams in clothing. Mother says I am old enough to help her and Maria make a special quilt for Maria's wedding, for she will be getting married next fall. But I have been warned by both that if I do not do my stitching well enough, I will have to take it out and do it over again! I do hope my quilting stitches will be up to their standards.

I have always enjoyed looking through the scrap basket and remembering what each fabric was left over from—this one a Sunday dress Mother made for me, this one a pinafore for Hannah, and so on. It seems that each scrap has its own story to tell. After our chores this morning, we brought out all the leftover fabrics, sorted them by colors, and looked through Mother's collection of quilt patterns and ideas that she has saved over the years. Maria chose a lovely star pattern and her favorite fabrics from the scrap basket for her wedding quilt. I can hardly wait for us to begin!

September 16, 1871

Dear Diary,

Something most dreadful has happened. My sister Hannah died yesterday from typhoid fever. I knew she was sickly ever since her babe Emma was born a few months ago, but I never thought she would die. I cannot believe that I will never again talk and laugh with her. Hannah was only twenty-three years old, and in addition to the new babe, she has another child Minnie who is eighteen months. Father explained that we don't always understand God's will and perhaps God wanted Hannah in heaven with Him. But do not her babes need her a great deal more? Because I have always been so close to my own mother, it makes me weep to think that her poor babes will grow up without a mother to love them.

Hannah's husband, Christian Stolt, brought the little ones to our house for my mother to care for, but they keep crying for their own mother. The babe refuses to drink cow's milk from a bottle, so Mother is taking her to a neighbor woman who is weaning her own babe, and hopefully she will be able to nurse Emma for a few months.

Losing Hannah brought back memories of my brother Henry's death when I was a child of five. At his funeral the preacher said Henry was in heaven with Jesus, but it was most confusing to me, as I could see his body in the pine coffin at the front of the church. I was purely puzzled how he could be in two places at once, or as I looked around the church, were we now also in heaven?

My dear mother is quite despondent, as this is the fourth of nine children she has lost, two as babes and two as adults. My father pretends to be stronger, but I noticed that his eyes were quite red when he came in from the barn last night after doing the milking. I wish people did not have to die until they were very old. It is so unfair to be taken away before having had a chance to live out one's life. Our house is filled with sadness and tears, and the tears are not only from Hannah's babes.

The little girls in this tintype photograph, circa 1870, appear to be about the ages of Hannah's daughters in this story.

October 28, 1871

Dear Diary,

In the midst of our mourning for Hannah, we have something happy to celebrate. My dearest sister Maria was married this morning to Albert Mattke, and we had a big celebration dinner here after the wedding. Mother, Maria and I have been cooking and baking for days and others brought food too. Everyone had a fine time and stayed until they needed to go home for the evening chores. When Hannah died a few weeks ago, Maria and Albert considered postponing their wedding. Father, however, insisted that life is for the living and that Hannah would not have wanted to spoil their wedding day.

Maria is quite pleased to be married, but I will miss her and it will be lonely here on the farm with only Father, Mother and myself. I sometimes shirked my work and let Maria do it because I wanted to play, but I will need to be more responsible now. It must have seemed strange for Maria to go home with Albert and to be sleeping in his bed in their new home, rather than sharing a bed with me as we have always done.

My body is changing and my dresses are becoming too tight in the bodice. When I began to bleed a few weeks ago, I was in fear that I was afflicted with some terrible disease and was dying. I did not want to tell Mother as she has not yet recovered from losing Hannah. However, she saw my soiled drawers when doing laundry and explained that I am turning from a girl to a woman. I find that a bit frightening. I wish I could just stay a child forever and not have to take up the burdens of being a grown-up woman.

Last year our little Trinity Lutheran Church hired its first pastor. After seven members left the church in protest within his first year, he was finally defrocked. I know only that he was described as a "wolf rather than a shepherd" and that his teaching was termed unscriptural and his walk of life offensive. I am still considered to be a child, so no one will tell me what he actually did to earn such contempt, but it must have been very bad!

November 17, 1871

Dear Diary,

My first cousin August Otto, the son of my father's brother Carl Otto, has arrived from Germany. He is nineteen years old, has dark auburn hair, and is very handsome! He will be living with us and working for Father and my brother, Frederick, for a time to earn enough money to start life on his own. Father is happy for help with the farm as he is getting older and also has his teaching work. I had hoped that August would be like a brother to me, since he is only six years older than I am, and my own two brothers were already grown before I was even born. But all he has done thus far is talk to Mother and Father about the family back in Germany and ask them questions about life in America. I imagine if he can leave his home and travel all the way across the vast ocean and this country by himself, then surely he is a man fully grown. So what use has he of a thirteen-year-old girl like me?

This unidentified handsome young man sat for his tintype photograph in about 1870.

Mother and I have finally finished stitching the quilt that we made for Maria's wedding. Because of Hannah's death and the extra work of caring for her babes until other arrangements could be made, we did not have time to complete the quilt before the wedding. It has turned out to be quite beautiful, and I am ever so proud that I helped make it. I only needed to take out a few of my stitches and do them over!

April 18, 1872

Dear Diary,

My cousin August has started to treat me more like a little sister, although we both feel a bit shy around each other. I love to listen to his stories about his family and life in Germany. He sometimes pulls my braids as he walks by and then feigns innocence. Yesterday we had a footrace to the barn and I won by just a hair. But I think he did not try his hardest in order to let me win. That shows he thinks me still a child, but also that he is a kind person.

We had much snow and bitter cold weather this long winter and could not even go to church many Sundays. That is often the only occasion I have to see other girls my age, since I am finished with schooling. I notice that some older girls like to hang around August, whispering and giggling and making sheep eyes at him. However, he does not seem to favor any one girl over the others. I surely hope that he does not marry too soon, as my life would be most lonely without him on the farm.

Mother and I completed another quilt over the long cold winter, but as much as we both love quilting, even that felt tedious after a while in our melancholy mood. But today the sun is shining and we saw our first robin, so spring cannot be far behind.

June 12, 1873

Dear Diary,

My cousin August and I have become great friends over the past year. We often work together in the garden, tending the animals or doing chores. He continues to tell me stories about his boyhood days in Germany and his voyage to America. We both love to read whatever books or newspapers we can put our hands on and spend hours discussing them. August has taught me to play checkers, and I do so enjoy a game in the evening, although he can almost always best me. He sorely misses his family, and he has written to encourage them to join us in this New World.

I baked a beautiful strawberry pie today, and when August tasted it he teased me that I would make some lucky man a fine wife someday. I do not know why I blushed so hard, as I am still but fourteen years and will not be marrying for some time. In fact, since I am the only one in our family not married, the duty of caring for Mother and Father in their old age may fall to me. I might not be able to wed until they have passed on and I am quite old myself.

October 5, 1873

Dear Diary,

The most amazing thing has happened! Last night August and I were outside sitting on the stoop to catch the evening breeze after a warm fall day, listening to the music of the crickets. I had leaned against him, and he rested his arm across my shoulders. I turned my head towards him to say something and he kissed me on the lips! He whispered that he had wanted to do that for some time. It quite took my breath and speech away! But then he apologized for kissing me, as we are first cousins, and told me to run off to bed. I could not sleep all night for thinking about it, and today I cannot meet his eye.

At church and social events I see how the older girls smile and talk so sweet to August, but he has never courted any of them. They are much closer to his age and several of them are quite attractive. Why would he kiss a plain fifteen-year-old girl who is his own cousin instead of one of them? My thoughts are quite in a jumble, and I am not sure what I am feeling—mostly puzzlement, I believe.

April 16, 1874

Dear Diary,

August and I sometimes steal secret kisses and hugs when we are alone. It feels so good to have his arms around me and to rest my cheek against his chest and smell the scent of him. We have discussed whether it could be sinful for cousins to kiss, but it feels so wonderful. Last night after supper Mother and I were piecing quilt blocks while Father was reading to us from the Bible. He read the story of how Jacob married Leah and Rachel, who were the daughters of his mother's brother. Fortunately, Father and Mother did not see the smile that August gave me when we both realized at the same moment that they were first cousins!

Sometimes I can think of nothing but August all day and night, and I imagine we exist in our own little world. When I try to look ahead into the future it is dark and empty, and I cannot imagine whatever will happen next in our lives. August is almost twenty-two, and it is sick-making to think he may soon have enough money saved to buy a farm of his own. I expect that he will then choose one of the young women his own age to marry. I will miss him something fierce when he leaves, and I will be quite jealous of his wife. I find myself wishing that nothing would ever change and that this happy time might go on forever.

October 1, 1874

Dear Diary,

Today is my sixteenth birthday and the happiest day of my life! Mother baked my favorite cake for dessert, and Father told the story of how I was born when they first lived in Chicago. But the most amazing thing happened after the dishes were washed and August asked me to walk with him to the meadow. Once we were well away from the house, he took me in his arms and asked if I would be his wife. Since I was now sixteen years of age, August felt he could honorably ask Father for my hand in marriage. Of course I said yes!

We ran all the way back to the house and burst in, surprising my parents. August told them that we wished to wed if they would give us their blessing and if it is permitted for first cousins to marry. Mother laughed, "We both knew from watching you that this day was coming." Father told us, "In Germany marriage between first cousins does happen, since in small rural villages there are not many single people from whom to choose a marriage partner. Sometimes it is preferable to marry a cousin rather than a stranger, as at least one knows the person comes from a good family!" Mother told August that they already love him like a son, but that they would ask us to wait a year until I am seventeen before we wed. We both happily agreed, and Father brought out his whiskey bottle, ordinarily used only for medicinal purposes, so that he and August could have a small drink to seal their agreement. Oh, I am so happy! I feel besotted with love. I know I will not sleep a wink this night!

November 25, 1874

Dear Diary,

This summer our church finally purchased a log cabin to use for a schoolhouse, so Father no longer has to hold classes in our parlor. Now that Mother and I are not helping him with the schoolchildren, we have more time to quilt. How excited I was last week when Mother suggested that we begin sewing a wedding quilt for myself and August. We settled on a rather elaborate pattern called "Carpenter's Wheel," but did not have enough scrap fabrics to make all the blocks the same. Mother decided since this is a very special quilt and much work will go into it, we should buy the fabrics—something we have never done before!

When we went to town yesterday to do our marketing, we chose fabrics of red, green and cheddar yellow that we will use on a bleached muslin background. The woman at the dry goods store remarked that this color scheme is very popular right now. She explained that it is impossible to obtain a colorfast green dye from plants or minerals. This green fabric is an over-dyed green, meaning that it is dyed with both blue and yellow, one over the other. Both are quite colorfast, although over time one color may fade faster than the other.

I have helped Mother make quilts before, but it is ever so exciting to know that this quilt will be for my marriage bed. It gives me a strange feeling in my stomach to think of sleeping beside August, as so far we have done nothing more than kiss, and I do not know much of what goes on between a man and wife. Of course, living on a farm I have seen animals mate, but that always looks quite disgusting. Surely marriage must be better than that or else no one would ever marry and the human race would soon disappear. When I asked my sister Maria to tell me about the private things of marriage, she demurred, saying that it is Mother's place to explain it before my wedding night.

February 15, 1875

Dear Diary,

What wonderful news! August received a letter today from his father saying that the rest of their family will be coming to America from Germany this spring. There have been crop failures and economic woes in recent years and their second son Carl will soon be drafted into the Prussian Army if they remain. Since I was born in this country, I have never met my uncle, aunt or cousins, and I am so looking forward to it, especially as I will also be marrying into their family.

Our Carpenter's Wheel quilt is coming along nicely, although it is proving to be more challenging than we had thought because of all the set-in seams. We will soon begin quilting it so that it will be finished when August and I marry in the fall. I still cannot believe that this handsome man has chosen to spend the rest of his life with me when he could have chosen from among many older and prettier girls from the neighboring farms and towns. I praise God for this miracle every night when I kneel down and say my bedtime prayers.

***CARPENTER'S WHEEL QUILT:** Antique quilt from the collection of Lanie Tiffenbach, done in Turkey red, over-dyed green and cheddar yellow on a muslin background. Hand-pieced and densely hand-quilted. Maker unknown. Estimated date 1850–1880.*

May 14, 1875

Dear Diary,

August's family arrived from Germany two days ago, and what a joyful reunion they had with him after four long years apart. August had written to them that we are to be wed. I did so worry that they would not approve of me, but my fears were for naught. Uncle Carl bears a striking resemblance to Father and so he felt familiar at once. Aunt Albertina is a dear person and immediately expressed her pleasure at having me for a future daughter-in-law.

The boys Carl and Albert, nineteen and eleven years, resemble August and have his mannerisms. I can see how they look up to him with all his experience in this new country. Carl has auburn hair like August, but Albert has flaming orange hair. I adore my two girl cousins, Friederike, at seventeen a little older than I, and Mathilda, at fourteen a few years younger. It seems strange that we are first cousins and have not met before, but what fun we are having getting to know each other! The two of them are sharing my bed, and last night we talked into the wee hours. Their family is staying with us for a few weeks until they determine where to settle, which I hope will be nearby.

July 30, 1875

Dear Diary,

We have suffered a major calamity, just when we were so happy. A plague of grasshoppers or locusts dropped from the sky above us, exactly like one of the ten deadly plagues that God visited upon the ancient Egyptians in the Bible. They relentlessly stripped the fields and every blade of grass and all the leaves from the trees, and they left everything as bare as January. The dreadful disgusting creatures were so thick on the ground that one could not walk outside without them crackling under one's feet. When they got inside the house, we had to be sure to destroy them before they chewed holes in our clothing or bedding. After a time our well water, the eggs our chickens laid, and even the milk from the cows tasted of those horrible hoppers. By the time they flew off in search of greener pastures, they had laid waste to our farm.

We are all terribly discouraged that our hard work has been for naught, and there will be little food for us or the animals to sustain us over the next year. Father believes this is a test of our faith, and we must trust in God to provide for us. As he is wont to do, Father quoted Scripture: "Man does not live by bread alone, but by every word that proceeds out of the mouth of God." It must be sinful, but when he said that I got an amusing image in my head of our family sitting around the table, chewing on pages out of the Bible because we had run out of bread. Of course, I did not dare tell Father that!

November 7, 1875

Dear Diary,

I cannot believe I am a married woman! Yesterday morning August and I were wed at Trinity Lutheran Church in Nicollet, with our family and friends present. I am seventeen and August is twenty-three years of age. We had hoped to be married after my birthday a month ago, but it is customary to hold weddings after the harvest is completed and farm families can take time off from their work. Following the ceremony everyone came to our farm for a noontime feast and afternoon celebration, bringing us gifts with which to start our own home.

Since August has worked on our farm for four years, Father has come to depend on him greatly. August searched for a farm to buy but found that he did not yet have enough money saved. Father asked if we would remain with them a while longer, and he will continue to pay wages to August. Perhaps in a year or two we will be ready to start off on our own. I am glad that things do not have to change too quickly, as it would be hard for me to be separated from Father and Mother.

This tintype photograph of an attractive young couple was most likely a wedding portrait. The woman's dress and hairstyle date it to about 1875.

It feels so right and good to be married to August, but it did seem quite strange last night when he followed me up the stairs and into my bedroom. I will not write here of what is sacred between a man and a woman, but I feel like I have joined a secret sisterhood of married women everywhere. The strange thing is that, as Louisa Otto married to August Otto, my married name is the same as my maiden name! Or, using both names as women often do, would Louisa Otto Otto now be my married name?

February 12, 1876

Dear Diary,

I am going to be a mother! I sensed that the very first time I lay with August on our wedding night, I fell with child. I have been very tired and sickly for the past three months, but am feeling better now. My belly is beginning to swell and our babe should be born at the beginning of August. Mother and I are working on a small quilt, and when that is finished we will sew little gowns and diapers from flannel. I am having mixed feelings about having a child so soon, as I am still getting used to being a married woman. I am quite fearful of the ordeal of birthing a child, yet I do so want to have children of my own.

August 25, 1876

Dear Diary,

My heart has been too heavy to write and my mind feels dull, like it is wrapped in a white flannel shroud just like our poor little Mina. She was born too early on July 10th and was ever so tiny and frail. I prayed constantly for her, but she just grew weaker. Only three weeks was she with us, yet she left such a large empty space in our lives. Mother helped me wash her and wrap her in a flannel shroud, and I then wrapped her in the beautiful quilt that Mother and I had made for her. I know it sounds foolish, but it was a small comfort to know that she was enfolded with warmth and love in her little pine coffin in the ground.

I have been so very amazed at and overcome by the fierce love that I felt for this tiny mewling bit of a being who caused me such pain in her birthing and made such demands upon my body and time and sleep. I sometimes think that this must be the kind of love that our Heavenly Father feels for us poor wretched human beings in spite of our many failures and misdeeds. I take some small comfort that my precious little babe is safe in heaven in the arms of Jesus.

In a tastefully posed post-mortem portrait, circa 1880, a baby wearing a crucifix and medal and perhaps its christening gown appears to be peacefully sleeping. In the late 1800s and early 1900s a portrait was often made of a deceased child as a remembrance.

Again this summer we were visited by the hordes of grasshoppers that wrought such devastation on our crops last year. What loathsome creatures they are! They once again devoured every bit of green in sight, destroying in days what it had taken us months of work to grow. Even August broke down and wept at the sight. I could scarcely deal with this calamity on top of birthing and losing our babe. I feel like everything goes in cycles. When August came to stay with our family, we were so happy and everything seemed so wonderful to me. Now I feel like we are caught up in a cycle of calamity. How will we endure it and when will it end?

September 30, 1877

Dear Diary,

I bore a beautiful girl child early this month. She is thriving, and I am recovered in body and spirit. We named the babe Hannah for my dear sister who died a few years ago. It was a much more difficult birth than my first time, with tiny Mina. This time I felt as though my spine would crack and my body would rip apart. I could not believe there could be such pain without damage or death to either or both of us. August sent for the midwife to attend to me along with Mother as soon as I went into labor. It seemed impossible that such pain could go on and on as it did for almost twenty-four hours. At first I was terrified that I would die, but later I almost wished for death as a release from the eternity of pain. Eventually our babe Hannah was born whole and healthy. I have such love for this little mite, but I cannot imagine ever going through such pure agony again.

I feel that our cycle of calamity has finally ended. This spring our state set aside a special day for fasting and prayer to beg God's mercy in removing the terrible scourge of grasshoppers. He did indeed send a miracle to save us, in the form of ice and snow that destroyed many of the grasshoppers just when they were hatching. The ones that remained did not do much damage before God commanded them to leave and they flew away. I truly believe that things have turned to the good again.

November 6, 1878

Dear Diary,

Today August and I have been married for three years. This fall we bought our own farm in Eden Township, Brown County, near to where August's parents live, and we are getting settled into our new life. Our little Hannah is past a year old and is walking already. What a joy she is to us! Although I have much more work to do, when the babe is napping in the afternoons, I take a little time to myself to sit down and quilt. In the midst of a busy day, I find that quilting soothes the mind and feeds the soul.

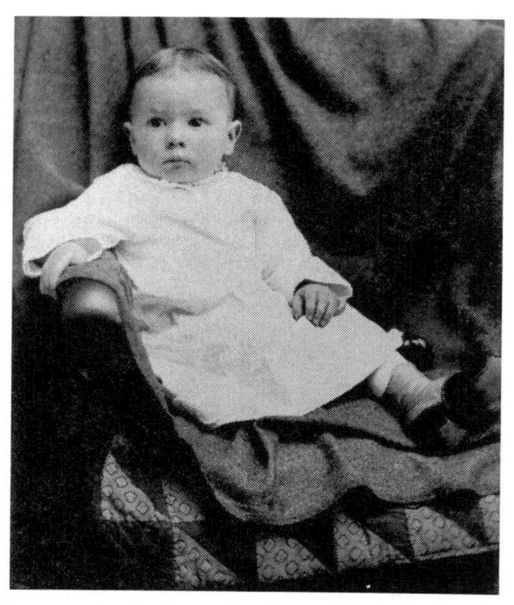

A sweet baby girl is posed on a plain blanket with a patchwork quilt peeking out beneath it in this tintype photo from around 1875.

September 22, 1879

Dear Diary,

I will write while my two little ones are napping. I birthed another girl babe three weeks ago, named Albertina but called Tina. Praise God, she is healthy and growing, as is two-year-old Hannah. I finished the babe's quilt only days before she came into this world. I think of myself as a fairly brave person. However, when giving birth I cannot help but cry out like a stuck pig! Although the pain of birthing is such hard physical pain, it is soon forgotten in the joy of a new child. I look at these two perfectly formed beings that somehow miraculously came out of my body, and I wonder is there any greater gift than being a mother?

March 29, 1880

Dear Diary,

The time of darkness has come upon us again, and I am so dreadfully frightened. A terrible diphtheria epidemic has hit our area and three of my sister Albertina Schwandt's nine children have died in the past week: Frank at four years, Lebrecht three years, and Bertha twenty months. The difficult thing is that no one knows how to treat or cure this devastating disease. Julius insisted on fetching the doctor from New Ulm, even though he admitted that he could do nothing to save the children. Father and the other men in our family built the little coffins and dug the graves in the church cemetery. We could not even hold a funeral service for the poor babes, as no one leaves their home unless absolutely necessary for fear of spreading the contagion.

As I had done when my little Mina died, Albertina wrapped her children for their burials with the cradle quilts that our mother had made for each of her grandchildren. How they had loved those quilts! They were really the only thing each child had that was truly theirs alone, as clothing was passed from child to child, and the few toys they had, such as wooden blocks and cornhusk dolls, had to be shared.

I have been so fearful for our two babes, but I praise God that he has thus far spared their lives. I cannot imagine how poor Albertina finds the will to go on living after losing three babes at once, and I fear I would not be as strong in her place. She says the only way she can bear it is to imagine her children embraced in the arms of Jesus in green pastures by still waters. She told our mother that she wishes to just take to her bed and pull the quilts over her head. However, there is much work to be done and the other children to care for, including her newborn Maria who cries to be nursed every few hours. Our dear father, ever the teacher, reminds her that God has left her with six other children and as she is still in her childbearing years, she may well be given more.

July 20, 1881

Dear Diary,

Another child has blessed us, a son named Paul, and August was ever so proud to finally have a male heir. Please, Lord, let this be the last one I have to birth! Now that we have our boy, I never want to go through that torturous pain again.

The babe was not strong at first, but he is a month old now and we feel assured that he will live. Our daughters seem to think he is somewhat of a doll or plaything. Hannah, who is almost four, wants to help me with everything, although she has to stand on a stool with a dishtowel tied around her to stir the pot or dry the dishes.

Three adorable children pose in front of a crazy quilt in this studio photograph from around the turn of the century. Crazy quilts were all the rage from about 1880 to 1910.

Since we bought this farm, we have attended informal worship services at various neighbors' homes. This past June my husband August, his father, brother, and other relatives and neighbors formally organized

Immanuel Lutheran Church of Eden Township. A church building is being erected, and we are being served by the pastor from Sleepy Eye. I am pleased to say that the first baptism performed was for our own babe Paul.

My father, Christoph Otto, has retired from teaching school, as it was becoming too difficult for him. He has reached the advanced age of sixty-nine years, having taught at our church's school for the past fourteen years. My brother Frederick has been working Father's farm, in addition to his own, ever since August and I moved away from there. Father and Mother continue to live on the homestead. I get lonesome for them and they love seeing the children, so we often take a trip with the horses and wagon to visit them on a Sunday afternoon.

September 16, 1881

Dear Diary,

We seem to be caught up in a constant cycle of blessing and loss. Tragedy always seems to be lurking just around the corner whenever things are going well, and it has once again struck our family. My eldest sister, Augusta Wicherski, died yesterday of influenza at forty-three years. She leaves motherless her four children: Emil, thirteen; Ernest, eleven; and the twins Otto and Olga, age five.

Why does everyone I love have to die? Poor Mother and Father! This is the third adult child they have lost and they are quite overcome with sorrow. It goes against the order of nature that a parent should outlive their children, and death is not as much expected once they are past the dangers of childhood. I just do not understand death at all. One day you are alive and walking and talking, and the next day your soul flies from your body and everything you had been just vanishes. Who can fathom a mystery as deep as that?

November 27, 1883

Dear Diary,

We had another girl babe born last month whom we named Bertha, which is actually my first given name. When I am in childbirth and feeling like I am being torn apart, soaked in sweat, afraid of dying, and purely worn out from pain, I regret ever marrying and wish I had remained a spinster! But when I am handed the tiny babe, all is forgotten in the fierce love I feel for that little bit of life. I guess the good Lord in his wisdom makes us forget just how dreadful the birthing is or else no woman would have more than one child and mankind would soon die off.

Our two older girls at six and four are a great help with minding little Paul and doing the dishes, but four children under the age of six do keep one busy. I cannot find time these days for my quilting pleasures, and I do so miss that. But I imagine I will have time enough to quilt when my children are grown and I am old. For now I must treasure their baby years and the joy they bring to me.

August 22, 1884

Dear Diary,

The dark days are here again. I cannot believe that I have lost yet another sibling, and it has quite knocked the wind out of me. My sister Maria, who has always been my dearest friend, died yesterday in child-birth and the babe with her. She labored so long and so hard for two days and nights. The little one was finally born backward and already dead. Poor Maria bled so heavily that she bled her life away. The fear of every woman since Eve who has fallen with child is that either she or the babe or both will die in childbed. Maria was but thirty-three years old, leaving behind her husband Albert Mattke and two children, Theodore, age thirteen, and Lydia, not yet two years.

I have now lost four adult siblings, and only Albertina and Frederick are left. I know that the Lord giveth and the Lord taketh away (Blessed be the name of the Lord!), but why, oh why, is He taking so many from my family? Mother has become quite hysterical with grief and has taken to her bed. My dear father, in spite of his own losses, reminds us that we are not alone in our suffering, as our Lord himself suffered too.

I find that I have fallen with child again, and with my sister just dying in childbed, I am in great terror that I too will die with this next babe. I cannot bear the thought of leaving my other children bereft and motherless, and so I do my best to claw my way out of the depths of despair, hand over hand, keeping occupied with daily tasks and reciting Bible passages to calm my soul. Oh Lord, save me from this fate for the sake of my dear children, and please, Lord, let this one be my last!

June 8, 1885

Dear Diary,

Life follows on the heels of death. Last December our newest babe Emil was born, and he is a plump and loud child, demanding constant feeding. I can scarce keep up with his needs, as well as tending to my other four children, preparing meals, and household chores. The laundry is never ending with two babes in diapers. They need to be changed every hour or two to keep their clothing and bedding, or the lap they are sitting on, from getting soaked. When the weather is cold or rainy, I have wash lines strung across my kitchen with diapers drying day and night to keep up. How I would love to return to my quilting, but even more I would love to sleep the whole night through or take an afternoon nap. But I must not complain, as the sun is shining and life feels sweet again.

My parents are getting quite elderly and frail, and they can no longer live alone. They have moved in with my sister Albertina, her husband Julius and their eight children. (God did indeed send two more babes after the three were lost to diphtheria in 1880.) Father often seems to be confused or forgetful and needs to have things repeated over and over to him. Mother denies there is anything amiss and tries to protect his dignity by calming him and speaking for him. It is quite difficult to see my father like this, as he was always such an intelligent and learned man.

August 26, 1886

Dear Diary,

I have fallen once more into the depths of darkness, and although I have been in dark places before, there is no place darker than the death of a child. Our oldest daughter Hannah passed away a month ago at eight years of age. She was in great pain, and we took her to the doctor in New Ulm, who diagnosed a kidney complaint but could not save her. I know it must be a grievous sin, and I dare not confide this even to August, but I am most angry at God right now. I have lost one brother and three sisters, all long before their expected time. It was difficult enough when our first babe Mina died, but to lose a sweet bright eight-year-old is too terrible to bear. How God can allow the deaths of innocent little ones is beyond my understanding, and I find myself unable to pray or worship God because I am so angry. I have even had the blasphemous thought that perhaps there is no God. I do hope that with time I will be able to let go of this fierce anger within me and be reconciled to the God I once knew and loved.

In the past when I was feeling low, I could always depend on Father to uplift my spirits with his kind and gentle words of wisdom and comfort. Now I do not have that, as he seems to have withdrawn completely into a world of his own. He was such a caring and kind man, intelligent and wise, with a vast knowledge of many subjects. Now he has become cranky and difficult to get along with, sometimes throwing violent fits.

He speaks of long ago events, but cannot seem to remember that he just ate his dinner or how to find the privy. The exertions of caregiving have begun to wear on Mother and on my sister Albertina and her family, with whom my parents are living, but there is no other sustenance available for the elderly. For those truly without blood relations, there is the unpleasant prospect of the County Poor Farm, or for those who are completely crazed and dangerous, there is the State Insane Asylum, neither of which bears thinking about. Lord, help us all!

An unidentified older couple posed for a carte de visite photograph in about 1880.

July 7, 1887

Dear Diary,

I birthed another fine boy babe in May, whom we named August after my husband. I admit that I still feel angry with God for allowing my sweet Hannah to die last year, but at the same time I feel that little August is meant to be some compensation for her loss. Besides, how can I marvel at the perfection of this child that came forth out of my body and yet think there is no God or that he is not loving? I am determined not to wallow in my sadness, but rather to be the best mother that I can to the five children that I have been graced with.

I feel as if I have quite lost my father. Dementia has taken his memory so that he has turned quite childish in his behavior and, indeed, requires the same care as a child. He had always loved to read his Bible, but now he cannot make sense of the words. It frustrates and angers him so much that he shouts and throws things. He alarms us when he can no longer remember common everyday things or when he wanders into the fields or down the road at any time during the day or night. His condition is gradually deteriorating, and it is getting more difficult for Mother, as she is not well herself. We have mentioned the possibility that he may need to be committed to the State Insane Asylum, but Mother will hear none of it. She insists that she married him for better or for worse and will continue in her duty to him as long as they both shall live. God help them both!

December 31, 1888

Dear Diary,

The person on this earth that I have known the longest (even before I was born) is gone. My dear mother, Sophia Otto, passed away on December 27th at the age of seventy-three years. Though I am filled with grief and it has been a sad time for our family, I realized that I am no longer angry with God as I was three years ago when our dear Hannah died. I expect my heart has thawed out bit by bit, the way the frozen ground gradually warms up after a cold winter. While I am feeling her loss greatly, she had been unwell and in pain, and I would not wish her to continue suffering. I truly feel that Mother lived a good life and that she has gone to her great reward in heaven. I know I have been greatly blessed, both to have been my mother's daughter and also to be a mother myself. I did not fully understand just how much my mother loved me until I had children of my own.

But even more difficult has been the care of Father. He does not seem to remember that Mother has passed and continues to call for her. He cannot care for himself, yet he does not want anyone else helping him. He is prone to violent fits, to wandering, and to taking off his clothing at the oddest times. Albertina and Julius can no longer care for Father, as they are kept busy with their farming work and their eight children. Yesterday we were forced to do the unthinkable and commit him to the Minnesota State Insane Asylum in St. Peter. It is a terribly sad and frightening place, but thankfully Father does not seem to know where he is any longer, and the people who work there seem to be capable and kind. May God watch over him!

September 12, 1889

Dear Diary,

I have been remiss in writing, as there are never enough hours in a day to do what needs to be done just to get through that day. I realized that I never recorded the birth of our latest child, Martha, born in April. Thankfully, she is a good and content babe and does not cry at all when attended to in a timely way.

Yesterday my dear father, Christoph Otto, passed over into the heavenly realm, being seventy-seven years of age. Unlike the anger and despair that I felt at the deaths of my sisters and daughters, I feel only a grateful sense of relief that Father is no longer locked away in the State Insane Asylum. I imagine him in heaven, once more gentle, wise and loving, as he was in years past before his affliction robbed him of his senses. It brings me a great feeling of peace to know that he is reunited with our mother and our dear ones who have gone on ahead.

A few members of our Immanuel Lutheran Church, including my husband August, his brother Carl, and their two sisters' husbands, are working to organize a "daughter" congregation in the town of Morgan. Our little country church is overflowing on Sunday mornings, and we also wish to serve those members who live in town. The new church is to be called Zion Lutheran and will begin holding services in January. This is the fourth church that members of our Otto family have been instrumental in founding in this country. What an honor and blessing!

March 8, 1891

Dear Diary,

Two weeks ago, in the midst of a terrible winter blizzard, I felt the familiar cramping telling me that my latest child was ready to leave the confines of my womb. I had an uneasy feeling in both my mind and belly all day, but I did not expect the babe to arrive for a few more weeks. I finished my evening chores and put the children to bed, all the while hoping the babe was not truly coming. The storm had been going on for two days and nights, and the wind was whipping the snow near to blinding and piling it into high drifts. I could not possibly send August out for a midwife or neighbor woman for fear he would become lost in the storm and freeze to death.

When the pains came on harder, I told August that the babe was arriving and he would need to help me. He went quite white with fear and said he did not know if he could manage it. But I told him that I had done this eight times before and would tell him just what to do. He is a farmer and has helped in the birthing of his livestock and how different could it be? I was glad that the children were asleep, and I held a knotted rag between my teeth so as not to awaken them with my cries.

After a long night of labor, our little Mary was born just before sunrise, with August and myself managing quite nicely to do what was necessary. When it was over, August declared himself to be purely worn out and exhausted from lack of sleep and worry! After the other children woke to the surprise of a new sister, he crawled into one of their beds to sleep. I do not have time to write more now, as baby is crying.

March 2, 1893

Dear Diary,

It seems that I record little but births and deaths. Our newest son George was born in January, the tenth child I have birthed, with eight still living. I am barely through nursing the latest one before I immediately fall with child again. I love my children but I have borne enough, and I wish I knew some way to keep from having more. Tina and Bertha, ages thirteen and nine, are ever so much help with the younger ones and the housework and cooking, and Paul at eleven has proven to be a good little worker alongside his father.

This photo from about 1880 shows a woman with seven children spaced at regular intervals. As women had little or no knowledge of birth control methods in earlier times, it was not unusual for them to have a child every year or two.

Last fall after harvest August declared that he was tired of farming and wanted to turn his hand to something else. The local wagon maker had just passed away, and August was able to buy the building and supplies from his widow for a reasonable sum. We therefore sold our farm and purchased a house in the nearby town of Morgan.

I was quite concerned and argued against making such an abrupt change in our lives and livelihood. We have eight children to feed and raise, the oldest being fourteen. I am thirty-four years old and, given my fertility, there may be more children yet to come. How will we feed and clothe our children if this business does not prove to be worth the risk? August, however, was determined to take the opportunity presented, and he firmly believes that he will be successful at his new craft. On a positive note, I do know I will enjoy living in town and not being as isolated as on a farm.

Without all the farm chores to be done, I hope to have time to return to my quilting, which I had once so loved doing. In recent years I have had time only to make simple utilitarian quilts for our family. I prefer the more creative process of piecing the quilt top, where I can choose colors and designs and create something original and truly mine. But of course that takes much more time and patience and energy, all of which have been in short supply for some years past!

January 27, 1895

Dear Diary,

August and I have been blessed with yet another son, William, born last month. All my children are precious to me, and I do not regret having many children, but I am getting worn down with the constant child-bearing and child-rearing. There is a saying that a woman loses a tooth for every child, and my mouth is proving the truth of it! But as women we submit to our husbands and to God's will, and we persevere through whatever hardships life holds for us. We know that family is what matters most in life. When I married August, I expected our lives would be filled with hopes, goals, and accomplishments, but I have found that so much of life is just getting through each day with its chores and routines.

Thankfully, August has been successful in his new livelihood as a wagon maker and his business is prospering. I am so enjoying living in the village of Morgan. Even though I have a large family to care for, I have less work than I had on the farm. I have returned to the joy of piecing quilt blocks from my overflowing scrap basket when I sit down to rest at the end of the day.

December 10, 1896

Dear Diary,

I am in the depths of despair. Tragedy has sought us out in our happiness, and death has visited our home once again. Our dear daughter Bertha is gone at age thirteen, just as I was beginning to glimpse the woman she would become. She had always been frail and tired easily, and the doctor said that she died of heart disease. Although she passed a month ago, I have been too despondent to write. While it is hard to believe that a loving God would take three of my young daughters from me, yet I will surely go mad if I do not believe that they are safe and happy in a better world.

Bertha was always such a "little mother" to her six younger siblings, helping them dress and eat and making up games to play with them. They miss her so and continue to ask for her, and it quite breaks my heart. I have had days where I just want to lie down and die from pure grief. If it were not for my eight living children that need me, I would wish to go where my three dead ones have gone. I console myself that although this world is a vale of tears, the next will be a paradise.

May 31, 1898

Dear Diary,

This month I bore my twelfth child, a well-formed son whom we named Erwin. As I am nearly forty years old, he may well be my last child, or perhaps I am just hoping that! As always, when I was in childbirth I thought that there was no greater pain that a woman could bear and still live. But after losing three children, I know very well that the pain of bringing a child into this world is nothing compared to the pain of seeing a child out of this world.

I have had much experience with death, but still it remains the greatest mystery to me. Strangely enough, we somehow feel that death will never come for us, even though common sense tells us that it most certainly will. And while we fear death as the end of life, yet still we believe that it will be the beginning of a far better life in heaven. What mysteries!

September 15, 1900

Dear Diary,

We have changed our church membership to St. John's Lutheran Church in Morgan, as it is more convenient for us. I am quite excited that it has a "sewing society" where twice monthly a group of women meet to work on quilts. Now that I am finally neither carrying nor nursing a child, I am able to leave the older children in charge of the younger ones and join in the quilting fun.

Sometimes we each bring our own hand-piecing to the sewing society, and at other times we all gather around a quilting frame and help a member hand-stitch her quilt. We share quilt patterns, techniques and fabric, and the beginning quilters learn from the more experienced quilters. I do not know which I enjoy more, finally being able to return to my quilting or having the close friendship of other women with whom to share the joys and sorrows of life. There is something so very special about women friends, as they can understand and relate to another woman in a way that even one's husband or children cannot do.

Colorful advertising trade cards, such as these for the Willimantic Thread Company and Milward's Helix Needles, became prized and highly collectible in the late 1800s.

June 1, 1902

Dear Diary,

Our oldest daughter Tina was married last November at the age of twenty-two to a neighbor man, Frank Seifert. It was a hasty marriage, with a fine healthy son born six months later. There is a saying that the first child can come at any time, although after that it takes nine months! But these things have always happened and will always continue to happen. Tina is most happy to be a wife and a mother. But, of course, this means that I am a grandmother at forty-three years, with my youngest child being but four years old.

Now that my children are a little older and I no longer have any in diapers, I am pleased to have more time for my quilting pleasures. Continuing the tradition of my mother, I made a little quilt for this first grand-babe. Although my life is still quite busy, and it is sometimes hard to find the time to do my quilting, I have found the secret to be a matter of simply making the time. If I sit down to quilt for an hour or two, the dishes and the dust will still be there waiting for me when I get up again.

A photo postcard from the early 1900s shows an older woman hand-piecing her "Drunkard's Path" quilt blocks, while her black cat sits in her sewing basket.

June 10, 1905

Dear Diary,

Another marriage between first cousins, such as August's and mine, occurred last year when my sister Maria's daughter Lydia Mattke was married to my sister Albertina's son George Schwandt. Although it is less common in this country and some may think it strange, the royal families of Europe have been intermarrying for many generations.

I am pleased to report that our daughter Tina bore a fine girl child three months ago, and I was happy to make a lovely cradle quilt for this second grand-babe.

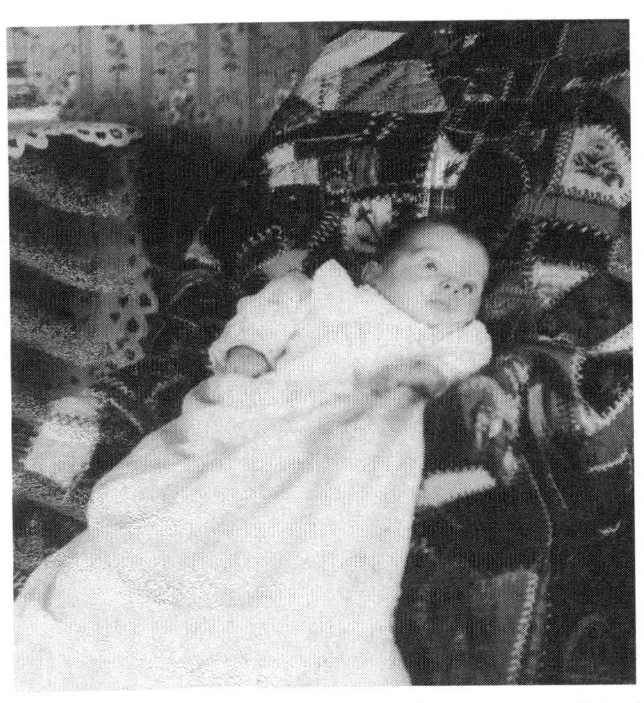

In this photo postcard dated 1908 a baby is posed on a crazy quilt in the family's Victorian parlor. Most crazy quilts were made from fabrics such as silk and velvet and were used as display pieces to showcase a woman's embroidery and needlework skills.

Many quilters have been caught up in the "Crazy Quilt" fad of recent years. They piece together odd-shaped scraps of colorful silk, velvet, satin, and fine wool fabrics, which they collect or buy in packets. They overlay every seam with embroidery, and add lace, ribbons, beads, and even more embroidery, which all seems a bit like "gilding the lily." Most are used only as display pieces in the parlor rather than as bed coverings. They are too extravagant for my taste, and I prefer to use my time and money to make something of function as well as beauty.

April 8, 1908

Dear Diary,

I have neglected to record events for the past few years. Our large family continues to grow ever larger. Our daughter Tina has just borne her third child, and our son Paul was married last year in June to Mathilda Ott. She is actually his first cousin, being the daughter of August's sister Friederike. It appears that our family is making a habit of marrying first cousins, just as August and I did some thirty years ago!

Our other seven children, still at home, range in age from twenty-four years down to nine years. So from our nine living children, I am looking forward to many more weddings and many more grandchildren in the years to come. Although the difficult losses and challenges in my life shook my faith at times, they could not destroy it. I have chosen to be happy and thankful for the great abundance that God has given me. I feel most truly blessed!

When August passed away in 1914, his children found Louisa's diary amongst his belongings. Enclosed between the final pages of the diary was a newspaper clipping of Louisa's obituary from the Morgan Messenger dated May 7, 1908.

Stricken Suddenly—Mrs. A. H. Otto Passes Away Without Warning Sunday Evening Shortly After Retiring for the Night.

A sad and sudden death occurred in this village Sunday evening about 9:40 when Mrs. August H. Otto was taken with a coughing and choking spell and survived but a few minutes afterwards. Mrs. Otto had been troubled with choking spells in a light form for the past two years, but her relatives never suspected they might finally prove fatal.

Sunday she seemed to be well and went visiting and received visitors. In the evening while the callers were there, she showed no signs of ailing. The visitors left about nine o'clock, and a half hour afterwards the Otto family retired. Only a few minutes elapsed, however, before she was taken with violent coughing and choking, which made breathing difficult. She passed away in a few minutes.

Mrs. Otto's maiden name was Louisa Otto. She was born in Chicago, Illinois, on October 1, 1858, making her nearly fifty years old at the time of her death. When she was two years, her parents moved to Nicollet, this state. On November 6, 1875, she was united in marriage with August H. Otto. They resided in Nicollet for three years and then moved to a farm in Eden Township, where they resided for fifteen years. The family moved to Morgan in 1893, where they have since resided.

Twelve children were born to them, nine of whom, together with the husband, survive to mourn the loss of mother and wife. They are Mrs. Frank Seifert, Redwood Falls; Paul, North Redwood; and Emil, August, Martha, Mary, George, Willie and Erwin, all residing at the family home. The funeral was held Wednesday forenoon, at ten o'clock, at the German Lutheran church. Burial was made in the Lutheran cemetery east of the village.

4

ALBERTINA'S STORY: TRADING A GOOD LIFE FOR A HARD LIFE

This story is based on the life of my great-great-grandmother Albertina Minx Otto (my maternal grandmother's maternal grandmother), born in 1822 in East Pomerania, Prussia, Germany. She and her husband Carl Otto and their children were the third Otto family to emigrate to America in 1875. Albertina was a sister-in-law to Sophia and Henrietta, whose stories were told in Chapters 1 and 2. My own dear grandmother quoted her grandparents as saying, "If we had known how hard life would be here, we would not have come!"

Carte de visite photographs of a fashionable couple from the 1870s. In this era women's hairstyles were less severe and they no longer wore hoop skirts. Men wore double-breasted frock-coats with contrasting collars and top hats.

PERSONAL JOURNAL OF ALBERTINA OTTO

May 1, 1874

This shall be my private journal where I can record my innermost thoughts and feelings that I dare not confide to anyone. This will allow me to express myself openly and honestly in a way that I cannot otherwise do. In our society women are taught to be submissive, put on a cheerful face and not complain, and keep any negative emotions inside. Sometimes I wonder why the good Lord gave us brains and mouths, if not to think and speak.

I was shocked to my very core today when I overheard my husband Carl telling a friend that he was thinking of emigrating to the New World in the near future. I could not believe my ears, as I have never heard a word of such foolishness from him. He does not know that I overheard, and I dare not bring up the subject for I fear I might begin weeping if that really is his intention.

We have a good life here in our rural village of Kratzig in Pomerania, Prussia, Germany. I have been greatly blessed with a fine husband and five living children: August, Carl, Friederike, Mathilda, and Albert, ranging in age from twenty-one to ten years. Tragically, five years ago we lost our youngest Heinrich at age three to scarlet fever. The death of our cherished babe plunged our whole family into deep despair, but was especially difficult for Albert, who at age five could not comprehend that his younger brother and playmate was gone forever.

Our family is relatively well off in an area where most people are quite poor unless they are landowners. My two daughters have pierced ears with gold earrings, which shows others that we are not landless peasants as are most in our village.

It is the custom here that the youngest son inherits the family farm. Older sons need to find work before their parents are through raising their large families and are ready to retire. The farms are too small to support more than one family or to be split up between children. When the youngest son inherits the farm, he also assumes responsibility for the care of his parents in their old age. Carl's three older brothers have found other occupations: Christoph and Georg as teachers and Gottlieb as a weaver. Their father, Juergen Otto, had deeded his land and cottage to Carl when we married, making us responsible for his parents' care for the remainder of their lives. They had married when Juergen was thirty and Carl's mother, Maria, was only sixteen, so Carl's father was quite old by the time we married and died five years later. Since it is her house, Maria has always insisted that I do everything her way and constantly tells me how to raise my children. She is still living, but with the infirmities of eighty-one years is nearly bedridden and requires constant care. I feel I have earned our inheritance several times over by living with and caring for my mother-in-law these past twenty-four years!

Two of Carl's brothers, Christoph and Gottlieb Otto, emigrated to America with their families in 1857 and 1861 respectively. They had low-paying jobs here in Germany and little with which to support their families or to leave as a legacy. They are prospering in their new lives and have acquired rich farmland and good livestock. They have written over the years of savage Indians and primitive homes and hardships, but mostly their letters have glowing reports of jobs to be found, money to be made, and especially the plentiful farmland just waiting for the taking. In an agricultural society such as ours, the highest ambition of any man is to be a landowning farmer. Then he is assured that his family will never go hungry, and he will leave that land as an inheritance for his children, and they for their children, and so on for generations.

Unfortunately, our oldest son August was seduced by the talk of money, farms, adventure and opportunity. Three years ago when he turned nineteen, he announced his plans to emigrate to America to seek his fortune. His uncle Christoph Otto offered him work on his farm in a place called Minnesota and off he went. It quite broke my heart to have my firstborn son leave us and journey to the other side of the world, with its dangers of a sea crossing, wild savages and untamed wilderness. My fervent hope is that he will enjoy his youthful adventure but eventually return home with money to buy a farm or business and then marry and start a family.

Whenever mail arrives from America, the villagers gather around to hear the letters read out that tell of a country where there are riches for anyone willing to work. The men are all intrigued by a nation said to have the richest farmland in the world, being both plentiful and cheap. In Germany land is mostly owned by the nobility or wealthy, is passed down in families, and is rarely for sale and then only at high prices. I remind Carl that we have our little farm that provides a good living here and have no need to risk everything to follow a dream like many others who are quite poor. Besides which, Carl and I are already both fifty years of age. We have many more years behind us than in front of us and are far too old to start off on any new ventures!

July 10, 1874

Our neighbor's son Franz Braun left for America six months ago with high hopes, but has returned home disillusioned and with empty pockets. He declares, "America is the promise of fools!" From what we have learned, he used all his money for passage and had no means to journey on from New York. He obtained a job on the docks, but was paid very little because of the many immigrants flooding into the country looking for work. He took an intense dislike to the large city with its masses of humanity everywhere. He shared a squalid room with other men and immediately began saving every penny he could in order to return home.

I overheard Carl talking of moving to America several months ago, but he has said nothing to me about it. I used this opportunity to point out that perhaps life is not so rosy in America as some claim and not everyone succeeds there. Carl scoffed, "Franz is a mama's boy and he probably cried himself to sleep every night! America offers chances and choices, and if he had been willing to take chances and make better

A stereoview card entitled "Letter from America" consists of two side-by-side images that combined into one 3-D image when viewed through a stereoscope. These were popular in the late 1800s and early 1900s.

choices, his trip need not have ended in failure." But thankfully Carl did not speak of our family emigrating, so I pray he has put this absurd notion to rest.

November 8, 1874

Oh, I am ever so upset! Our son August has written from America that he has fallen in love with Louisa, the youngest child of Christoph and Sophia Otto, and they plan to marry. As she is but sixteen years, her parents have asked that they wait another year before they wed. Of course, August and Louisa are first cousins, but they did not meet until they were grown. They were not raised together almost like brother and sister as cousins often are in a small village. Here in Germany first cousins do sometimes marry, as living in rural areas there are only a limited number of possible spouses. I do not mind that August is to marry his cousin, but it is unbearable to think that he may not return to Germany and we may never see him again.

Yesterday after reading August's letter for the tenth time, Carl proposed that we consider joining his two brothers Christoph and Gottlieb and our son August in this young and prosperous America. He reminded me that since his mother passed away in July, we no longer have family obligations to keep us here. I was quite upset as I never had any thought to leave our home and kinfolk and everything familiar for the vast unknown of a raw and unsettled frontier. Only about ten years ago Carl's two brothers' families barely escaped being massacred during an Indian uprising that killed hundreds of settlers in the very area where we would be going. I let Carl know that I was greatly opposed to this idea and he should put it out of his head at once. It makes me quite ill to even think about taking such a journey, not knowing what fate awaits us at the other end.

December 8, 1874

I am so angry that I could spit! Carl has become obsessed with learning all that he can about America and has had more correspondence from his brothers Christoph and Gottlieb, which only adds fuel to the fire. He has calculated how much money we could expect from selling our land and cottage and whatever furnishings we could not take with us, and has gathered information on what it would cost to buy land and livestock and equipment to start over in America. He has heard that the average immigrant arrives in America with less than twenty dollars in his pocket. Carl asks, "If people like that can be successful with only a little hard work, how much easier would it be for us if we arrived with a substantial amount of money with which to make a start?"

I always assumed that I would live and die near where I was born, just as our ancestors have done for many generations. I have no wish to leave behind my kinfolk, friends, belongings, and comfortable life, and I have made my feelings known to Carl, but he just pretends not to hear and persists in studying on this subject. To make matters worse, my children have all caught this "America fever" too. Last night our second son Carl, who has turned nineteen, announced that regardless of what our family decides, he plans to follow his older brother to this great land of opportunity next spring.

How will I ever prevail if my husband Carl as the head of the household decides that we should make this move to America? I will have no choice but to submit to his will. It has always been hard for me to bite my tongue and not say what is in my mouth, but I know that God has set husbands over their wives. It seems that just because God is a man, he intends for women to be meek and obedient and not give their husbands any problems. I have said as much to Carl as I have dared on the subject of America, and I am now biting my tongue until it bleeds!

January 12, 1875

It has been determined that our family will leave this spring to start a new life in the New World. I feel much as Sarah in the Bible must have felt when God commanded her husband Abraham, "Get thee out from thy country and from thy kindred and unto a land that I will show thee." And like them, we will soon be strangers in a strange land.

It has been a painful negotiation on my part, but Carl persuaded me in the end. Our oldest son August intends to stay in America, our middle son Carl plans to leave with us or alone, and by the time our youngest Albert is of age, he may also decide to follow his brothers. In all likelihood our sons would not return to Germany, and we would not see them again on this earth or know our future grandchildren. Our two daughters Friederike and Mathilda are approaching marriageable age, and there are only poor laborers or peasant farmers to choose from in this area. And who knows whether their future husbands might take them far away also?

Carl insists that we must look ahead beyond the end of our noses and consider the future. It would be unthinkable to grow old without our children and grandchildren around us. In the end I was convinced that the best hope of keeping our family together is for all of us to join our son August in America.

In addition, it has always been Carl's dream (like most men in our agrarian society) to be a large landholder, and if he is to fulfill this ambition, it cannot be put off any longer. We are both past fifty and the children, being twenty-two to eleven years, would be a great help to us. Within a few years they will be grown and on their own, and we surely cannot accomplish this goal without them.

Carl is in the process of selling his land and our lovely cottage. I am heartbroken at the prospect, as I have only been able to think of it as truly my own home since my mother-in-law passed on six months ago. I will soon have to decide which belongings to take with me and which I will need to sell or give away. How difficult that will be! My boys are quite excited by the adventure of going to the New World, but my girls are torn between the excitement of a new life and leaving their friends behind. I am still unhappy at having to do what I did not want to do. However, I must put on a good face and be a dutiful wife, as the Bible says that a woman must obey and cleave to her husband.

May 29, 1875

I have not had time to write in my journal since we decided to come to America. There was much work to pack what we were taking and to dispose of what we could not take. It was utterly heartrending to say our farewells to our friends and family, as we all knew that this would be the last time we would ever see each other.

We left the port of Hamburg, Germany, on April 16, 1875, aboard the steamship *Hansa* of the North German Lloyd Line. It employed three masts of sails to supplement the steam power during fine weather and carried almost a thousand passengers. When we first laid eyes on this huge hulking mass of iron, young Albert's eyes grew as big as saucers at the excitement of traveling on such a marvel. My first thought was of disbelief and wonder that such a heavy vessel could remain afloat and not sink to the bottom of the seas from the sheer weight of it.

The ocean crossing was a miserable and wretched affair, with too many people crammed into too little space. We felt like we were packed in like cattle being shipped off to market. There were the ever-present sounds of others talking, laughing, crying, coughing, and snoring at all hours of day and night, the constant pitching and rolling of the boat making many sick, the stench of unwashed bodies, seasickness and dysentery, and the howls of those in misery or fear. What a nightmare it was to be packed in the belly of the ship with hundreds of strangers for weeks on end!

Carl spent much of his time comparing stories and information on America with the other men, and the children quickly made new friends. I went up on deck when weather permitted to wash and dry our family's clothing, visit with other women, and enjoy the sunshine and fresh air. It was a terrifying feeling to realize that our little boat was but a tiny speck in a vast undulating ocean. A small boy died during the passage over and was buried at sea. It quite broke my heart to watch the tiny body disappear into the endless deep, with no place for his family to mourn him. Although we were all seasick at times, we managed as well as most to endure the crossing.

We landed on the shores of this alien country on May 2, 1875, entering at Castle Garden Immigration Center in New York. After crossing the vast country by train, we finally arrived in the town of New Ulm, Minnesota. We hired a man with a wagon to take our family and our trunks to the farm of Carl's brother Christoph Otto in nearby Nicollet County. Our son August came running from the fields when he saw us arriving. Oh, how I wept with joy to see his face again after four long years! I felt almost shy with him as he had changed from a boy to a man, having filled out and grown muscular from physical labor.

We had a happy reunion with Christoph and Sophia and met their lovely sixteen-year-old daughter Louisa, who is to be wed to August this fall. It is obvious that they are in love, and I am happy for my son that he has found a good wife even if she is his cousin.

We are staying here for a short time while Carl searches the area for a farm to buy. Meanwhile, I am greatly enjoying renewing my friendship with my sister-in-law Sophia. She has taught me much that I will need to survive in this new land, including ways of coping with the isolation and loneliness of living on the open prairie. She has also shown me the beautiful quilts that she makes from leftover fabric scraps and has even given me some patterns and instructions on how they are made. If the winters are as long and lonesome as we are told, the girls and I may need some such diversion.

Christoph's son Frederick Otto came by one day in his role of census taker to collect information for the 1875 Minnesota Census. He was supposed to do this as of May 1st, but because of heavy rains, he did not get out until a few weeks later. He first entered the information for Christoph's family into his ledger and included August as he had been living with them for four years past. After some discussion between the men, they decided that it would be a fine thing for our family to be included also. So even though we were not actually here on May 1st, we were proud to be enumerated in the census record of our new country.

June 24, 1875

Unlike most immigrants who are very poor, we were fortunate to arrive with enough money to immediately buy land. Carl purchased a quarter section containing about 150 acres in Eden Township, Brown County, Minnesota, on June 8th for the sum of $1,050. This land was formerly part of an Indian reservation which was reclaimed by the government following the Sioux Uprising of 1862. Most of the Indians were driven out of the state into the Dakotas in 1863, and this land was opened for white settlement in 1864.

The area is called Eden Township, named after the Garden of Eden by the first settlers for the beauty of nature and the fertile soil. We are pleased there is a small settlement of Lone Tree Lake nearby with a post office, hotel, and general store so that we do not have to travel a great distance to receive mail or purchase basic supplies. The tree for which the lake and the settlement are named is an extremely large old cottonwood tree measuring more than five feet in diameter and so tall that it can be seen for many miles across the open prairie.

Our farm is very large compared to most farms in Germany. The farm was owned by another family for about ten years, and they had built a house and barns and fences on the property and planted some trees. I had been overmuch worried how we would live if we bought open land, and I am so thankful that we were able to find an established farm. I shudder to think that my poor sister-in-law Henrietta was not so fortunate and had to live in a house made out of sod when they first moved onto their land. Carl is most grateful that the virgin sod has been turned for the fields, as they say that is backbreaking work, and so he and the boys were able to begin planting at once.

Since we were already into June, our first priority was to get the crops and gardens planted, but there is still much hard work to be done to get this farm provisioned. So far we have only bought beds and a table and chairs, and there is much that I am lacking in the way of furnishings and supplies for the house. Carl purchased a team of horses and a wagon, two milk cows, and a flock of chickens, and he plans to acquire a hog to fatten for next winter. Tomorrow we will make a trip to New Ulm to purchase more food and household goods and supplies.

What I miss most about home is the social life of a village, where one could not step outside without engaging in a conversation with a neighbor or someone passing by. Here when I step outside, I see only skies and prairie in every direction and lots of work needing to be done. The most important thing I have learned so far in this new land is that establishing a farm is very hard work.

August 26, 1875

Words cannot describe the terrible disaster we have suffered! Our summer was filled with endless work planting and tending the fields and gardens and getting our farm started. We had just finished harvesting the oats and what a huge job that was. The stalks were cut with a hand sickle and then bound into bundles. The bundles had to be stacked on end to dry and then the grain had to be threshed by flailing it by hand to separate the grains from the stalks. The girls and I also had to help in the fields, and it was very hot and exhausting work. We were not used to doing such labor in Germany, as there were always landless peasants willing to work for low wages. The girls complained how their hands and complexions were absolutely ruined and how they would never be able to find husbands looking as they do now.

We were about to start on the wheat harvest, when at the end of a hot day we were outside to catch the breeze and heard a queer buzzing sound. We looked behind us at the sky and saw a strange-looking thick dark cloud moving towards us. It was quite frightening and at first we thought it was a dust storm, but as it moved closer the buzzing grew louder. Friederike and Mathilda clutched at each other in fear. Then as the cloud suddenly descended on us, we realized it was a huge swarm of grasshoppers, and the girls ran screaming to the house.

The hungry pests settled on the crops in the fields and gardens and soon chewed them down to the dirt. Before they were done they had consumed everything we had grown and everything green. Next they chewed on wooden hoe and shovel handles and horse harnesses and anything that tasted of sweat and salt. Carl lamented, "To add insult to injury, those wretched creatures are not content with devouring the crops that we have grown by the sweat of our brows, but they wish to consume our very own sweat as well!"

This sketch showing farmers capturing grasshoppers during the grasshopper plagues in Minnesota was published in Frank Leslie's Illustrated Newspaper in 1888.

We are all feeling much depressed and discouraged at having been defeated in our first year here. It was quite easy to believe in the divine providence of God when all was going well. After suffering so from the forces of nature, I find myself questioning God. How fickle is our weak faith! As he is wont to do, Carl quoted Scripture reminding us that even the winds and the sea obey our Lord, so surely He must be able to control a swarm of insects. He concluded, "As long as we have faith, we will survive. We may have our faith shaken, but that is not the same as losing it."

I hope this is not an omen of what our life in America will be like, or we will soon be sorry that we ever came. In talking to those who have been here longer, this grasshopper plague has not happened before and, God willing, it will not again. Thankfully, we do have oats stored to feed to the livestock over winter, and we have enough money to buy food and supplies to see us through the coming year. I am healthy and strong and though I had no wish to come here, I am committed to caring for my family and maintaining some kind of order out here on the frontier. I put on a good face and do what needs doing, but I often find myself pining away for my former home and friends. Carl knows I am not happy here, but he says it is still early days and we must give it time.

November 11, 1875

Our son August was wed on November 7th at Trinity Lutheran Church in Nicollet to our niece Louisa Otto. After the wedding we had a wonderful celebration at her parents' farm. Louisa is only seventeen years to August's twenty-three years, but she is a sweet and hardworking girl, and we do know that she comes from a good family. When August came over to help with harvesting our oats, Louisa generously offered to come along to assist with the cooking, baking and dishwashing involved in feeding the extra hands required at harvest time. I was touched by her offer, and it was lovely to get to know her better before their marriage.

Since August has been working for his Uncle Christoph for four years and is saving money to buy his own farm, it has been decided that they will continue to live there for another year or two, which made Sophia quite happy. I am pleased that my firstborn son has found a soul mate and I am looking forward to having grandchildren soon.

Carl purchased fourteen acres of wooded property along the Minnesota River for $288 for cutting firewood for cooking and heating and trees for lumber. Carl and the boys often hunt deer and go fishing there as well. In fact, this game and fish make up a large part of our sustenance as we have not been settled long enough to raise animals of our own for meat, other than one hog and a few chickens. Carl and the boys are much enjoying these outdoor pursuits and will be busy over the winter months keeping us supplied with firewood and food.

We had a lively discussion over dinner today after Carl mentioned that following the grasshopper ravage some farmers have given up heart and hope and are moving or finding other jobs. He posed the question, "What is the main difference between those who endure in hopes of better times and those who give up at the first adversity?" Some of the suggestions were character, stubbornness, daring, luck and intelligence. Mathilda jokingly suggested that perhaps it was lack of intelligence! In the end we agreed on determination as being the most important factor. We are determined not to let one setback defeat us, and we vow to make a success of our farm.

January 8, 1876

Life is so much harder here than we had anticipated. In Germany farmers live in small villages and work the fields surrounding it. We had the services that a village provides, such as a butcher, grocer, blacksmith, shoemaker and brewery, as well as friends and family nearby. Here in America farms are sold in large plots, usually 160 acres, and the homes are located on the individual farms rather than in a central village. We feel so isolated out on the open prairies with the farms spread out and must go some distance to a town or to visit friends or relatives. The roads are often no more than dirt tracks and are sometimes nearly impassible due to rain, mud or snow.

We are having a bitter cold winter, but far worse than the cold that freezes the body is the lonesomeness that freezes the soul. I had known that I would miss my kinfolk and friends left behind, but I did not realize how very lonely I would be in this New Country. At times I feel desperate for "woman talk," to share with someone else the trials of raising children, dealing with a stubborn husband, the endless meals to be prepared from meager supplies, and even our hopes and dreams.

It is said that many women when removed so far from civilization suffer from an extreme depression known as melancholia, leading to erratic behavior, violent acts or even taking their own lives. A woman in the next county with a number of small children recently hanged herself from the barn rafters in her desperation. It is not hard to imagine that a woman could go quite mad living out here on the prairies, especially if there were no other women to talk to and only a taciturn husband and the wind howling across the vast open spaces to keep her company.

I was doubly saddened to learn that the poor woman was buried in the "suicide row" outside the hallowed ground of the church cemetery because of that last unpardoned sin. When we are in a loving relationship with our children, we readily forgive them any trespass committed in a moment of weakness, whether repented or not. I cannot believe that our loving heavenly Father would do any less for his children of faith. Is there any sin so large that an all-powerful God would be unable to forgive it if He so chose? Who are we as mere mortals to put limits on God's abundant love and mercy?

Most of our neighbors and others we have met are also from northern Germany and speak Low German like we do, and so we have not needed to learn the English language of this country. As there is at present no church established nearby, on Sunday mornings Carl reads from the Bible and leads us in prayer and a favorite hymn or two. But it is not the same as attending a real church, and I do so miss the social life that a church provides. Sometimes I must pretend to pray so my family does not know how much I hurt and grieve for what I have lost.

In the Old Country most men did not have farms of their own or large enough farms to support their families, so there were always ready workers to hire. Here everyone owns or rents their own farm, and it is difficult to find extra help. Our entire family is kept desperately busy and often has to labor under the hot sun or in the rain to plant, tend and harvest our crops. Friederike and Mathilda miss their friends and social life and complain, "There is nothing here but work, work and still more work!" I myself am not any happier, and the farming is exhausting and backbreaking for all of us. I try to console the girls and tell them that it will get easier with time. I am not afraid of a little hard work. However, it is my belief that so far this country has not lived up to its promise!

April 5, 1876

The winter was very long and lonely out here on the prairie. Often we did not leave home or see anyone else for weeks on end because of the cold and snow. During blizzards we all became a little "stir-crazy" after days of being housebound. Sometimes surrounded by the barren white wilderness we got to imagining we were the last people left on earth!

Fortunately, my two sisters-in-law, Sophia and Henrietta, had shown me the beautiful patchwork quilts they had made using leftover scraps of fabric. They explained how they were sewn and sketched out simple patterns for me. Their enthusiasm for quilting was contagious and awakened a creative urge in me. I am an accomplished seamstress and have taught my daughters to sew, and we are not afraid to try something new. So this winter Friederike and Mathilda and I decided to make a quilt of our own to occupy our time.

Our little general store at Lone Tree Lake had some double-pink calico fabric that we all admired, and we bought what yardage was left on the bolt. My girls chose a pattern called "Crosses and Losses." They thought it an apt description of our life so far in America, with the crosses we have to bear and the losses we have suffered. We used the double-pink fabric for the background of the pieced blocks and the alternate whole blocks, and we used scraps of leftover black and dark blue fabrics in the blocks. Unfortunately, we ran out of pink fabric before we were through and had to substitute other fabrics for the backgrounds in some of the blocks. Then we ran out of black and dark blue scraps and had to use other colors instead. By the last few blocks we were down to the bottom of our scrap basket and devised some really scrappy blocks. So rather than the uniform look we had planned, we ended up with a scrap-basket look. But I understand that is how quilting is done, as you just "make do" with what is at hand. In fact, we were even rather proud of how creative we were with what little we had.

CROSSES AND LOSSES: Primitive quilt from the collection of Lanie Tiffenbach, made with a "double-pink" background. Hand-pieced and hand-quilted. Maker unknown. Estimated date 1875–1890.

When the blocks were pieced together we bought a thin wool batting and a wonderful black print for the backing. Carl was able to fashion a quilting frame, and the girls and I spent many a long winter afternoon sitting around it and stitching. I suppose our stitches are not the finest, but we were ever so proud of our first effort at quilting. As they have not had many pleasures out of life in this new land, I told the girls they could have the quilt for their bed. Their faces lit up and they both gave me a hug, which made me quite happy as well.

October 25, 1876

This country has more tragedies to inflict on us. Sadly, we lost our first grandchild without having seen her. On July 12th August rode over on his horse, ecstatic that Louisa had borne a daughter. Carl and I were thrilled with the news, and I could hardly wait to see and hold her. Unfortunately, we were in the midst of harvesting the oats and did not have an entire day to spare to make a visit. But the tiny babe did not live long, and August was most downhearted when he returned to deliver the sad news. Carl and I both had tears in our eyes when he left, as we had both happily anticipated becoming grand-parents. We also knew too well the grief of losing a child, and our hearts ached for August and Louisa.

This summer we were once again invaded by a huge plague of grasshoppers of Old Testament proportions. Carl had many discus-sions with others over the past year on possible ways to defeat these horrible pests, should they return. In anticipation of their arrival, he and the boys dug up a small strip of ground alongside the fields and gardens, and we all carried dry hay and straw and laid this alongside these acres. This was much hard work but our livelihood was at stake. When the dreaded insects appeared in the skies, we all ran to set the hay and straw afire. The smoke soon drove off the grasshoppers and they left in search of better fields before they had done too much damage to our crops. We were able to harvest enough for our living and for seed for next year, and we are most fortunate to have that.

Carl and the boys raised a large litter of pigs and two beef calves this year, so we will have meat for the winter and also to sell to others. After having lived in a village all my life, one thing I cannot get accustomed to on the farm is the smell of manure. I told Carl that I did not care for the pigs for that reason, but he replied, "The fattened hogs will bring a good price and they smell of money!"

Last evening as I was gazing out the window at the endless flat landscape and feeling particularly blue, I wished out loud that we could go back to Germany. Carl put his arms around me and said that he was proud of how brave I have been and how hard I have worked. He reminded me that we had sold our house and land and there would be nothing to go back for. "We just need to stick it out a few years and everything will turn out right. Besides, our sons are enamored with this new country and would stay here, and how could we leave them behind forever?" I have finally accepted that we are here to stay, for better or for worse. I am determined not to pine any longer for that which is behind us but rather to turn my face forward.

May 15, 1877

Praise the Lord! We have been saved from the pestilence of grasshoppers this year by a miracle. The people joined as one from every town and every religion in this state and sent up fervent prayers for deliverance from this plague. And God heard and answered our prayers! He sent freezing snow a few days later that killed the grasshoppers, and so we are saved from this calamity. Finally this year we can hope for a bountiful crop from our labors and sweat.

We have been in America for over two years and have learned that farming is much like fighting a war. In addition to the difficulties of getting established in such a primitive area, we also have to fight for our very existence against the forces of nature. We suffer with extreme cold in the winter and extreme heat and humidity in the summer. We struggle with times of drought and times of flooding. We fight constant battles against mosquitoes, grasshoppers and other bugs. The winds whip fiercely across the open prairie, sometimes bringing hail, tornadoes or blizzards. With such vast prairies covered with tall grass, the threat of prairie fires is a constant fear in dry seasons. Winter blizzards can strand us for weeks and can be deadly if one is caught unawares outdoors.

We do not yet have a church in this area, but when weather permits we meet most Sunday mornings with other Evangelical Lutherans at our homes. The men take turns reading from the Bible and leading us in hymns and prayers. Occasionally we will have a pastor come from a nearby community to give us communion, baptize babies or perform a wedding. Our children have become friends with some of the other young people in the area, and our girls in particular are much happier now that they again have a bit of a social life.

On April 24th Carl declared his intention to become a naturalized citizen of the United States in the District Court of Brown County in New Ulm. Women and children become citizens along with their husbands or fathers, and so we will all soon be citizens of our new country. Of course, we all feel very proud of this, but even though I am resigned to life here, I still cannot help missing my former home in Germany.

The girls and I finished stitching our second quilt over the past winter, and we are improving with practice. There are endless varieties of patterns and color combinations that we can use, and we have more ideas than we have either time or fabric. I feel that everyone has a creative spirit that needs to be nourished and fed in order to keep life interesting.

October 30, 1878

Our son August has purchased a farm here in Eden Township, close to our farm. Louisa bore a healthy daughter a year ago, and it

The women in this vintage photograph are all doing hand sewing with the exception of one lucky woman who has a sewing machine. The photographer posed the ladies in a garden, as lighting conditions were better outdoors.

will be wonderful to have them nearby so we can visit often and spoil our precious grand-babe.

Some of the neighbor women have formed what they call a "quilting bee," and I have been invited to join. We have twelve members and will meet once a month at each other's homes. Since the most time-consuming part of making a quilt is stitching the layers together, we will share this work and at the same time be able to socialize together. Our first gathering was yesterday and what a wonderful time we had! Each woman brought food to contribute for a noon meal. We sat around the quilt frame and stitched for the entire day, until we had to go home to cook supper for our families and do our evening chores. The fortunate woman who had the quilting bee at her house had her quilt nearly completed in just one day. I will need to have a quilt top ready for quilting when it comes my turn to invite the women to my house.

I did so enjoy the company and conversation of other women who likewise have come from the Old Country and are going through the trials and tribulations of life in this new country. We talked of Germany and America, husbands and children, recipes and gardening, ailments and cures, and the joys and sorrows of life. I realized how much I have missed the simple friendships of other women since we came here. How I am already looking forward to next month's bee!

We have had yet another letter from our relatives in Germany, asking us to send them money. The common misconception is that all Americans are wealthy, and they expect us to share our riches with them. They have no idea of the great hardships we have suffered and how much backbreaking toil we have had to invest in making a living in this undeveloped country. After reading this latest letter Carl became upset with our relatives' constant begging, and he finally admitted, "If we had known how hard life would be here, we would not have come!" I could have responded that I had felt that all along, but I managed to bite my tongue.

December 10, 1879

We had the joyful occasions of two weddings in our family this past year. We had become good friends with the neighboring Ott family, and we had joked that with our surnames being so similar, perhaps we were relatives. But now that two of our children are married to two of their children, we truly are related. Our second son Carl married Amelia Ott in June, and our oldest daughter Friederike married Ernest Ott in November. Both young couples have rented farms nearby in Eden Township, and we are most pleased to have them well married and close at hand.

I gave two of my handmade quilts as wedding gifts, and I will need to continue making quilts for my two youngest, Mathilda and Albert, for when they decide to marry. I greatly enjoy our monthly quilting bees, with the conversation and laughter of other women as we stitch away. When I had the quilting bee at my house early this year, Mathilda helped us quilt. The other women admired the evenness of her stitches and invited her to join our group. Even though most of the women are around my age, she is nevertheless enjoying their company and friendship. I think she is also learning much about life from hearing their thoughts and experiences.

Until recently food staples and supplies were transported and sold in wooden barrels, but with the invention of sewing machines, cotton bags have replaced barrels. We accumulate many of these cotton bags because everything from flour and sugar to seeds and chicken feed is sold in them. The bags are stitched with string that can be unraveled and reused for household purposes or for tying quilts. Unfortunately the companies print their logos on the bags, and it usually takes soaking in kerosene, scrubbing with lye soap, and boiling in an iron kettle to remove the printing. Once this is done, however, the cloth is very useful and can be used to make dishtowels, sheets, aprons, underwear, nightgowns and everyday shirts. When making a quilt I sometimes use a number of these bags sewn together for the backing, and it saves me the expense of buying fabric.

August and Louisa now have two little girls, Hannah and Albertina (named for me!), and Carl and I delight in being grandparents. Even though I was opposed to moving to this country, our children have thrived and are happy with their lives. I have to admit that it turned out for the best in spite of the disappointments and hardships that we endured in getting settled. I have learned to enjoy such simple pleasures as the sound of the wind singing through the grass, the infinite blue dome of sky stretching from horizon to horizon, the fresh smell of spring rains, the taste of the first tomato of summer, and the satisfaction of a day's work well done.

September 18, 1880

Yesterday was such a beautiful fall day that Carl decided to go to New Ulm to sell a wagonload of wheat, and I went along to shop for supplies. One of the stores had received a shipment of the new-fangled mechanical home sewing machines, and a salesman was demonstrating how they operated. We had seen these machines before but the price had always been too dear. They have since become more affordable, and Carl was quite intrigued at how quickly a seam could be sewn on it. He had money in his pockets from selling the wheat and decided right then and there that I should have one of these labor-saving devices.

When we arrived home, nothing would do but that I sit right down and try it out. We were both pleased that I was able to learn to operate it so quickly and that it sewed such a fine tight seam. When I expressed my concern over spending money on such a luxury, Carl told me that I deserved it and much more, as I have been hardworking and long-suffering through the trials of recent years. If this machine could make my life easier, then he was pleased to buy it for me. I was quite overcome with feelings of gratitude for such a caring and thoughtful husband. I am eager to try piecing my quilt blocks on this new machine. It should work well as long as the pieces are not too small or the pattern too complicated. I can just imagine how envious the other women in my quilting bee are going to be when they see it!

Advertising trade cards, such as these for the Domestic and Household Sewing Machine Companies, were highly collectible and often pasted into scrapbooks.

November 3, 1881

Praise God, we finally have a church to call our own! This summer thirteen men in our area organized Immanuel Lutheran Church of Eden Township. Among the charter members were my husband, our two older sons, Carl's brother Gottlieb Otto, and Gottlieb's son August. Our church building was erected with the help of the members over the summer and fall. It is wonderful to once again have a place to come together to worship and socialize with like-minded Christians.

When it was my turn to host the quilting bee early this summer, I asked all the women to bring food for an evening meal. The day was spent in quilting, conversation and laughter. The men and children did the evening chores and then joined us for a feast and frolic. Several men brought fiddles for music and dancing, while the children ran about and played games into the night. The anticipation and preparation for the quilting bee, then the excitement of it, and afterward the memories to replay in my head all put me in a fine state of mind.

It was fortunate that we had such an enjoyable time, as it later turned out to be a most dreadful summer of diphtheria epidemics and very destructive tornadoes in the area, with much loss of life and property. Although my niece lost three young children, thankfully the Lord protected and spared our own family from these two dire calamities.

Last week we did our fall butchering of a hog, always a great deal of work. At dawn a fire was started under the big kettle outdoors to boil water. The pig was killed, scalded, scraped and dressed. The hams, shoulders and bacon were soaked in brine and then later hung in the smokehouse where a fire will be kept smoldering for several weeks. The lard was rendered in big kettles on the cook stove and put into stoneware crocks. The German sausages and blood sausages were mixed and stuffed into the cleaned intestines and also smoked. Some of the meat was salted and some was cooked and put up in canning jars. We all worked from dawn to dusk for days to accomplish this, but what a good feeling it is to have provisions put by for the winter!

I was recently reflecting that we have been in this country for over six years. I was surprised to find that I no longer have any desire to return home to Germany, for this land has now taken over my heart and become my home.

November 14, 1884

I note that it has been three years since I last wrote in this journal. There is always work waiting to be done on a farm, and it does not leave much time for reflection. Our younger daughter Mathilda was married a week ago to Theodor Mattke in a lovely ceremony at our country church, being respectively twenty-four and twenty-six years. Theodor is also from East Pomerania, Prussia, Germany, and he immigrated to America on the *Elbe* in December 1882. His two older brothers, who had come over earlier, both have farms in Eden Township, and Theodor has been working for his brother Albert for the past two years. Mathilda and he met when Theodor joined our church, and they were immediately attracted to each other. Theodor, however, felt he needed to get his feet under him in this new country before he could wed.

Mathilda Otto and Theodor Mattke posed for their wedding photograph on November 7, 1884. Dark wedding dresses were practical, as they could later be worn for other occasions.

Like many young couples, Theodor and Mathilda will live with us for a time until they have saved enough money to purchase a farm of their own. Carl will welcome Theodor's help as he is now sixty-one years old, and I will also depend greatly on Mathilda's help and companionship. My neighbors and I continue to hold our quilting bees and make quilts in our spare time, and Mathilda was pleased to choose the colors and design and work on her own wedding quilt.

It is wonderful that all our children and their families live nearby, as the men are able to help each other. This means that my life and the lives of my daughters are much easier because we no longer have to do much outdoor farm work. We have a fertile family, as all three of our other married children are producing babes every year or two. August has four, Carl four, and Friederike three little ones. I am so thankful that I can see my grandchildren often and spoil them as grandmothers are meant to do!

December 17, 1886

The time that the newlyweds Mathilda and Theodor lived with us seemed to fly by. In May 1885 Theodor bought an eighty-acre farm close by in Eden Township for $750, and he and Mathilda moved out of our home to begin life on their own. I was grateful to have kept my youngest daughter with me for that extra time.

After renting a farm for a number of years, our son Carl and his wife have purchased their own farm in nearby Three Lakes Township, Redwood County. We are proud of how well our children are doing in this new land.

Our youngest son Albert was married last month to Caroline Ott. He is the third of our children to marry an Ott, as Caroline is a first cousin to both Friederike's husband Ernest Ott and Carl's wife Amelia Ott. Since Carl and I cannot manage the farm by ourselves, Albert will continue working alongside Carl, and the farm will someday be his. I am pleased that he and Caroline will be living with us, for it is lonesome to be the only woman in the house and have no one to talk to all day while the men work outside. Caroline was overcome by the beauty of the wedding quilt we gave them, and she is eager to join in our quilt making.

We have had both life and death in our family. August and Louisa are devastated by the loss of their eight-year-old Hannah, as are Carl and I. They are left with four children but are expecting another babe. Carl and Emilie have five healthy children, Friederike and Ernest now have four daughters, and Mathilda and Theodor just had their second daughter. I think often of the joys that I would be missing had we remained in Germany and our children and grandchildren were here in America. After all the challenges of being transplanted from one world to another, I admit that I am happy to be where I am. I truly feel that God sent us across the ocean in order to give our children a new destiny, and I believe I have finally acquired the gift of contentment.

December 1, 1889

We have been in America for nearly fifteen years, and all of us from one generation to the next still have not learned the English language of this country. Almost everyone we know are also German, our church services are held in German, and the schools our grandchildren attend still use German as their primary language of instruction, although they do teach English as well. Sometimes it is hard to believe that we are so far from the land of our birth, as we continue in our German traditions.

This woman chose her lovely "Rocky Road to Kansas" quilt for a backdrop when she sat for her portrait with her children about the turn of the century. Women were proud to display their handiwork and often included quilts in their photographs.

Albert and Caroline have produced three children in the three years since they married, and Carl has teased Albert that Caroline may soon make him start sleeping in the barn! Carl and I are happy to have them living with us, as we so enjoy being grandparents, although three babes manage to keep us all busy. I have tried to make a small quilt for each grandchild, but there have been times when I just could not keep up and the new babe had to make do with a piece of an old soft blanket or an older child's quilt until I could find time to sew another. I like to feel that my quilts warm both their bodies and their spirits.

March 21, 1891

Of all the losses we have suffered in this new country, this has been the hardest to bear. Our thirty-two-year-old daughter Friederike Ott died two weeks ago of bloody flux or dysentery, which the doctor blamed on contaminated food or water. She had been ill for a week with stomach pain, severe diarrhea, fever, weakness, and delirium. I helped Ernest nurse Friederike in the last days as she began to slide slowly towards death. She would whisper, "Help me, Mother," but I could do nothing except sponge her face, hold her hand and care for her children.

Friederike leaves behind her husband, four daughters ages ten to four, and little George not yet two years. We have taken the children into our home until their father can find someone to help with them. How lost they are without their mother and how they cry for her! It is difficult caring for the needs of these five motherless children, plus helping Caroline with her four babes under the age of four. I have scarcely had time to sleep, let alone grieve for my dear departed daughter. At sixty-eight years of age I do not believe I can raise five more children, and both Caroline and I already have our hands full with her four little ones. I greatly hope another solution can be found for their care.

In this lovely cabinet card from about 1890, a little boy is surrounded by four older sisters. They appear to be about the ages of Friederike's children when she died.

December 30, 1893

A year after our daughter Friederike died, her husband Ernest Ott remarried. As is necessary sometimes after a mother's death, the five children had been split up and shuffled around between various relatives and friends to be cared for during that interval. Not only did they grieve the loss of their mother, but they also suffered with the separation from their father and siblings. I cannot imagine how difficult it must be to take on the raising of five children that are not one's own, but Johanna is being a loving and patient stepmother to my daughter's children. We are all so relieved and happy to see the children reunited as a family.

Sadly, Mathilda and Theodor lost a newborn boy a year ago—their only son. They were much disappointed as Theodor wishes for a son, both to carry on the family name and to help with the farming. Grieving with my daughter Mathilda brought back some of the pain of losing my own young son many years ago. However, Mathilda has been much cheered by the recent birth of their fourth daughter whom they named Emma, although of course they had hoped to have a boy instead.

In September Carl and I sold our farm as well as our wooded lots along the river to our son Albert for the sum of $1,400. However, we will continue to live on the farm with Albert and Caroline and their growing brood of children. They already have six little ones, with the oldest being but six years old. I love having a house full of little ones, and I love being a grandmother.

"Stairstep children" were common in large families, as illustrated by this charming photo postcard from the early 1900s.

December 1, 1896

It has been a year of great loss and sadness for me. Some mornings I am so weighed down with melancholy that I can scarcely force myself to rise from my bed. The first loss was in January when Mathilda and Theodor's five-month-old son died. They had been so thrilled to finally have a healthy son, after losing their first one a few years back. However, when the babe became feverish and listless, they took him to the doctor in Morgan, who diagnosed him with tubercular meningitis but could not save the little one.

The next loss was in November when August and Louisa's thirteen-year-old daughter Bertha died of a weak heart. She had always been somewhat frail, but we never thought that she would die. This is the third daughter that they have lost, each ten years apart. This has been especially hard on their whole family, as Bertha was such a help to her mother. The younger ones cannot understand that she is gone forever and continue to ask for her.

But the hardest loss for me was on November 23rd when Carl, my dear husband of forty-six years, passed on to his great reward at the age of seventy-three years. He had been in declining health for a few years, but it was still a shock to me when he died. On occasion I think to myself that I must remember to tell him something when he comes in from working outside, before I realize that he is truly gone. I am so thankful that I can live here with Albert and Caroline and their seven children (with the eighth on the way). If I had to live alone, I think I would die of pure lonesomeness.

December 16, 1900

I have blessed with a great abundance of grandchildren. August and Louisa are the parents of nine living children. Carl and Emelia had their twelfth child in last summer, thankfully all surviving. In addition to their four girls and after losing two boy babes, Mathilda and Theodor rejoiced to finally have a healthy son born last year. Of course, there are Friederike's five children that she left behind. And, finally, Albert and Caroline had their tenth child born this past January, and Caroline is already carrying another babe. Living in a household with ten children is quite a challenge at my age. My family teases me that I am getting forgetful, but is it any wonder that I sometimes get all those little ones confused and call them by the wrong name?

Caroline is such a wonderful mother, and I marvel at how well she manages to provide care and love to every one of her many children. Albert is an unusual father, too, in that he is not afraid to pitch in and change a diaper, wash the dishes or get up in the night to rock a crying child. Of course, most men consider those chores to be women's work and depend on their wives to do everything concerning the children and the house. Although I am seventy-eight years of age, I still do whatever I can to help Caroline, as I certainly do not wish to be a burden on her and Albert.

As I often told Carl when he was still alive, he was indeed right all those years ago when he insisted that we needed to come to America in order to keep our family together. All of our children have farms nearby and so they can share labor and equipment and support each other through the good times and bad. Our children escaped the limited destinies they would have had in Germany, and they have thrived on the opportunities that this new country presented. I fully expect that our grandchildren will reap the benefits also, along with their children and their children's children.

September 11, 1903

Our family has once again been visited by the angel of death. Our son Albert's wife Caroline died a few weeks ago from pneumonia, having been unwell with complications of childbed since her last child Amanda was born a month previous. Albert, the children and I are all grieving so deeply for her as she was the heart of this large family. Caroline was only thirty-six years old and Amanda was her twelfth child, with all of them still living. The rest of the children range in age from sixteen to two years of age, and the older children will need to help Albert and myself care for the younger ones. Fortunately I am in fair health and can still be of some use, even though I have almost attained the age of eighty-one years.

This compelling photograph, circa 1900, of a family with ten young children (and perhaps more still to come) illustrates what little control married women had over how many children they bore in those earlier times.

A newborn babe was more than Albert and I could handle with eleven other children to care for, so Amanda was taken in by Caroline's sister and brother-in-law. They have two older children and are pleased to add a babe to their family. I fear they may be reluctant to return her when she gets older, and they may end up raising her as their own. But it cannot be helped as it will take every bit of energy and life that I have left in my body to help Albert raise his other motherless children. Poor Albert is stunned by the loss of Caroline and goes about his work as if he were walking in his sleep. I can scarcely sit down before one or two little ones crawl into my lap for comfort, but I take my own comfort from their sweet faces and loving hugs.

October 14, 1907

Today I have reached the great old age of eighty-five years, a milestone that not many people attain. I know I am not long for this earth, but I am not afraid of death. After all, that is what happens next when life is over. I have waiting for me on the other side of the great divide my husband, two children, parents, siblings, and many other loved ones. While I have no idea what happens after our final breath, it does not seem frightening but rather like a new experience just waiting to happen. When one has lived as long as I have, death is an expected guest.

As I look back and count all my blessings and all my losses, it is apparent that overall I have been greatly blessed. I birthed six children and even though I did lose Heinrich at age three and later Friederike as an adult, I still have four children remaining to me. I also now have forty-one living grandchildren and eight great-grandchildren.

My three sons had twelve children each, although August lost three and Carl lost two. My daughter Friederike had five children before she perished. My daughter Mathilda had four girls and three boys, although two of the boys died as infants. Arthur, the only surviving son, is presently eight years of age and his parents' pride and joy.

I sometimes think of what God told Abraham and Sarah in the Book of Genesis, "Look now toward heaven and tell the stars, if thou be able to number them; so shall thy seed be." When I look up at the stars and think of how our family has multiplied with children, grandchildren and now great-grandchildren, I feel that someday our descendants will also be too numerous to count. I can truly say with the Psalmist, "My cup runneth over."

This family portrait of Theodor and Mathilda Mattke and their children Martha, Minnie, Arthur, Helen and Emma was taken about 1914. Tragically, Arthur died in 1915 of kidney disease at age sixteen.

This is no longer Albertina writing, but I wish to add a note to finish out her journal. I am her granddaughter Emma, the youngest daughter of Mathilda and Theodor Mattke. I inherited my Grandmother Otto's journal a few years ago after my mother passed on. I have since spent many hours reading and re-reading her story of challenges, hardships and blessings.

Albertina Minx Otto died on January 7, 1910, at the very advanced age of eighty-seven years. All told, living and dead, she had born to her six children, forty-eight grandchildren, and one hundred eleven great-grandchildren, with many more generations yet to come.

My grandmother left behind a wonderful legacy of courage and perseverance in the face of changes and adversity. Her story will stay with me forever. I will strive always to follow and honor her example.

Signed: Emma Mattke Meyer

5

MAGDALENA'S STORY: AN ARRANGED MARRIAGE

This story is based on the life of my great-grandmother Magdalena Helget Tauer (my father's maternal grandmother), who was born in 1855 in the Pilsen Kreis District of Bohemia, then a crown colony of Austria-Hungary and now part of the Czech Republic. In researching her immigration record and marriage record, both from 1876, it was surprising to find that she was married within days of arriving in Minnesota.

This lovely portrait from about 1875 shows an unidentified young mother holding her child.

LETTERS FROM MAGDALENA HELGET TAUER TO HER FRIEND IN BOHEMIA

Natschetin
Pilsen Kreis District
Bohemia
Kingdom of Austria-Hungary

June 12, 1874

My Dearest Friend Elizabeth,

I am so thankful you still love me as before and do not judge me by my mistakes, as many do. It was wonderful to see you when you returned to our poor little farming village to visit your mother. Growing up next door, we were always as close as sisters, running in and out of each other's homes. I have greatly missed you since you married and moved away, but I am overjoyed that you are with child. My seven-month-old Maggie is the joy of my life, though I have to endure the shame of bearing a child out of wedlock.

Georg Fleishman has not acknowledged her and asks, "How can I be sure she is even mine?" How could she not be his when I thought I loved Georg so much that I would not even look at another boy? At age eighteen he still has eight long years of military service in the Austrian army ahead of him, and even then he must find work and establish himself before the authorities would give us permission to marry. I had clung to the hope that little Maggie would charm him, and he would claim her as his own and promise to marry me when he was able.

Georg came to see me last month to say that he was leaving to begin his service. "I am too young to be a husband or father," he told me, "and I cannot say what I will do many years from now when I might be in a position to marry. This is your problem, not mine. I want no part of you or your babe, so do not expect me to ever marry you!" I had to turn away to hide the tears that sprang to my eyes. How could he be so cold and uncaring after what we had been to each other? I am devastated by his rejection and cannot stop weeping.

Oh, Elizabeth, how will I manage to raise a child by myself? As you know, everyone in our village is quite poor and life is very hard. Do you realize that it has only been twenty-six years since our parents and grandparents were serfs bound to the land? Of course, life is not much improved, burdened as we are now with heavy taxes. With our high altitude, rocky unfertile soil, and harsh climate it is difficult to make a living from the land. There is little work to be found by men and practically no way for a woman to earn an honest living.

If only my Mother had not died at my birth, I could turn to her for help and wisdom. My two older sisters, who were twenty and sixteen when I was born and who helped raise me, feel that I have shamed the family name. But they stood by me when I gave birth and acted as godmothers to my babe. My dear father has been nothing but kind to me and he absolutely dotes on his little granddaughter. As you know, he is a farmer without any land of his own and works wherever he can. He has just turned sixty-one years and thankfully is still in good health. But what will happen when Father can no longer work to support us or after he has passed on? I dread to think of what the future may hold for me and my little Maggie.

Sending my love,
Magdalena

March 10, 1875

Dear Elizabeth,

I was overjoyed to hear that you were safely delivered of a son. My precious Maggie is sixteen months old and walking and talking. Although I did not want her or love her while she was growing in my belly, now I cannot imagine being without her and would lay down my very life for her. Is not a mother's love amazing?

My brother Wenzel Helget has been in America for five years already, living and working on a farm near New Ulm, Minnesota. He writes and tells how he is prospering in his new homeland and saving money to buy his own farm. If I were a man, I could go to America where no one knew me and start life afresh. But it is not easy for a woman to travel alone, and where would I get the money for the voyage? Who would care for my babe while I worked to support her and myself?

Some village women shun me and others hiss and call me bad names, but the men are the worst. I cannot count how many have made rude offers to me, and I had to threaten to tell their wives or girlfriends if they did not leave me alone. They think because I made a mistake once, I am willing to lift my skirts for any man, no matter how old or ugly, whether married or not. I was only eighteen and ignorant of men when I let Georg have his way with me. I now know him to be a coward, and perhaps it is best that we do not marry.

I confessed my sin to our priest often while I was with child. Each time he pronounced absolution for my wickedness, made the sign of the cross, and intoned, "Go and sin no more." However, it was not until I held the miracle of my perfect child in my arms that I felt God's forgiveness descend on me. Although no man may want me for a wife now that I have brought this shame upon myself, I am determined to hold up my head and make a life for myself and my child.

With love,
Magdalena

April 28, 1876

Dearest Elizabeth,

I received the most surprising letter from my brother Wenzel in America! You will recall that he and Josef Tauer from Trohatin were great friends growing up. Do you remember when Josef Tauer wed Margaretha Kiefner seven years ago at our church in Berg, and how at fourteen years of age we dreamed to someday have such a wedding? The Tauers soon left for America, and Josef's letters convinced Wenzel to join them a year later. Now Wenzel writes that Margaretha has died in childbirth, leaving Josef with two young girls to raise. He is in immediate need of another wife to care for his house and children.

My brother knows of my situation and suggested that Josef ask me to marry him. Josef enclosed a short note with Wenzel's letter, "Will you come to America to be my wife? I do not have much money, but I swear to be good to you and your babe. If agreeable, come at once." They seemed so sure of my answer that they sent money for our ship passage and expenses.

Oh, Elizabeth, what shall I do? Shall I leave the only home I have known and journey to another world to marry a man fifteen years older than myself whom I scarcely remember? My cousin Anna teases me, "You will work like a slave, receive no pay, and have to bed the old goat in the bargain!" Or shall I stay in this village where I know what life has in store, as little as it may be? However, Maggie will then bear the stigma of being illegitimate all her life, and I may never have a chance to marry or have more children and may end up being a burden on my family.

When I asked my sisters how I could possibly marry a man I scarcely knew, they just laughed, "Well, that is what marriage is for!" Of course, I am not a fool and I know love is not necessarily a part of every marriage. Women marry for many reasons, some because they want children and others because they need a roof over their heads and food for their table. Only a lucky few are able to marry for love.

My father says that Josef is a good man and I may not have another such offer. But I do know that he depends on me and will greatly miss Maggie and me if we were to go to America. Dear Elizabeth, please help me make this most momentous decision!

Love and affection,
Magdalena

Lafayette Township
Nicollet County
Minnesota, America

August 1, 1876

Dear Elizabeth,

You must be eagerly awaiting my news. I finally have a few moments to pen a letter. How frightened I was to leave behind my family and homeland forever and set out for the uncertainty of a new life! Thankfully, another couple from our village was traveling to the same town in Minnesota, and so I was not alone with my babe.

We took the train to Bremen in Germany, where we boarded a ship called the *Nurnberg*. The sea voyage seemed a nightmare, lasted sixteen days, but felt like an eternity. Oh, Elizabeth, just imagine one large dark room below deck, crowded with several hundred people, noisy with talking, crying, praying, snoring, and retching. Then imagine the smells of the privies, unwashed bodies, vomit, and dysentery. Imagine, too, the ship constantly bucking and rolling making us seasick, and everyone's terrors of the boat being swallowed up by the sea during storms.

It was most difficult to care for an active babe in such confined quarters, especially when I was so seasick I felt I would surely die. During the worst storms I could do nothing but hold Maggie down with one hand and hold onto the side of the berth with the other to keep from falling out. At times we both heaved up everything in us down to our toes. Oh, the terrible sounds and the awful stench of every soul on that boat retching during storms—and then the washing and scrubbing to be done after! As homesickness and remorse consumed me, I asked myself over and over, "What have I done to myself and my child?" I wrestled day and night with how I could swear a sacred vow to "love, honor, and obey" until my dying day a man that I did not even know.

We finally landed in the port of Baltimore on June 30th and passed through inspections, which did not involve much more than checking our identities against the passenger list. We then took a number of different trains and many days to reach our destination in New Ulm, Minnesota. I had written to my brother Wenzel from Bohemia to let him know of my decision, and I posted another letter from Baltimore telling when to expect us. I gave him strict instructions not to let my future husband see us until we had time to rest and clean up after the long journey.

I stayed with Wenzel and his wife Barbara for several days, and then Josef and his two daughters came to supper. Josef looked older than I remembered, as it had been seven years since I had last seen him, but he still remained quite handsome. His girls, Margaret and Barbara, ages six and eleven, were delighted with my two-year-old Maggie, and she in turn was enamored with Wenzel and Barbara's lively eighteen-month-old twins, Joseph and Maria. Things were a bit awkward between Josef and myself at first, but the antics of the five children made us all laugh and put us at ease.

Josef and Wenzel went to see the priest the next day and the wedding date was set two days following. Everything was happening much too quickly for me, but as it had all been agreed to beforehand, there was no reason to wait. Although it was only five months since Josef's first wife died, no one will fault him for a hasty remarriage. Everyone knows that life is short and life is hard, and a man needs a wife to care for his home and children.

And so Josef and I were married on July 17, 1876, at Holy Trinity Catholic Church in New Ulm. Wenzel and Barbara hosted a dinner for us with a few Bohemian friends that evening, after which we left for what would be my new home. Josef is thirty-six years to my twenty-one, and we have begun our life together.

With love,

Magdalena

September 15, 1876

Dearest Elizabeth,

Josef and I were a little shy around each other at first, and I was quite nervous about getting into bed that first night with a man who seemed a stranger. But unlike the few times when Georg had forced himself on me back home, I found that the act could even be pleasurable. Josef is a good man and kind to me so we are feeling more comfortable now.

Josef's two daughters, Margaret and Barbara, have been starved for a mother's attention since their mother died, and they took to me immediately. They treat my two-year-old like a favorite doll, and they are so sweet and eager to please that I cannot help but love them. There is a small house on Josef's farm, and I am sure that he has done his level best to cope with caring for it and his girls. However, it is obvious that things have been neglected in past months, and I am busy putting the house in order again.

We suffered a great devastation this summer from an invasion by a mighty army of grasshoppers, as I was told had also happened last year. They landed in huge buzzing swarms and stripped everything green within a short time. It was heartbreaking to watch the hungry pests devour my garden and Josef's crops in the fields. They even chewed holes in clothing that I had drying on the wash line! With little else to eat, our chickens then ate the grasshoppers, giving their eggs such a disgusting taste that we could scarcely force them down.

In an effort to defeat the plague, Nicollet County offered a bounty of three dollars per bushel of grasshoppers as soon as the pests arrived. We are told that there are something like 20,000 grasshoppers to a bushel. But so many sacks of grasshoppers were brought in the first few days that the county officials reduced the bounty to one dollar a bushel. Inside of a week over $30,000 had been paid out, and the county treasury had been drained down to its last dollar.

Josef and I spent an exhausting several days trying to collect these dreadful creatures and stuff them into sacks, but we only managed two bushels. We learned too late of the methods that a few had used to take advantage of the bounty. It is said that a man with a scoop made of a bag of cloth stretched over a barrel hoop could walk through a field and catch grasshoppers at a rate of a bushel an hour. We have also heard that two men with a wheeled hay-rake lined with cloth could capture as many as fifty bushels of locusts a day.

Josef is anguished at the loss of his crops and will not be able to make a payment on the farm for a second year. We will need to borrow money to get through the next year and for seed to plant in the spring. Some are selling their farms and moving away, but Josef asks, "How can we go elsewhere with no money? At least here we have a roof over our heads." We pray that this pestilence will soon pass and the land will again prosper. In spite of our troubles, I feel so greatly blessed to suddenly have my own house and a husband and three children!

Sending my love,

Magdalena

This tintype photograph of a young mother with three daughters was taken about 1880.

January 11, 1877

Dear Elizabeth,

Your letter arrived safely, and it gave me a great deal of pleasure to hear news from home. I am overjoyed to share with you that we will have another child this summer. If it is a girl, I have decided to name her after you, as you have always been my dearest friend.

Josef and I had never discussed the fact that I had borne an illegitimate child, and it has been nagging at me for some time. In a tender moment last night I finally asked Josef if he thought less of me for it. He gently reminded me that he and Margaretha had their first child four years before they married. The differences between our situations were that he claimed the child as his and they were betrothed to be married when he had finished his military service and could get permission from the authorities. "You are a good wife to me and a good mother to my daughters, so how could I in return not be a good husband and a good father to your child? I feel that all three children belong to both of us, and I am happy to claim Maggie as my own." You can imagine how relieved this made me feel, but Josef could not understand why I was crying. I truly believe I made the right choice in coming to America to marry Josef, and I do not think I will ever regret it.

My sister-in-law Barbara and I have become good friends. She has shown me several patchwork quilts that she has made, rather like the goose-down comforters we made at home. The women here make the top piece by cutting colorful fabrics into certain shapes and stitching them together in a pleasing design. They use a thin layer of cotton or wool between the top and the backing and secure the layers together with hand stitches. The quilts are fascinating but they seem so much work to make. I admired the one Barbara is working on, and she said it is to be a belated wedding gift for Josef and myself! She has also promised to teach me to quilt, and I am looking forward to spending more time with her and learning to make these beautiful quilts.

Love,
Magdalena

August 6, 1877

Dear Elizabeth,

I bore a healthy daughter in July, named Elizabeth after you as I had promised. Our three girls are delighted with their new sister, and she is much spoiled with all the attention. Sadly, Wenzel and Barbara suffered a great loss when their two-year-old twins died from croup on the same dreadful February day. But God has heard their cries of grief and Barbara's belly is beginning to swell with a new child.

I wrote last year of the terrible plague of locusts that destroyed our crops. We are told that they are called Rocky Mountain locusts and have come to this region because of droughts further west in the past few years. They do not lay just a single egg, but rather about a hundred eggs packed snugly together, each the size of a grain of rye. If a blade of wheat or a stalk of corn escapes the parents, it will certainly be consumed by the children. This spring when the eggs began to hatch, a day was set aside for prayer and fasting. Our prayers and penance were pleasing to Almighty God, and he sent a freezing sleet and snowstorm to destroy the newly hatched locusts. We truly feel that God has tested us and delivered us from this dreadful pestilence.

Josef says it will probably take us several years to pay off the debts that we have incurred during this hard time. We have very little money and often have to barter garden produce, eggs, or chickens at the general store to obtain necessities such as flour and sugar. Somehow, though, Josef manages to find a few coins for beer or liquor at the saloon whenever he is in New Ulm or St. George. I desperately wish I had that bit of money to spend on food or household goods, but I realize that Bohemian men have a great love of drink. Josef works hard and has very few pleasures, and so I hold my tongue.

While cleaning the house after I arrived, I found a trunk containing new fabrics as well as scrap fabrics left over from clothing Josef's first wife had sewn for her family. Barbara told me that Margaretha wanted to learn to quilt but felt she needed to accumulate more variety of fabrics and wait until her children were a little older. She had vowed that after her newest babe was born and weaned, she would not let anything stand in the way of having time for her own pleasures. Tragically, she and the infant died together before that time came. Barbara and I agree that every woman must have something of beauty and enjoyment in her life, and we are both determined that I will learn to quilt.

With love,
Magdalena

August 12, 1878

Dear Elizabeth,

What a joyful reunion we had when my sixty-five-year-old father Georg Helget arrived from Bohemia to spend his last years with us. He was very lonely after little Maggie and I left, and my brother Wenzel and I both begged him to join us in America. Because our house is quite small and Josef and I have four daughters with another babe expected, Father is making his home with Wenzel and Barbara. They have only one child, six-month-old Joseph, named after my husband as his godfather.

Wenzel is now working as a laborer at a flour mill. They live in the "Goosetown" section of New Ulm where many Bohemians have settled, being named for the flocks of geese that our people raise. I love to visit as the people speak our German-Bohemian dialect and keep the old traditions. The men have formed bands that play the familiar Bohemian polka music featuring concertinas and horns in the evenings or on Sunday afternoons. Father already knows some of the people from the Old Country, and he is quite happy there.

As promised, Barbara began her quilting lessons with me. She has taught me how to make paper templates, cut fabric using them, and sew the pieces together with tiny stitches. With a new babe she does not have as much time for lessons when we visit, but I am diligently working on my piecing when I have a few minutes of quiet after the children are in bed. Fortunately, my older sisters taught me how to sew clothes, and so I am not finding it difficult, only time-consuming.

I am using some of Margaretha's fabrics and patterns that she had saved, and as I go through her belongings I try to piece together the life and personality of the woman who was Josef's wife before me. I wonder if he loves her still and if I am merely a replacement or second best. Barbara's opinion is, "Men are not as complicated as women in their feelings. A man is generally happy with any woman who warms his bed, cooks his meals, and bears his children." I could never ask Josef directly, but I hope I mean more to him than that!

Affectionately,
Magdalena

August14, 1880

Dear Elizabeth,

The months pass so quickly and there is always much work to be done on a farm. Just to feed my husband and children three meals a day requires a lot of time spent cooking, baking, churning butter, gardening, and perhaps killing, plucking and frying a chicken or preparing game that Josef has hunted. Likewise, keeping a family of growing children properly clothed is never-ending when the clothes have to be sewn by hand and washed by first scrubbing on the washboard, rinsing, wringing them out, and pegging them on the line to dry, plus ironing and mending them. There are also the outside chores such as milking cows, feeding chickens and geese, gathering eggs, planting and tending gardens, as well as the seasonal chores like preserving fruits and vegetables in the summer, butchering animals in the fall and preserving the meat, and making soap from ashes and tallow.

Our two oldest, Margaret and Barbara, at fifteen and ten, are a great help to me with the housework and chores. Maggie at six is good at minding the little ones, Elizabeth three years and Maria eighteen months. Maria is a plump and agreeable babe, always smiling and such a joy to us all.

To add to my good fortune, I have again fallen with child. I do so hope this one will be a boy for Josef. He loves his daughters, but I think every man wants a son to carry on his name. Josef likes to tease me, "I am a good farmer and I sow my seed in a fertile field!" And I tease him back, "I am so fruitful that you have only to look at me and babes spring from my womb like grain spilling from a sack!" I praise God every night that He led me to this new land and has so richly blessed me with a good husband and a houseful of children.

Love,
Magdalena

October 14, 1881

Dearest Friend,

I write with grief lying heavy on my heart. Our beloved Maria died in August at two and a half years of "black diphtheria," named for the dark leather-like membrane that blocks the windpipe. A number of children have died from this dreaded disease in the past three years, but this summer a terrible epidemic hit our area. It is all the more fearsome because we do not know what causes it or how to prevent it. It is mostly a children's disease and nearly all that are stricken die.

Maria first complained of a sore throat and quickly progressed to burning up with fever and struggling to draw breath. We had the doctor come out from New Ulm, but he was exhausted from traveling day and night to visit the sick and he could do nothing to treat her. It was the most helpless and heartbreaking feeling to watch our child die in my arms. I think somehow little Maria was Josef's favorite (even our Lord had his favorites!), and he broke down and wept along with the girls and me at her passing. And then how we feared for our other children! But God was merciful and spared their lives. I should be grateful that Maria is in the arms of Jesus, but I do sorely miss her.

We had only recently changed our membership from Holy Trinity in New Ulm to St. George Catholic Church in that little village. It was closer for us to travel, and we feel at home as many members are also Bohemians. When Maria died we bought a double plot in their cemetery with room for four graves so someday we can be buried there also. We did not have money for a stone marker so Josef carved a handsome wooden cross to place on Maria's grave.

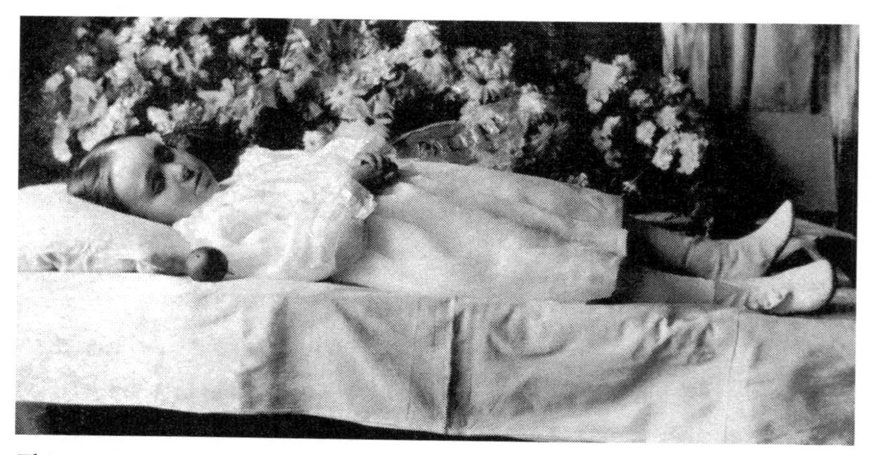

This post-mortem photograph was taken to memorialize the short life of a young girl around the turn of the century. This might be the only photograph the grief-stricken parents would have of their child.

Still others have been much more tragically affected. Fred Gerboth and his wife from Sleepy Eye had a sixteen-year-old boy and five younger girls. The diphtheria suddenly came into their home, and in a matter of days they buried all five girls with only the boy left to them. Fred was a candidate for the state legislature, but the tragedy so affected his mind that he had to withdraw. The Jacob Koschnick family, belonging to our church, has been dealt the most terrible blow of all. Within a six-week period they lost all seven of their young children to this dread killer. I do not know how those poor parents can bear to go on living. We have lost but one of ours and, oh, how we mourn that one!

It was a frightful summer of destruction and death. A series of violent tornadoes struck this very area and also demolished much of nearby West Newton and New Ulm, including Holy Trinity Catholic Church. There were a dozen lives lost and many injured, homes and barns carried away, trees and crops uprooted, livestock killed and property destroyed. We huddled in fright with our children in the root cellar several times as the roar of the storms passed over us, but always God's hand protected and spared our lives and our farm.

But in the midst of death there is life. We had a fine healthy son born to us last March, whom we named Michael. How happy and proud Josef was to finally have a son after five daughters! When he next went into St. George to buy supplies at the general store, he stopped in the saloon to announce the arrival of the babe and bought a round of drinks for all. We could ill afford his generosity, but I could not deny him his celebration of fatherhood.

With love,
Magdalena

November 30, 1882

Dear Elizabeth,

I am sorry to hear that you have lost a babe. I, too, a few weeks ago lost a daughter, who was born before her time and taken five days later. She was perfect in every way but ever so puny and frail. Josef went into St. George to bring Father Mon to baptize her, but he had gone to St. Paul and by the time he returned the babe had passed. He could not baptize her after her death and neither could she be buried in consecrated ground. We had not yet chosen a name, and it is said to be bad luck to name a dead babe. I had bought flannel to make diapers but had not yet accomplished that task. I used it to wrap the babe and to cushion the little box that Josef made from wood scraps. We buried her under the pine trees behind our house, and Josef made a wooden cross to mark the tiny grave.

I am mourning the daughter I will not have a chance to know and love. Such is the lot of women all the way back to Eve who ate of the forbidden fruit and was told by God, "I will greatly multiply thy sorrow and thy conception; in sorrow thou shall bring forth children." My own mother lost five of her ten children as infants, and then she herself died bringing me into this world. I was the namesake of two dead sisters and the third daughter to be called Magdalena. I will mourn with you for your lost child, as I know you will mourn with me.

In happier news, my brother Wenzel has purchased a farm of eighty acres in Cottonwood Township, Brown County, across the river from where we live. Just imagine that in only ten years he saved enough money for a farm! In Germany a man can work his whole life and never be able to afford land. My father lives with Wenzel and Barbara and is happy to be living on a farm. We continue to make payments on our little farm and hope that soon it will be ours in full.

I find little time for my quilting pleasures these days, as we are busy just scraping a living from the soil. I also raise chickens in order to have eggs to trade at the general store for groceries. I did manage to finish my first quilt even though it took me several years. Last winter was long and hard, and quilting helped to fill the lonely days. I was quite proud of the completed bedcovering, and Josef and the children all agreed it was a thing of wonder.

With my love,
Magdalena

September 20, 1884

Dear Friend,

I have not put pen to paper in some time, as I never seem to have a moment to call my own. I am pleased to have only good news to send you this time. We had another child in February named Katharina, but we call her Katrina. She is thriving and the four older girls dote on her and our little Michael. I thank God every night for answering my prayers when I was not much more than a frightened child myself, with a babe to raise on my own. I could never have imagined then that I would be so richly graced with a husband and many children.

My oldest stepdaughter Margaret was married in July to a Bohemian man, John Hanslick. She is only nineteen to his thirty-six years, but a man often needs time to establish himself before he can support a family. The wedding was held at our church in St. George, and what a fine party we had, with everyone bringing their favorite dishes from the Old Country. After dinner we moved most of the furniture outside, and the men played their Bohemian polka music with concertinas and brass horns for dancing until long into the night. The younger children fell asleep in a heap like tired puppies, while the older ones ran about playing games. I will miss Margaret at my side, but she loves John and is eager to start her own family. I wish God's blessing upon them.

Love,
Magdalena

June 22, 1886

Dear Elizabeth,

The Bible tells us, "The Lord giveth and the Lord taketh away." This was never truer than with Josef and me. We lost our precious two-year-old Katrina in March to that terrible plague called diphtheria, which afflicts us every few years. The doctors are saying now that it is passed from person to person rather than carried on the wind or caused by filth. So when our Katrina was struck down ill, I forbade the other children from going near her. When Father Beinhart came to give her last rites, he saw that her cheeks and neck were swollen and insisted that she had the mumps. He even wrote this in her burial record, but I knew that it was the diphtheria.

I nursed Katrina myself for two days and nights until what they call the "strangling angel of children" came for her. How bravely she fought to breathe, but what a hard death it was! It is law that every village or township must have a health officer, and we were placed under quarantine to keep the contagion from spreading. We were not allowed to have a public funeral, and so Josef built a small coffin and buried her in the St. George cemetery next to our Maria. We all know that life holds many hardships and sorrows, but the cruelest of all is to lose a child. I could not stop myself from weeping for days and nights afterward. It hit Josef hard too, but he just spent more time in the fields and barns where he could grieve alone.

As I said, God seems to be giving with one hand and taking with the other. Only twelve days after we lost Katrina, I birthed another wee girl. I greatly feared that her birth was brought on by shock and grief and that she was arriving too early into this world. But I believe God knew I could not bear another loss so soon and thankfully the babe was born fully formed. We named her Katharina, feeling she was sent as a gift to compensate for the child we had just lost, but we are calling her Kate instead of Katrina. Of course, there are no replacements for some things and so we are still mourning our first Katharina.

Not only am I a mother again, but I am also a grandmother, for Margaret and John had a boy babe last fall. I wonder why God gives women a childbearing span of about thirty years, as towards the end of that time their older children are often grown and bearing children of their own. But as women we take whatever children God sees fit to send us, whether many or few, whether early or late in our lives. We must be grateful for the ones that survive.

Much love,
Magdalena

November 24, 1889

Dear Elizabeth,

We are now truly "bauers" or landowning farmers in this great new country of ours. How wealthy we feel! Last week Josef made the final payment on our little farm in Lafayette Township, Nicollet County, which he began purchasing in 1874 for the sum of $210, and yesterday he received the deed to it from the Winona & St. Peter Land Company. It took much longer to pay off the loan than Josef had planned, but for a few years the grasshoppers ate most of the crops. Instead of making payments on the farm, Josef had to borrow money for us to live on and for seed to plant the following year. Then those loans had to be paid off before money could be applied against the farm.

We have a small farm of only twenty acres, compared to most farms of eighty or one hundred sixty acres, but with most of the work being done by hand, it is about all that Josef can manage alone. My brother Wenzel is very ambitious and has been buying up nearby land. He now owns over 300 acres! He has some advantages, as our father Georg can still lend a hand with chores and his son Joseph is old enough to help. Wenzel has also sponsored friends and relatives from Bohemia who have worked for him to pay off their passage. Josef has only what little help I can spare and what small chores our children are able to do. Still we marvel at how much better off we are than if we were in Bohemia. There if one's parents are poor, there is little chance that your life will ever be any different.

Back in January 1888 we lost a son, departing this life even as I was laboring to bring him into it. It grieved Josef greatly, as he is hoping for more sons to help with the farm and continue the family name. We buried the infant under our pine trees, next to the one lost in 1882. I feared that Josef blamed me for the loss, as if somehow I could have stopped the bleeding, or as if I could have not worked so strenuously. But how is a woman with a houseful of children and endless work supposed to take to her bed and rest?

I started piecing another quilt last winter after I lost the babe. I often felt melancholy and it helped to sit for a spell and let my mind wander as my needle wandered across the cloth. On occasion I despair that my children are taken from me as punishment for my long-ago sin in bearing a child out of wedlock. I asked this of our priest the last time I went to confession. He assured me that our God is a loving God and would not bear a grudge for a sin that was confessed and forgiven long ago. He said that I am but suffering the sorrows of women ever since Eve ate of that apple.

However, once again my belly is grown round with child, and indeed I am so large that either the infant will be born sooner than I had calculated or else I may be carrying twins. Every woman goes to childbed with a certain fear that either she or the babe or both may die in the process. I worry most of what should become of my other children if I were to die. Pray for me as my time comes near!

Blessings,
Magdalena

December 2, 1890

Dear Elizabeth,

Almost a year ago on Christmas Day I was delivered of boy and girl twins. The weather and the house were ever so cold at the time. In order to keep them warm, we wrapped the babes in blankets, put them in a dresser drawer, and set the drawer on the open oven door of the wood-burning stove. I did not get much sleep, as I had to get up every few hours to nurse them and add more wood to the stove.

The boy babe first cried much of the time and could not seem to feed properly, then he became too weak to cry or suck, and after nine days he crossed over. Our current priest is not so strict, and he allowed Josef to bury the tiny coffin in our cemetery plot even though the babe had not been baptized. (It was much too cold to take the tiny ones out to church in the open sleigh.) We had earlier discussed names for the children, including Martin or Albert for the boy, but had not made a choice. When the priest asked Josef for the name for the burial record, all Josef could remember was Albert, and the priest just wrote Al in his book. But I already thought of him as Martin. Our little Theresa was baptized on April 15th, when it was finally warm enough to take her out to church.

Each time I am with child, I promise myself I will not love this one so deeply in order to spare myself the terrible pain should I lose it. But I cannot help myself, as I do love them all something fierce from the time they take hold in my womb. When I must bury a child, a part of my heart is buried with it.

On a happier note, we had a busy year with two weddings. In June my Maggie was married to Fritz Wendinger at our church in St. George. Because she was only sixteen, Josef and I had to sign a consent to allow her to marry. We tried to persuade her to wait another year or two, but Maggie has always been a headstrong girl. She was so much in love and so eager to be married that we finally agreed. I sometimes ponder that had I remained in Bohemia, Maggie would have had to bear the shame of my sin and be called illegitimate all her life, while here she was as loved and accepted as any of our children.

In November Josef's younger daughter Barbara married Joseph Lessner, also at our church. She has just confided to me that she missed her monthly, and Maggie's belly is already swelling with a babe. So even though I have lost another child, I still feel God's blessings on me.

Love,
Magdalena

August 2, 1891

Dear Friend Elizabeth,

Death has visited us once again in the guise of diphtheria and has taken away another precious little one, as in 1881 and 1886. Nearly every family in the area has lost at least one child to this dreadful plague that passes through every few years, although the quarantine laws seem to be having some effect. Our sweet Kate died a hard death on April 20th, having just passed her fifth birthday, and she was buried with our other three children at the St. George cemetery. Our sixteen-month-old Theresa cannot understand that Kate is gone, and she continues to look in the corners and under the beds as if she thinks Kate is playing a game with her. But sadly, as you and I know, when death comes for you there is nowhere to hide.

This memorial photograph of a young girl taken about 1890 is a reminder of a time when it was all too common to lose babies and young children.

I was two months from birthing another child, whom I felt would be some compensation for the one I had lost, just as Kate came so soon after we lost Katrina. I fear that my grief and sorrow caused the babe to leave my womb before her time. She did not tarry long enough for us to name her. Josef buried her under the pine trees where two of our other unnamed babes are resting. I feel weighed down with melancholy and wish I could crawl into my bed and turn my face to the wall. But as long as there is someone on this earth who loves me and needs me, I manage to keep going. Even if I count Josef's two daughters as mine, I now have more children in heaven than I do on this earth, seven gone and six living.

I do have one piece of good news. This past spring Josef purchased an adjoining forty acres of land from the Winona & St. Peter Railroad for $420. To raise the money he sold our twenty-acre farm to a neighbor for $500. Josef feels very clever as he doubled our acreage and has $80 into the bargain. Because there are no buildings on this new land and because our neighbor already has a home on another farm, he is allowing us to remain living on our original farm.

Our only son Mike is a good sturdy boy of ten years and already much help to Josef with the farm and animals. Elizabeth is fourteen and of great assistance to me, especially with little Theresa. I must remember to praise God for what I do have and not weep for that which I do not have.

Much love,
Magdalena

June 18, 1892

Dear Elizabeth,

I am again mourning children gone too soon, this time both a grand-babe and a daughter. Our only granddaughter, Margaret's little Maria, died in May at almost two years old. I gave birth to another daughter on May 26th, whom Josef insisted we name Magdalena after myself. Alas, she was born sickly and struggled for eight days, her tiny body cramping up in pain. Even though she had not been baptized, we were permitted to bury her at the St. George cemetery. I am still weak from childbirth and misery and find it hard to keep going, but what choice do I have?

When we women are in childbed, our babes seem to know that they are going forth into a hard life and they are reluctant to leave the safety of the womb. Having carried a child for nine months and having to endure the pain of birthing, it seems most cruel when the babe is taken away. Each time I lose a child I find my faith in God shaken, but I cannot allow it to slip away for long. Life is just too hard to bear without a strong faith, and I try my best to pray, "Thy will be done, Lord."

While I was mending an old patchwork quilt today, I reflected that life is much like that old quilt. When one piece wears out or unravels, it affects all the pieces around it. Even so the loss of one of our children leaves a large hole in the fabric of our family.

Sending love,
Magdalena

November 18, 1893

Dear Elizabeth,

The babes just keep coming! I have either been with child or nursing a babe for most of our married life. After losing my last two because they were born too early, I vowed that I would be more careful the next time. So when I became plump with child earlier this year, I tried not to work like a field hand. I decided to return to my long-neglected quilting to force myself to occasionally put my feet up and rest. I enjoyed piecing the scraps when I could spare a few minutes between chores or while I was waiting for a pot to boil. Even now I try to escape the day-to-day drudgery and find a bit of time for my own pleasures.

This past July I was once again delivered of boy and girl twins, whom we named George and Franzis. Since they were so small and we feared they might not survive, Josef sent for the priest to baptize them two days later. Our little George suffered with cramps and did not thrive, and he was taken from us at barely two months into this hard world.

In this vintage photograph girl and boy twins are posed in front of a small whole-cloth quilt. This quilt is not pieced, but rather the beauty of the quilt comes from the quilting stitches.

I know that the Lord giveth and the Lord taketh away, but I still do not understand why he would give me so many children, just to snatch them back again! Why not spare me the pain of bringing them into this world if I am not to be allowed to keep them? Josef reminds me that the Good Book says, "Who can know the mind of the Lord or understand His ways?" We must remember that God's ways are higher than ours, even if we cannot wrap our feeble minds around them. We are grateful that our little Franzis (called Francy) is growing strong at four months.

When I last went to confession I asked our priest if there was some way to prevent myself from falling with child every time Josef hung his pants on my bedpost. He just scolded me and told me to take as many children as God gives me and be thankful for them. When I asked how I was supposed to feed more children, the priest replied, "That's easy! Just add more water to the soup." What does a man such as he know of the pain of bearing babes, caring for them night and day, hearing their cries when they are hungry, or burying their tiny caskets?

I have some sad news to share with you. My dear father George Helget died on October 24th at my brother Wenzel's farm. He had attained the great age of eighty years, but was in poor health and had told us that he was ready to meet his Maker. We do miss Father but are comforted to know that he is finally reunited with our long-departed mother in heaven.

Love,
Magdalena

October 14, 1895

Dearest Elizabeth,

God be praised! I birthed a fine son last December. We named him Joseph for his father, but everyone calls him "Sep." He may be our last as I am near the end of my childbearing years at forty, and Josef is fifty-five years. It seems strange to still be having children when I am also a grandmother of ten children, my daughter Maggie's three and my two stepdaughters' seven children.

But as ever God gives with one hand and takes with the other. My stepdaughter Margaret Hanslick died in August at age thirty years from tuberculosis. She wasted away in the last months, and because of the contagion her children had to be kept from her. It quite broke her heart and theirs to be thus separated. Her four boys are ages one through nine, and their father John cannot care for them alone. Their neighbors have taken the baby in, while the three older boys have been parceled out to live with various relatives until such time as they are older or John can remarry or hire help.

Last week our Elizabeth, your namesake, was married to John Wendinger, who is a brother to my daughter Maggie's husband, Fritz Wendinger. They are a good match even if John is twenty-seven to Lizzie's eighteen years. They have been sweet on each other for several years, but Lizzie knew that I depended on her help and promised that she would wait until she was eighteen to wed. She helped complete the quilt I had started several years ago and was happy to have it for her marriage bed. I have many more ideas for quilts in my head, so I am anxious to start on another one over the coming winter.

Blessings,
Magdalena

Wedding portrait of Elizabeth Tauer and John Wendinger, married on October 8, 1895, at St. George, Nicollet County, Minnesota.

December 6, 1896

Dear Elizabeth,

I am sending you a photographic image of our family showing Josef, myself, and our four youngest children, Mike at fifteen, Theresa six, Francy three, and Sep two years. Our older daughters Barbara, Maggie, and Elizabeth are all married and have families of their own and so are not shown with us, and Margaret is deceased. I had long wished to have such a family portrait made but did not think that we could afford one.

This family portrait of Josef and Magdalena Tauer with their youngest children, Michael, Theresa, Joseph, and Franzis, was taken in about 1896 in New Ulm, Minnesota.

However, last winter Josef stopped in New Ulm with the Wilfahrt brothers after they had been out cutting wood nearby. Our Bohemian men are very fond of their drink, and the three of them began sampling beers in a number of local establishments. As they were passing by Anton Gag's photographic studio, they stopped in to visit, for Anton is also a Bohemian. He convinced the men that it would be a good occasion to have a portrait made, and so they posed in their dirty work clothes, one wearing a coat of muskrat skins and all of them holding cigars.

Josef Tauer (left) posed with two friends at a photography studio in New Ulm in about 1895.

When Josef brought the photograph home, I decided that if he could spend good money on such pure foolishness, then I would indeed have a family portrait made. So one day this fall when we went into New Ulm for supplies, I had everyone dress in their Sunday best and we sat for our portrait. I treasure it ever so much!

Love,
Magdalena

November 28, 1899

Dearest Elizabeth,

I am exceedingly heartsick with sorrow. Our dear Francy died on October 17th without any warning. When she suddenly went into convulsions, Josef mounted a horse and raced to New Ulm for the doctor, but she died in my arms before they returned. The doctor called it apoplexy, which I understand is a hemorrhage in the brain. Josef took this death very hard and sat for hours afterward clutching Francy with tears streaming down his face. It took a lot of persuasion before he would give her up so we could prepare her for burial.

It is hard enough to lose a tiny babe that is born too soon, but to lose a lively six-year-old is almost enough to destroy one's faith in God. I remember when I had lost the second of my babes I took comfort in imagining Jesus carrying the two of them in his arms. But now that he has taken ten of my little ones, how am I to imagine Him carrying all of them? It is just too much for a soul to bear. I wish I could take to my bed, pull the quilts up over my head, and sleep forever to forget my sorrows. Little Sep and Theresa look at me with their sad eyes and tears, but I have no answers to give them. I can only hug them and cry with them as we look at Francy's image in our family picture.

We buried Francy in the cemetery beside her brothers and sisters. When we lost our first child, Josef and I bought a double plot with space enough for four adults, thinking that we also would be buried there someday. Since then we have filled it with seven of our little ones (another three were buried on the farm), and there is no longer room for us. Besides my daughter Maggie that came with me from Bohemia, I have borne fourteen children to Josef. Ten of those have died between birth and age six and only four are left to us. Josef had four children with his first wife, two of whom died at birth. So between the two of us, we have had a total of nineteen children, but only six are living still: Josef's Barbara, my Maggie, and our Elizabeth, Michael, Theresa and Joseph. Sometimes when I am in deep despair over my lost children, I wonder how I will survive yet another day. At times it feels as if my whole life has been nothing more than a struggle to survive. But surviving is all I can do, as I expect the Good Lord is not ready for me just yet.

With love,
Magdalena

9 North Valley Street
City of New Ulm
Minnesota, America

August 21, 1901

Dear Elizabeth,

Josef and I have retired from farming and moved into New Ulm. We sold the farm to our son-in-law John Hanslick, who has four sons to work alongside him. Our older son Mike was not ready to manage the farm on his own and wanted to try his hand at something else. Josef is almost sixty-two, suffering from health problems and worn out from hard work. He does some odd jobs around town and some seasonal work on nearby farms to support us, and we also have money from the sale of the farm left over after buying this house.

Mike was married in June to Marianna Zischka at the church in St. George, both being twenty years of age. Marianna is already well known for making her beautiful Bohemian bobbin lace. Mike says that farming is too much hard work, and he has obtained a job as a drayman, driving a horse and wagon and making deliveries for local businesses. Josef and I have only the two littlest ones at home now, Theresa eleven and Sep six years.

I finally have time to return to my quilting, which has been sadly neglected over the years. Two-color quilts have been popular for some time with those who have the means to purchase their quilting fabrics rather than using leftover scraps. I had always hoped to make one someday. I already had a sufficient quantity of muslin on hand to use in a quilt top and for backing and binding. When I found an especially pretty double-pink fabric in the dry goods store last week, I knew that with the purchase of a few yards of it I could make a lovely two-color quilt. I bleached the muslin from a tan color to a more attractive off-white color. I found just the right pattern among the ones I had saved, which is really quite simple but appears more complicated. The quilt is called "Jacob's Ladder" for the Bible story in Genesis 28 where Jacob sees ladders set up on the earth and the angels of God ascending and descending from heaven. I am most excited and hope to start on it tomorrow!

Your dear friend,
Magdalena

JACOB'S LADDER QUILT: Designed and pieced by Lanie Tiffenbach using vintage double-pink fabric and bleached muslin. Long-arm machine quilted by Barb Simons.

June 30, 1905

Dear Elizabeth,

Our son Mike decided he did not like working for others and returned to farming in Lafayette Township. He and Marianna have a lively two-year-old boy named Joseph after my husband. Our Theresa is now fifteen and working as a maid for a well-to-do family, and Sep is ten with a few more years of school ahead of him.

Theresa Tauer at her First Communion at Holy Trinity Catholic Church in 1902

I have greatly enjoyed returning to my quilt making. I can usually piece two quilt tops during the spring and summer months and then set up my quilt frame to quilt them over the fall and winter. Oftentimes the Bohemian women in my neighborhood stop by to visit, bringing along their piecing, mending or other handwork. We don't feel guilty wasting time sitting and talking if we can do something productive at the same time. Making quilts for others allows me to express my creativity and at the same time show my love for family and friends.

With love,
Magdalena

Traveling photographers often used quilts as convenient backdrops to create a studio setting outdoors, as in this postcard photo from the early 1900s. These are probably the backs of the quilts, with the mother hiding behind the chair to hold the baby in place.

April 18, 1908

Dear Elizabeth,

My daughter Theresa is naive and foolish when it comes to men, just as I myself was so many years ago. She met a young farmer from Renville County at one of the dances regularly held by the Bohemian bands on Saturday nights. After some months of courting, Theresa began to show signs of morning sickness and confessed her fear that she might be carrying a child.

As is the way of men, Ernest had earlier promised to marry her in this event. However, his parents are Lutheran and would not allow him to marry a Catholic girl unless she would agree to convert to their Lutheran faith. We felt that since Ernest had caused the problem he should be the one to convert. Finally when Theresa was about seven months gone, a compromise was reached. It was agreed that they would be married posthaste, and Theresa would raise their children in the Catholic faith, but that Ernest would remain in the Lutheran Church.

On February 26th Theresa was married to Ernest Schefus at Holy Trinity Catholic Church here in New Ulm, at the respective ages of eighteen and twenty-three years. Tragically after all of that, the tiny boy was born too early and lived only one day. Theresa feels that it is her fault that the babe died, as under the difficult circumstances she did not want it when it was first growing in her. I comfort her that losing a babe is the will of God and that nothing she did affected it. If she is anything like me, she will soon be with child again.

Affectionately,
Magdalena

Ernest Schefus and Theresa Tauer posed for their wedding portrait on February 26, 1908. Their attendants were Mike and Marianna Tauer, Theresa's brother and his wife.

February 12, 1909

Dearest Elizabeth,

I send my sympathies to you on the loss of your husband, along with the news that I am also a widow. Josef was ill for some time suffering from bladder problems, and I was quite worn out with caring for him. On November 15th of last year at the age of sixty-nine years, he died in his own bed as he wished, having refused to stay in the hospital.

Josef and I shared thirty-two years of joys and sorrows. I never once regretted my decision to come to America to be his wife, even though I was leaving the familiar and stepping off blindly into the unknown. In spite of our many trials and losses, we made a good life for ourselves.

I have only Sep at home now to keep me company. He will soon be finished with eighth grade and will need to find some type of work to help put food on the table. My youngest daughter Theresa and her husband Ernest Schefus are renting a farm in Camp Township in Renville County and will soon welcome a little stranger into their family.

Love,
Magdalena

November 15, 1912

Dear Elizabeth,

As I predicted when my daughter Theresa lost her first babe, it was not long before she bore a healthy boy and two years later another one. They are called George and Mike and are quite an active pair. I have been blessed with twenty-one grandchildren and expect there are more still to come.

My youngest son Sep is eighteen years old, has a job as a carpenter's helper, and is making enough to support the two of us. I am proud of him, as he is a quiet and good boy and does not get into any trouble. I am slowing down somewhat at age fifty-eight, but I still plant a large garden behind our house and preserve much of the produce. I try to work on my quilting for an hour or two each day, and that helps pass the time and gives me pleasure too.

This postcard photo of George and Mike, the oldest children of Theresa and Ernest Schefus, was taken in 1913.

As I was recently piecing small scraps together for a patchwork quilt, I thought of how I had constructed a new life bit by bit after I came to America. I also imagined that our family was something like that patchwork quilt, composed of Josef and his two daughters, myself and my daughter, and the children from the two of us. Just as in a quilt, the different parts of our family blended together well to make a pleasing whole. How greatly I was blessed!

Your dear friend,
Magdalena

July 1, 1917

Dear Elizabeth,

I am sorry to hear about your trials during this great "War to End All Wars," but I am relieved to hear that you are managing to hold on and survive. My son Joseph at age twenty-two obtained a deferment on the grounds that he is my sole support, and he is currently working as a bricklayer. We do not know what will happen if this war continues, but I pray he will not be drafted into the army. He is a gentle and shy person and would not make a good soldier.

My brother Wenzel Helget died last month at age seventy-three. His wife Barbara had died a year previous, and Wenzel so mourned her that he purely wasted away from grief. Joseph Helget, their only child to survive to adulthood, had died in 1909 at age thirty-one from typhoid fever contracted from drinking contaminated water, leaving a wife and three daughters.

Elmer, the youngest son of Theresa and Ernest Schefus, is shown in this studio photograph from 1917.

In happier news, I have been greatly blessed with more grandchildren. Barbara now has six children, Maggie and Elizabeth each have four, Mike and his wife have two, and Theresa has three little boys. I am enclosing a picture of her youngest, Elmer, age two. He was supposed to sit in the chair but is quite an independent little fellow and insisted on standing.

Hoping you are well,

Magdalena

March 15, 1920

Dear Elizabeth,

My son Joseph was eventually drafted into the Army in May 1918, but the Great War ended soon after that and he was honorably discharged in June 1919. I was so thankful that he did not have to take up arms, but was engaged by the Army as a cook at Camp Dodge in Iowa.

Joseph (Sep) Tauer, son of Josef and Magdalena Tauer, served in the US Army during World War I.

We have read in the newspapers that Bohemia is officially no more. As we understand it, Austria-Hungary has been stripped of much of its territory, with the country of Czechoslovakia formed out of some of its former colonies including Bohemia. We are happy to hear that it is a democratic country, and we hope that life will finally be better for you after enduring the difficult years of war.

You said in your last letter that you married for love and that your love lasted throughout your marriage. You asked since mine was an arranged marriage to a man I could hardly have loved at the time, did Josef and I ever come to love each other? Not having had much experience with men, it was a bit difficult at first to live with a stranger and learn his ways. But we soon formed an easy friendship, shared a sense of humor, and grew close in our shared joys and losses.

Josef's greatest fault was, like many Bohemian men, his love of beer and strong drink. I often wished I could have the money wasted by him on those pleasures to spend for food, fabric, or new shoes for the children. But never did he beat me or the children when he came home from town smelling of drink, as do many men. Yes, I can say I truly loved Josef and I miss him greatly. Of course, we never spoke of such things directly, but he treated me with kindness and never raised a hand to me, and I do believe he loved me too.

Love and affection,
Magdalena

Sigel Township
Minnesota, America

March 16, 1926

Dear Elizabeth,

Once again I write of both blessings and loss. First the blessings: My youngest daughter Theresa had a baby girl named Irene two years ago. The two older boys are a great help to Ernest with the farm work, but Elmer at eight years is assigned to watch the baby. He has a pair of pet goats and he hitches them to a little wagon with the baby in it. Sometimes the goats give the poor child a wild bouncing ride, and my heart nearly stops with the fear of it!

This snapshot photo from 1924 shows Irene, daughter of Theresa and Ernest Schefus, in a wagon pulled by pet goats.

Another blessing: My youngest son Joseph was married in September 1923 to Cecelia Donnay. They have a daughter and are expecting another child in the fall. Sep is currently working as a carpenter in New Ulm. I had, some time ago, gone through what little money Josef left to me, but while Sep was living with me and working, he was able to support the two of us.

Since his marriage I have made my home with my older son Mike and his wife on their farm in Sigel Township near New Ulm. Cecelia is an independent woman, and I suspect she did not want to take on my care when she married Sep. I have always gotten along well with Marianna, and she made me feel welcome in her home. However, I still find it difficult to accept that I need help, even if it is from my own children. Fortunately, the money that I have from selling the house will last the few remaining years I may be allotted on this earth.

Now the loss: Mike and Marianna suffered a most terrible tragedy last August and are still in deep mourning. Their sixteen-year-old daughter Lillian was accidentally shot by her boyfriend when he was showing her his father's gun. He did not realize that the gun was loaded and is much consumed by guilt and remorse. Marianna had doted on her daughter, and she tells me she cannot imagine how I could lose ten children and still go on living. I tell her that the Lord never sends more troubles than you can bear, but I guess He must have lost count of just how many of my babes He had taken from me. Mike and Marianna's only other child, Joseph Michael Tauer, is married, and his year-old son is the only one who can make them smile these days.

With love,

Magdalena

This photograph of Lillian and Joseph Michael Tauer, children of Michael and Marianna Tauer, was taken in 1910 in New Ulm, Minnesota.

City of New Ulm
Brown County
Minnesota, America

June 28, 1931

Dear Elizabeth,

Mike and Marianna have retired from farming and have moved to New Ulm to live, and I have moved along with them. I am now seventy-six years old and I sometimes need help with certain tasks. All my life I was the one taking care of others. Now that the tables have turned I find it hard to ask for help, as I do not wish to be a burden on anyone. When Josef and I were on the farm and the children were young, there was never enough sunlight in the day to accomplish all my tasks, but now that I am old I seem to have more time than tasks to keep me occupied. I try to do some quilting each day but my eyesight is failing, and I do not think that I will be able to either quilt or write letters much longer.

However, I have found that there are certain benefits to growing older. I can rise up when I want, lie down and take a nap in the afternoon, or be wakeful in the night keeping company with God or reliving my past days. I lived through many days of darkness, but they were spread out over my allotted lifespan and somehow I endured them.

I think oftentimes of how empty my life might have been if I had remained in Bohemia and not found a husband and had more children. Even though we never had much money and I had to work hard, I did have a happy life with Josef and our children. I was greatly blessed to have so many babes and even the ones that I lost brought me much joy while they were with me. How I loved to sniff their sweet baby smell as I nuzzled their necks, and how I loved to nurse them, feeling the gentle release in my breasts as they looked up at me with their trusting eyes! When they smiled and cooed at me, when they hugged my neck with their chubby arms, when they took their first wobbling steps, I would feel my heart overflow with happiness. Yes, I would suffer the heartbreak of losing those babes again just to have them for the short days, months, or years that they blessed me with. Yes, I would do it all over again, every bit of it.

Your dear friend,
Magdalena

April 30, 1939

Dear Elizabeth,

I am your namesake, Elizabeth Tauer Wendinger, writing to let you know that our beloved mother, Magdalena Helget Tauer, has passed. She departed this world on April 21, 1939, at the great age of eighty-six years. She had been ill only four days and died at the home of my brother Mike Tauer in New Ulm. We rejoice that she is reunited with our father and their many lost children in heaven.

Mother always said that you were her dearest friend. She so treasured your letters and shared them with us. I feel that I know you well, although I do wish I could have known you in person.

God bless you,
Elizabeth Tauer Wendinger

6

CAROLINA'S STORY: COURAGE IN THE FACE OF THE UNKNOWN

This story is based on the life of my great-grandmother Carolina Schroeder Schefus (my father's paternal grandmother), who was born in 1855 in West Pomerania, Prussia, Germany. She immigrated to America in 1880 with her husband and four children. I grew up on the farm that Carolina and my great-grandfather purchased, which was passed down in the family for several generations.

This lovely vintage photograph of an unknown young farm woman was taken in Germany.

RECORD BOOK OF CAROLINA SCHEFUS

October 12, 1880

Today I was given this record-keeping book by my cousin Martha as a parting gift when we said our tearful farewells. Tomorrow my family shall leave our home in the village of Dorow, Pomerania, Prussia, Germany, forever. Martha and I have been inseparable since we were babes in arms, and I cannot fathom that we will never see each other again on this earth. Martha has always teased me about my great love of books, and she has charged me with writing my own book about the journey we are about to undertake and the adventures ahead. She thinks it is very brave, that I, who have never been further than an hour's journey from my birthplace, should travel across the wide ocean and the broad new country of America to the very ends of the frontier.

In truth, I am not brave at all and greatly fear leaving the known, as poor as it may be, for the vast unknown. I am terrified that we may all perish on the dangerous ocean crossing. How will I care for four little children under the age of six, one but a new babe, on such a difficult journey? I fear to think of keeping them fed, clothed, and protected in this place called Minnesota, which sounds like a wild unsettled place. I know I worry overmuch, but we are risking our lives and those of our precious children. What if the tales of riches in this new world prove to be false and we do not have the money to return?

Georg is the head of our family and makes all the decisions for us, as he rightly should, and he has sufficient courage for the both of us. He is still young enough to long for some adventure out of life, and he is excited about the challenges of a new country and hopeful of a better living. Like many men in these poor economic times who do not own land or have a family trade to inherit, he has not been able to find work other than as a day laborer or seasonal farmhand. We can barely scrape by enough to put food in our mouths and clothes on our backs and keep the wolf from the door, especially as our family grows. There is little opportunity to improve one's status here, and as the saying goes, "If you are born poor, then you will certainly die poor."

Only the knowledge that we will be reunited with my father and mother (Fritz and Sophie Schroeder), my two younger sisters Friederike and Wilhelmina, and my older brother John, his wife and children at the end of the journey makes this undertaking bearable. When they departed for America a year ago, I had grieved so, believing I would never see them again. Georg wanted to accompany them, but I was in terror of leaving the only home I had known and risking our lives and those of our precious children. In any event, we did not then have the money for the ship passage and that settled the matter.

My parents and brother have penned letters to us, telling of the great opportunities to earn money and own land in the New World. In Germany a man can toil all his life and never be able to save enough to obtain that all-important patch of soil to call his own. Georg is most excited at the prospect of owning a farm, and we have now put aside money for the journey by scrimping and saving, selling some meager possessions, and receiving small gifts from well-wishing kin and friends. I wonder if I am strong enough to endure the hardship and sacrifice involved in getting there and establishing a new home in an alien land, even with my parents and siblings ahead of us. Georg has no such fears and prepares to venture forth with an explorer's courage from one world to another, full of ambitions, hopes and dreams.

So I begin my tale: My maiden name is Carolina Sophia Schroeder and I am twenty-five years of age. In 1873 I wed Johann Joachim Georg Schefus (known as Georg), now age thirty. We have three young daughters, Friederike (Rike), Wilhelmina (Minnie) and Johanna (Hannah), being six, four and two years old, and a newborn son, Wilhelm (Willie). Tomorrow we leave our tiny village and travel to the great unknown awaiting us in America. There are not enough pages in this book to write often, but I will try to record the large events in my life and my feelings so that someday my children and grandchildren will be able to read of the great adventures before us, whether good or bad. Have courage! May God protect us on this long and frightening journey!

A tintype photo from about 1880 shows four young siblings who appear to be about the ages of Carolina's children when they emigrated to America. Many women were blessed with a child every year or two throughout their childbearing years.

November 5, 1880

Praise God we have safely landed in America! We traveled by train to Hamburg and boarded the steamship *Allemania*, departing on October 19th and arriving in New York on November 3rd. There were seventeen first-class and 728 steerage passengers on our ship. How difficult it was to live in such close proximity to strangers in the dark and dank hold, with the reeking odor of unwashed bodies, seasickness and dysentery, and with the ever-present noises of babies squalling, children shrieking, and people talking, weeping and snoring. When weather allowed, we took the children above deck to breathe some clean air. Seeing nothing in any direction but mighty waves, I felt that we must surely be swallowed up or lost at sea!

It was difficult to tend to four little ones among so many people, to keep them occupied and quiet when they were well or care for them when they were sick, often being sick myself as well. The girls became cranky and restless confined to their bunk for large stretches of time, with nothing more to entertain them than my stories and the little dolls I had made out of old socks for each child. When the ocean was not too rough, I allowed them to run about and play with other children. Then it seemed one of them was always losing her balance from the rocking of the boat, falling and crying from a bumped head. Of course, with a babe I had the necessity of constantly washing diapers by hand and finding somewhere to hang them to dry. As caring for children is considered "women's work," Georg was not much help and spent most of his time with the other men, comparing information on our new homeland.

My nineteen-year-old brother Friedrich Schroeder decided at the last moment to join us on this voyage. Our parents had wanted him to accompany them last year, but he fancied himself in love with a neighbor girl. She wept and clung to him so that he promised he would not leave her. Since that time Friedrich has sorely missed our parents, and he recently had a falling-out with the girl. We are looking forward to surprising our family when he arrives with us.

Yesterday we were processed through Castle Island Immigration Center and thankfully passed the medical inspections and questioning. We were concerned as the children had all developed colds on the voyage, but that was not sufficient to turn us back.

The children and I are at a boarding house while Georg determines the best route and means of travel to Minnesota and buys some food to take with us. I am purely worn out from traveling and caring for four little ones, and we have yet another long journey ahead of us. However, I am resolved to be strong and brave (or at least not show my fear and weakness) as at this point there is no alternative!

January 1, 1881

How strange life is! Who could have imagined that I would find myself on the very edge of civilization? The open prairies we passed on the train were like waves of the sea, with grass undulating to the flat horizon. Every day of our journey I kept asking myself, "What have we done? How will we feed our children? Can we survive in this land?"

But what a wonderful reunion we had when our train finally arrived in New Ulm, Minnesota. Georg had posted a letter from New York, and so my parents and the rest of my family were at the station to greet us. Mother and I could not stop hugging and crying with joy, and everyone exclaimed over our little Willie and how the girls had grown. Of course, they were ever so surprised and happy to find Friedrich with us.

We were soon whisked off to a justice of the peace, where in a quick ceremony my fifteen-year-old sister Friederike was married to twenty-two-year-old Julius Schiffman. She was thrilled to have her favorite brother Friedrich there to stand as a witness. I cannot fathom that my little sister is married, but she was ever so headstrong and determined to have her own way. Mother later confided that Friederike was so dizzy with love that she and Father feared for her virtue and that she might bring shame to our family if they did not allow them to wed.

We spent a few weeks with Mother and Father at their home in New Ulm while Georg searched for a job and a place to live. He finally found work on a farm in Le Sueur County near St. Peter, which had a small primitive house for us to occupy. We have settled in with the few possessions we brought with us or that our families or the owner of the farm were able to spare. This farm is about thirty miles from where the rest of my family lives, which is most of a day's journey by horse and wagon. This means, unfortunately, that we will not have many occasions to visit them or for them to visit us. I am quite terrified to think of having to feed, clothe, and care for our children while trying to build a new life in this lonesome distant land, so far from everything we once knew. God be with us!

January 15, 1882

How quickly our first year in this new country has flown! It was most difficult to get a home established with very little money or provisions. Essentials had to be made, begged, bartered or purchased to set up housekeeping, and a garden had to be planted, tended and harvested. We had to borrow money from Father to buy a few chickens and a cow so that at least we had eggs and milk to feed the children when there was little else to put on the table. Some days I had to pretend I was not hungry so Georg and the children could have enough to eat.

I have been very lonesome tucked away on an isolated farm in a new country, but to tell the truth, most of the time I was so overwhelmed with work and children that I did not have time to dwell on it. Although the rest of my family live at some distance, it is a comfort just to know that they are in this same country and we are able to see them on the rare occasion.

Last month I gave birth to another son, whom we named August. Until I married I had no idea of how babies got started, but now that I have had five children in eight years, I have no idea how to stop them coming! What a blessing it was to have my mother stay with us for a few weeks to help in the birthing and care for me and the children. Rike, my oldest at seven years, is a reliable and cheerful helper with small chores such as drying dishes. Minnie at five years is too energetic and would rather play, but can usually be trusted with keeping an eye on the younger ones. I want my children to enjoy their childhood, but with a growing family and a farm to manage, all hands are needed to do what they are able, even small hands.

Besides the everyday struggle to find and prepare enough food, I have to keep house, wash laundry and diapers on a scrubbing board, sew and mend clothing, milk the cow, tend the chickens and garden, as well as seeing to the constant demands of five little ones. I always feel as if I have barely laid my head down on my pillow at night when it is time to rise and begin all over again.

Georg filed a declaration of intention to become a naturalized citizen in the district courthouse in St. Peter on November 3, 1881. This was exactly one year to the very day after our arrival in this country and the very earliest he could file such a declaration. He is so proud of our adopted country and how well we have managed here. Georg is earning good wages as a farmhand, and we are saving as much as possible in order to begin farming on our own. I am feeling hopeful that the worst is behind us, and the future is beginning to look much brighter.

April 1, 1883

After completing the harvest last fall, we relocated to a farm that we are renting from John Lane in Ridgely Township, Nicollet County. This farm has good fields and a snug log cabin set back in the woods. The small cabin consists of one large room with a kitchen on one end, a table and benches in the middle, and our bed tucked into the back corner. There is a loft under the eaves where the children sleep, except for the youngest who is in the cradle near the fireplace. I am especially pleased that we are now living closer to the rest of my family and can see them more often.

The newest child added to our family is Anna, born one month ago. There is scarcely a mother who does not lose one or more babes. I am so blessed to have six healthy children. As our family grows, I fret about keeping them fed and clothed, but my wise mother tells me, "If God gives you children, he will provide for them."

We have become friends with our nearest neighbors, Rudolph and Christina Braun. Christina makes wonderful patchwork quilts from leftover fabric and has shown me how it is done. I am starting with simple four-patch blocks made from scraps. Some are pieces of new fabric but some are of used fabric. When Georg's or my clothes are worn out, I can usually salvage some of the lesser-worn parts and sew clothing for the children from these pieces. I do not like to throw anything away, and so I can use up all the scraps that are too small for any other purpose to make my quilts. I am so enjoying arranging the fabrics to make pleasing color combinations, and the piecing keeps my hands busy in the evening when I am through with chores and the children are put to bed.

We have joined St. John's Lutheran Church of Ridgely Township, which is only two miles away. This small country church began in 1869, when this area was first being settled. Since all the preaching and teaching is done in the German language, we feel comfortable there. Most everyone in this area is German, with those from southern Germany generally being Roman Catholics and those from northern Germany being Lutherans. Also, the climate in Minnesota is very similar to where we lived in northern Germany, and sometimes it is difficult to believe that we have moved halfway around the world from our birthplace.

November 1, 1884

Georg and I were blessed with another son on October 8th and we christened him Ernest. Having borne seven children in ten years, I asked my Mother if there was a way to stop the babes from coming every year or two. Somewhat embarrassed she replied, "The only known way is to refuse your husband's attentions, but that would surely destroy his affection for you and would be against God's will." She scolded me, "Do not complain of too many children too fast. God gives us women lots of children because we lose so many young ones. Count your blessings!"

I do love my children, for they are each and every one precious to me, but I get so weary of the endless feedings, the soiled diapers, and their constant need for care and attention, in addition to the cooking, washing, cleaning and all that needs to be done to just get through the day. Sometimes I wish I could just go off by myself and sleep and sleep and sleep!

Raising children was an all-consuming job in the 1880s, when this picture of a large family was taken. The endless tasks of keeping so many children fed, clothed, warm and dry were enough to tire out any woman.

I did finish my first quilt and I am quite proud of it. The four-patch blocks made a cheerful top. I bought inexpensive muslin for the alternate blocks and the backing, and I used a worn blanket for the filling. I wanted to use it this winter so instead of stitching it, I tied the layers together with knitting yarn. It looks lovely on our bed, and the children delight in looking at the various patches and remembering the clothing that was made from the fabrics in the quilt. I love to hear them exclaiming, "I remember wearing this dress!" or "Here is my shirt!" or "Look, this one is Mother's apron!"

November 22, 1885

Today my youngest sister Wilhelmina was married to Anton Seesz at the nearby Bethel Methodist Church. Our Lutheran pastor would not marry them because Anton is a Roman Catholic. Likewise, Wilhelmina refused to be married in his church, for she would have been required to sign an oath promising to raise her children as Catholics, and she plans to raise them in our church. I had tried to warn my sister against this marriage, because Anton is also a Bohemian and they are known to be drinking men. Father and Mother were not so happy with her choice either, as Anton is fourteen years older, but Wilhelmina at eighteen years believes herself in love and could not be dissuaded.

My other sister Friederike Schiffman is only twenty, but already has three little boys under the age of three, with yet another babe on the way. She is quite overwhelmed in caring for them. I took pity on her and sent my Minnie, who was then eight years old, to stay with her most of the past summer. Minnie has an outgoing nature and thought it was wonderful to escape her daily chores, visit her aunt, and play with her little cousins. She proved invaluable to Friederike in minding the babes, so she could then tend to her household chores and gardening.

I could not spare my oldest, Rike, as she is such a responsible worker and a great help to me. She was, however, a little jealous that Minnie had an adventure, while she had to stay at home and do Minnie's chores as well. I tried to make it up to her by letting her bake cookies (or eat an extra one) or by allowing her to fill a washtub with cool water on hot days to splash in with the younger children. Hannah at six had to take on a few extra chores too. She always expects the same privileges as her two older sisters, but is of an impetuous nature and does not take her share of work seriously.

My parents Fritz and Sophie Schroeder have used their savings to purchase a farm in Severance Township, Sibley County. I am so pleased that they are now living closer to us. They have also joined our little country church, and I do enjoy visiting with them on Sunday mornings—even though the visits are all too short.

I have started piecing another quilt from fabric scraps. Rike, Minnie, and even Hannah help me by tracing around the paper templates and cutting out the pieces. I allow them some creativity in choosing colors and fabrics, so this is an enjoyable pastime for them as well. Rike also keeps needles threaded for me, so this quilt top is progressing nicely. I am putting a few pennies away regularly so that I can buy a wool batting for a nice warm quilt. I will need to tie it, as there just is not time for fancy quilting now. Someday I hope to have money to buy new fabric for a quilt and also time to stitch a quilt together instead of tying it. But that may be some time yet with my ever-growing family and all the clothes that need to be sewn for them.

November 11, 1886

When I began this book I imagined it filled with exciting happenings, but instead I am mostly recording the births of my children. Our eighth child, a daughter named Emma, arrived a few weeks ago and is growing strong. No matter how many children we have, I am always amazed at just how quickly they change. It seems I have only been holding a helpless infant when suddenly I have a heavy lump riding on my hip, next a busy little thing crawling about, and then a small person who can walk and talk. What a miracle!

Our little log cabin is getting quite crowded with children and Georg had to make a larger table and more benches for it. Upstairs in the loft the three boys sleep in one bed and the four girls sleep crosswise in another, while baby Emma is in the cradle downstairs. Children do not remain babes for long when the next one comes along so quickly and crowds them out of the cradle. I wonder how many more children God has waiting for me, as I am but thirty-one and have many more fertile years ahead. Thankfully, my three older daughters at twelve, ten and eight years are good with the smaller household chores and minding the younger children, although they do tend to squabble over the work.

Even the smallest ones are taught to be helpful and useful as soon as they are able.

December 21, 1888

My dear father, Fritz Schroeder, died twelve days ago at his home, and I will miss him greatly. He would have been sixty-four years old today, but had been in poor health some months suffering from stomach pain. He had sold their Sibley County farm to my brother Friedrich when he married last year, but our parents continued to live on the farm with them.

Mother took this loss quite hard and has now gone to make her home with my sister Friederike. Both are pleased with the arrangement, as a mother would rather live with her daughter than a daughter-in-law, and Friederike will be most happy for our mother's company and help with her children. Poor Friederike lost her only daughter last year to scarlet fever on the occasion of her first birthday, and her oldest son Willie the year previous. However, she has since birthed another son and is once again with child.

With all the clothing that I sew for my large family, I have long wished for the luxury of a home sewing machine. They are said to cut the drudgery of hand sewing to a tenth of the time. We had bountiful crops this year and one October day when Georg took two fattened hogs to Fairfax to sell, he arrived home with a treadle-powered sewing machine. As he is not much given to displays of affection or gift-giving, I was quite overcome by his thoughtfulness. He in turn seemed pleased with the excitement the new machine caused in our household. The older girls and I have all learned to operate it, and what a time-saving device it is. Once we get caught up on our sewing, I plan to try stitching my quilt pieces on it.

This photo of a young girl sewing with a treadle machine dates to the turn of the century, by which time sewing machines had become affordable for many households.

July 25, 1890

I birthed yet another infant earlier this month, a girl named Augusta but called by the pet name of Gustie. I was glad to have four years between babes so that I do not have two in diapers at once. With nine children we have outgrown this small log cabin, but Georg believes that after harvest we should have sufficient money saved to buy a farm of our own. I do hope it will have a larger house.

Last winter I taught quilt-making to Rike, Minnie, and Hannah, now ages fifteen, thirteen and eleven. Of course, they had already learned to sew, and they were quite excited to be allowed to participate in my favorite pastime. Rike and Minnie decided it was much more enjoyable than doing the normal chores around the house and farm, and they begged for time to quilt each day. Hannah, being of a more flighty nature, had trouble sitting still long enough to get much accomplished.

The girls pieced a variety of simple blocks on the sewing machine, which were then sewn together for a top. This was layered with a batting and backing, and they sewed simple running stitches through the three layers. Some of their stitches were a bit large and uneven, but I told them this was their "learning quilt" and with practice they will improve. They are very proud to have the quilt on their bed. With Emma moved from the cradle to make room for Gustie, the girls are now sleeping five to a bed crosswise. Rike and Minnie complain their feet hang off the edge, and we have promised them a bed of their own when we buy our farm. The three boys share a bed but do not care about quilts and so any old blankets will do for them.

January 4, 1891

I am excited to record that last fall we purchased our own farm of 160 acres in Cairo Township, Renville County, for the great sum of $3,000. Of course, we did not have all the money to put down, but our contract allows us to make payments over the next ten years to pay it off. It is situated about five miles southeast of the village of Fairfax, and it is a wonderful farm with rich black soil and fine buildings. After ten long years of toil and sweat in this new world, we are finally landowners!

Our farm was homesteaded in 1872. The original house and barns were located near the south property line, near a slough that was wet and muddy most of the year. The buildings were all destroyed in July 1881 when violent tornadoes left a great path of destruction in the area. Although six people were killed right here in Cairo Township, fortunately no one was living on this farm because it was in mortgage foreclosure. After the tornado destroyed the farm site, it was rebuilt in a better location along the north property line, close to the township road and on higher ground. As a result, all of the buildings are fairly new and in good condition.

The house, while small, is still larger than the log cabin where we lived for the past eight years. We have the kitchen and a separate bedroom downstairs for us, and upstairs is a small room at the top of the landing for the boys, with a bedroom behind that for the girls. There is a large red barn for the horses, cows and pigs, as well as a chicken coop, a granary and corncrib to store crops, and a machinery shed for the wagon, plow, and other equipment. Georg has promised to build a summer kitchen for me to use during the hot weather. This will be a small building separate from the house where we can move the wood-burning cooking stove over the summer. That way I will not need to heat up the entire house when I am cooking, baking, boiling water for laundry, or canning produce from my garden. How proud we all are to have such a wonderful farm of our own!

July 30, 1892

I am grieving as my dear mother, Sophie Schroeder, departed this life on July 6th at the age of sixty-two years. I never appreciated the depth of her love until I had children of my own. I realized then that it was because of her fierce love that Mother was so strict and protective in the raising of her brood. She was ever an example of courage, caring and wisdom and I do miss her sorely.

We have become friends with many neighbors, including the Kolb family. Their five boys ages twenty-five to fifteen get on well with our three oldest girls at eighteen to fourteen years, and they like to visit on Sunday afternoons. Georg has cautioned the girls, "Do not get too enamored with these boys, as they are Roman Catholics and not Lutherans like us. I will not allow you to marry outside our faith." We have tried to steer them towards boys from our church, but there are not many to choose from. Our girls laugh and say, "We would rather kiss a pig than those boys!"

Rike, Minnie and Hannah have grown to be tall and large-boned young women, and they fear that they are not attractive and will not be able to find husbands. Georg says that back in Germany the Schefus men were tall broadly-built men and likewise the women were referred to as "big Schefus women." I myself am a tall woman, but I am slim rather than stout, as are my girls. Georg tells them, "A farmer is wise if he chooses a large strong wife rather than a small weak one, as farming is much hard work." He also says that a man should choose a wife with wide hips in order to bear him many children. The girls blush and titter to hear their father talk so, but they know there is truth in it. Of course, as their mother, I think my daughters are beautiful just as they are!

The older girls and I have been hand-stitching more of our quilts instead of tying them with yarn. They all love to choose patterns and fabrics to make something unique. However, it is sometimes difficult to find designs or colors that we can all agree on, as each one has her own ideas. With four of us working together, we can get several quilts pieced and quilted in a year. I am still making quilts from fabrics left over from sewing clothing, but I no longer put worn fabric into the quilts. There is too much labor involved in making a quilt for some of the pieces to wear out sooner than others, and we are not as poor as when I first began making quilts.

December 26, 1892

What a happy Christmas we had! I bore a fine son three weeks ago, our tenth child. I do hope he will be my last, as my body is getting quite worn out with both the bearing and the caring for children. I am almost thirty-eight years old and have borne ten children in eighteen years. It is quite a demanding job to keep such a large family properly fed and clothed, not to mention the expense of keeping all those children in shoes! Any spare time I have in the evenings or on Sundays is spent sewing, trying to keep up with my growing children. The older girls have all become good seamstresses and help with sewing, but there still is always a basket of clothes waiting to be mended or altered for a younger child. However, I thank God that we are ever so blessed not to have lost a single child, which is uncommon in a large family.

It required a great deal of time and work to keep a growing family properly attired. In this charming photo, circa 1890, the mother used the same bolt of cloth to sew dresses for four of her six daughters.

When Georg and our two older sons, Willie and August, were collecting firewood along the Minnesota River last week, they brought home a small pine tree. On Christmas Eve Georg set it up and the children decorated it with pinecones and strings of popcorn. We attached a few small candles to the branches (with a bucket of water standing by) and sang our favorite German hymns. The children woke on Christmas Day to find in each of their stockings an orange, a stick of hard candy, and a small wooden toy, rag doll, or a scarf or mittens that I knitted after they were asleep at night.

The weather was sunny and fine, and we took the sleigh to church in the morning for Christmas services. We had the new babe well swaddled in quilts so he could barely peep out. He was baptized during the service, with Fritz Meyer who lives next to our church and two neighbor women standing as godparents. We had not yet settled on a name, but it is a German custom to name a child after a godparent. We all agreed that Fritz was as fine a name as any for our babe, and so he was christened.

When we returned home from church the girls and I prepared a feast with roast duck, potatoes, gravy, peas that we had canned, and a pie made with the last of the apples from our root cellar. Everyone agreed that it was the best Christmas we had ever celebrated. How blessed we are to have such a large happy loving family!

March 3, 1893

The oldest Kolb boy, John who is twenty-six, has been courting our sixteen-year-old Minnie, and she has been quite flattered and overcome by his attentions. Rike also has become fond of Joseph Kolb, who is twenty to her eighteen years. Minnie confided to me recently that she is quite crazy with love for John, but Rike is more reserved and keeps her thoughts to herself. I have tried my best to persuade them to consider other boys, but there are few suitable ones from whom to choose.

Our brash and impetuous Minnie announced last night that she and John are in love, and he will marry her if she agrees to convert to the Roman Catholic faith. Georg became quite riled and upset, and he absolutely forbid her to marry John. Rike took Minnie's side and retorted, "It is not fair that two people cannot marry just because their parents are of different faiths." But Georg silenced her, and Minnie burst into tears and ran from the room. I am a dutiful wife and rarely express an opinion contrary to Georg's view. But I later tried to reason with Georg, "In this new country things are more free and we must let our children choose their own husbands and their own futures." But he is adamant that his children will not leave the Lutheran faith that they were raised in, and so our home is not so happy now.

May 14, 1893

Last Sunday afternoon without our knowledge or consent, our daughter Minnie accompanied John Kolb to the priest's house at St. Andrew's Catholic Church in Fairfax, where they were married in defiance of our wishes. When they returned and announced what they had done, Georg was very angry. "You have both behaved deceitfully and disrespectfully. If you are expecting my blessing or any inheritance from me, you can put that right out of your heads. Now be gone from here!" Minnie fled upstairs in tears, packed her few belongings, and left in haste to live with John's family.

I, too, am disappointed that Minnie did not choose someone of our faith, and I wish that she had waited until she were older to marry. I am sad that we could not give them a joyful wedding celebration and our blessings on their marriage. When Minnie ran to gather her things, I followed and hugged her. We had a quick cry together and I told her, "I understand that you are in love and felt you had no other course, but now you must follow the path you have chosen, for better or for worse. As your mother I will always love you, and in spite of his anger, your father loves you too." Just as Minnie and John were leaving the house, I recollected that I did not have a wedding gift for them. I grabbed up the last quilt we had made, ran outside, and handed it up to Minnie in the buggy. Both she and I had tears in our eyes as they pulled away, and I wondered when we would next see each other again.

December 15, 1893

Georg has steadfastly refused to see Minnie and John since their marriage, and I am sorely missing my daughter. Our Rike continues to keep company with Joseph Kolb, but she is more dutiful, and I think she fears her father's anger too much to make plans to marry him. We had news through Rike that Minnie is expecting a child next summer and very much desires to return home for a visit. George remains displeased with Minnie and will not allow me to have any contact with her. I am torn between my duty to my husband and my love for my child. I do not often exert my will over Georg's, but I was very adamant in telling him that when Minnie's time came, I would be there to help with the delivery. He did not respond to this challenge, but I believe he realizes that he cannot hang onto his anger forever and that a daughter needs her mother beside her when giving birth.

July 30, 1894

I am a grandmother! It feels strange, as my youngest child Fritz was only eighteen months old when my first grandchild was born a month ago. When John sent word that Minnie's labor had begun, Georg drove me to their farm in the buggy and waited in the barn with John and his father during the birthing. When little Anna, his first grandchild, was placed in Georg's hands, his eyes teared up and his resolve seemed to melt. I believe he is now somewhat reconciled to this marriage. Minnie and John are still living with his parents, trying to save enough money to begin farming on their own.

Last summer St. John's Lutheran of Ridgely erected a new white church building with a fine steeple pointing heavenward. Since ours was the first German Lutheran church in the area, it is considered to be the "mother church" of many neighboring congregations. St. John's Lutheran of Fairfax was one of the daughter churches, organized in 1890, the year we bought our farm. Both are about equally distant, but we have chosen to remain with the Ridgely church for now.

August 12, 1895

Threshing time is the busiest time of the year on a farm. First the stalks of grain have to be cut and tied into bundles and then the bundles have to be "shocked" in the fields, that is, stood on end leaning against each other to dry. The removal of the grain from the stalks is accomplished by a threshing rig that moves from farm to farm doing custom work. A great noisy monster of a steam traction engine provides the power, with flywheels and drive belts attached to the grain thresher.

Neighbors and relatives gather to help, just as others will help them when their turn comes. Several men operate the machinery and haul water for the engine to provide steam. Some take their horses and wagons to load up the bundles in the fields and haul them to the threshing site. Others pitch the bundles into the machine where they go into a cylinder and are beaten to separate the grain from the stalks. The grain falls to the bottom of the machine where men are kept busy shoveling it into sacks, sewing the sacks shut, loading them onto the wagons, and hauling the sacks to the granary and unloading and stacking them there. The straw and chaff are propelled out of the machine by a fan through a blower, which one man operates to form a compact straw stack.

Threshing time is hard work for farm women too, as we spend days beforehand cooking and baking food for the hungry crews. Threshing day starts early and by mid-morning the men are ready for a lunch of coffee, sandwiches and cookies. These are brought out to the threshing

Georg and Carolina Schefus and their four youngest children (center) stand in front of the threshing rig on their farm near Fairfax, Minnesota. Their other six children appear elsewhere along with other workers in this circa 1895 photo.

field and served by the women, so the men can take turns eating and not have to shut off the machinery. At noon the men all stop their work, wash up at the pump outside, and then come into the house to sit down for a big meal. The women try to outdo each other, for the men will report back to their wives what was served. The usual meal consists of meat, potatoes, gravy, several vegetables, bread, jam, pickles and always pies for dessert. By the time we are through washing and drying all the dishes, it is time to prepare and carry a mid-afternoon lunch to the field, usually coffee, lemonade, sandwiches and cake. Those men surely can eat!

When we were threshing oats last month a photographer was following the threshing rig from farm to farm, offering to take pictures of the threshing operation. Georg thought such an image would be a fine thing indeed. After the noon dinner the photographer had all the men, women and children pose on or around the horses, wagons and machinery. Although it appears that everyone is dressed too warmly for a hot July day, the men wear long sleeves to keep off the dust and chaff and as protection from the sun. Being from northern Germany, we are generally a fair-skinned people. Naturally, women and girls wear dresses with long sleeves and long skirts for decency purposes. The photograph is a thing of wonder and we are all quite proud of it.

September 3, 1895

Our oldest daughter Rike was married to Joseph Kolb last week, and Georg was as opposed to this marriage as he had been to Minnie's. He is a leader in our Lutheran church and entrusted with offices, and he feels embarrassed that his daughters are marrying outside our faith. I wish it were otherwise, but feel they must be allowed to determine their own lives. Rike was envious that her younger sister had married before her and already had one babe with a second on the way. She was afraid of Georg's temper, but did not feel it was fair that she could not do what her sister had already done. She has waited for over two years and is now twenty, with Joseph being twenty-two years, and they were determined to marry. I finally managed to persuade Georg that it would be better to give them our blessing than have them go against our wishes and marry anyway as did Minnie and John. He reluctantly agreed, and so Rike and Joseph were married privately by the priest at the Catholic Church in Fairfax, after which they had a studio portrait made.

Wedding photo of Joseph Kolb and Friederike Schefus, who were married on August 27, 1895.

As I had given Minnie a quilt when she married, I let Rike choose her wedding quilt from among the recent ones that the girls and I have made. The Kolb men are not big men and both our daughters are their husbands' equal in height. But they are good men and my daughters are happily married. All I want from life is for my children to be happy and then I am happy too.

November 30, 1896

Last March our third daughter Hannah was married to Mathias Huss, whose farm is directly across the road from our farmstead. She was only seventeen and he was ten years her senior, but Hannah was ever impatient to do whatever her older sisters had done and not let them get ahead of her. When Mathias first came to call, I pointed out that he was too old for her, and besides he is a short man and Hannah is quite tall. Mathias was her first suitor and Hannah was afraid that if she turned him down, she might be "left on the shelf." Alas, after only a short time Hannah developed baby-sickness in the mornings and so they had to be married in haste. Mathias, being Bohemian, is also a Catholic, but I think Georg is getting resigned to our daughters choosing their own husbands regardless of religion. He voiced his displeasure and disappointment, but knew that under the circumstances he could not afford to make such a fuss this time. After less than eight months of marriage, Hannah presented us with a fine granddaughter.

Hannah had chosen the fabrics and pattern for the quilt we made last winter. It is a red-and-white quilt in a pattern called "Chimney Sweep," which looked deceptively simple. However, we found that the blocks were set on point and required many setting triangles, which are always difficult, and so it required more time than we had anticipated. We purchased the red fabric special for this quilt and used it with bleached muslin, as our scrap basket was getting low after all the quilts we had made. Red-and-white quilts have been popular for several decades, ever since colorfast Turkey-red fabrics became available. The contrast between those two colors is most striking and pleasing to the eye. I hope this special quilt will bring Hannah and Mathias warmth, comfort and the promise of more children to come!

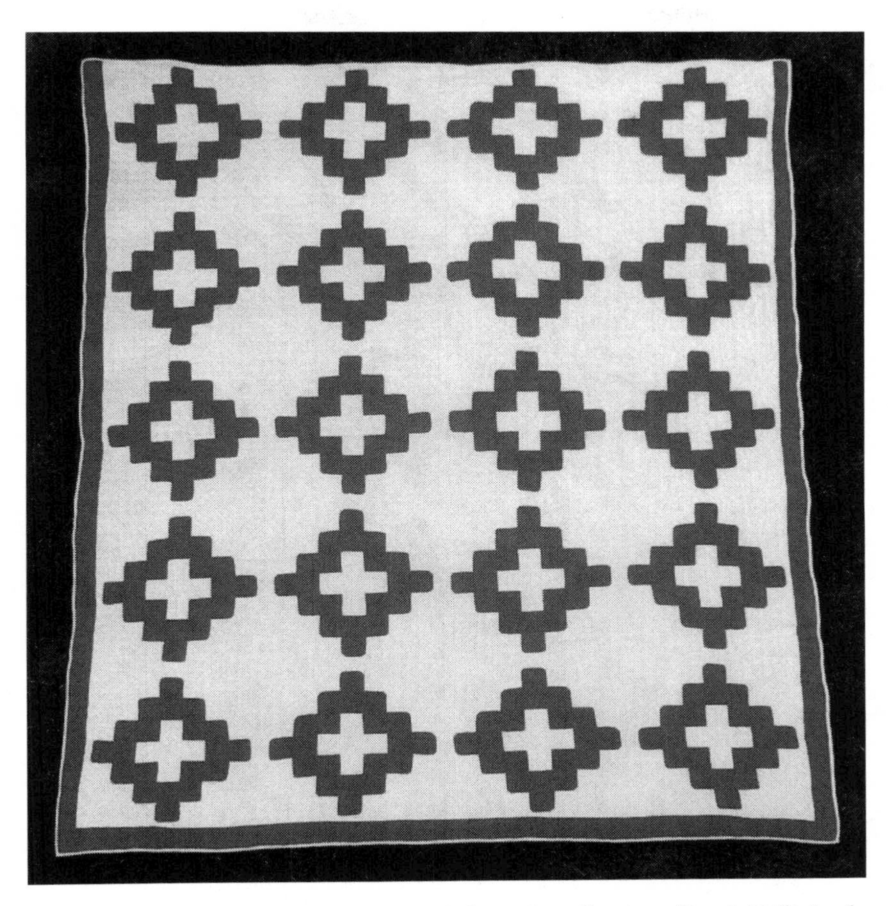

***CHIMNEY SWEEP QUILT:** Vintage quilt from the collection of Lanie Tiffenbach, made in red and white. Hand-pieced and hand-quilted. Maker unknown. Estimated date 1880–1900.*

June 17, 1897

After putting it off for a long time, Georg went to the courthouse in New Ulm today to file his final papers for naturalization, and he was granted United States citizenship. As his wife, I automatically became a citizen, as did the children born in Germany. I baked a cake topped with thick whipped cream and ripe red strawberries for a celebration.

With my three oldest girls married, I have less help around the house. Our three oldest boys, William at seventeen, August at fifteen and Ernest at twelve, are kept busy helping Georg with farm work and outside chores and are sometimes hired out to work for others. William and August are constantly shoving and punching each other, as boys like to do, and they often argue about whose turn it is to do a certain chore or who is slacking in their work. Ernest is big for his age, but can't quite keep up with his brothers, and being younger, would rather make a game of things than work.

Anna at fourteen years is a sweet child and a good helper to me with cooking, cleaning, laundry and chores. Emma at ten is reluctantly learning these duties too, although she often runs off to play with the younger ones. Gustie at seven can do a few small chores but is most useful in watching little Fritz aged four, who can get into mischief if he is left unattended for long. I am not finding time for my quilting these days, but I hope to return to it in a few years when my children are a bit older.

October 6, 1899

This is indeed a big event to mark down in my book! Today Georg made the final payment on our farm and had the deed recorded at the Renville County Courthouse in Olivia. In less than twenty years since we arrived in this country, we have purchased a large farm while also raising ten children. How richly God has blessed our toil and labor with good weather and abundant crops!

We have often heard how those immigrants who arrived in the 1860s were terrorized by the Sioux Uprising, and those who arrived in the 1870s suffered from terrible grasshopper plagues. However, since our arrival in 1880 this has been a land of plenty. As this precious soil of ours feeds our bodies, so the pride of accomplishment feeds our hearts.

August 14, 1901

Since we now own our farm free and clear and our little house was crowded, last summer we built a large addition onto the house. Georg and the boys did most of the work, with neighbors, relatives and friends helping when they could spare time from their own work. We used what was formerly our bedroom to enlarge the kitchen and then added a sitting room and a bedroom for us. Above that is a nice large bedroom for the three girls still at home, Anna eighteen, Emma fourteen and Gustie ten, along with a small storage room. The four boys, William twenty, August nineteen, Ernest sixteen and Fritz eight, now use what was formerly the girls' bedroom above the kitchen instead of the upstairs landing for their room. It is wonderful to have more space for our large family.

Family photo of John and Minnie Kolb with their children John Jr., Anna, Edward, Lucy and Alfred, circa 1901.

I am thankfully through with bearing children but still our family continues to grow. Minnie is kept busy with five little ones under the age of seven, and Hannah has two little girls. Rike, however, remains barren after six years of marriage, and it is a great sorrow in her life.

Studio portrait of Mathias and Hannah Huss with their daughters Caroline and Katherine, circa 1900.

As I did with my older daughters, I have begun to teach the younger girls to quilt. I am pleased to get back to my quilting and the girls are enjoying it too. It is a joy to let our imaginations take flight in the many shapes and patterns. Anna has become quite skilled and I have promised her that next fall we will begin making her wedding quilt. Now that we have a little money to spend on extras, we may even splurge and buy the fabrics!

August 28, 1902

Rike gave me a large photograph that was taken a few weeks ago when they were threshing grain on their farm. Two newspapermen and a photographer arrived to take photos for their paper. Rike had just carried the mid-afternoon lunch to the field in her wicker laundry basket, and the photographer posed her and her husband Joe Kolb in front of the threshing rig. Georg and our sons Bill, August and Ernest are also in the photo, and there sitting on the top of the tall blower stack is that little scamp, my ten-year-old son Fritz. He looks quite pleased with himself indeed! They must have been a thirsty bunch, as I note there is a keg of beer sitting in the shade of the huge tractor. These German men can drink quite a bit of beer on a hot day, and they enjoy their beer almost as much as they enjoy their food!

A happy occasion occurred a week ago when our Anna was married to Adam Wenigar. Georg is delighted with this marriage, as Adam is also a Lutheran, and we were finally able to have a proper church wedding and celebration. Adam's father died when he was a babe and his mother was remarried to William Bakeberg. They subsequently had a large family in which Adam was raised, although he never took the Bakeberg name. The Bakebergs were neighbors when we rented the Lane farm and have remained good friends.

The farm adjacent to ours on the west came up for sale last spring, and Georg purchased it outright for $5,500. With four sons from age twenty-five to thirteen to help with the farming, he reasoned that our family could easily work more land. Also, those sons will someday marry and need farms of their own. Georg feels most wealthy to be the owner of two farms! It remains an unending miracle to us how we have prospered in this new country.

We transferred our church membership to St. John's Lutheran in Fairfax this year, as the roads were better and it was easier to get there. Augusta had already begun her confirmation instructions at the Ridgely church, so we waited until after that event. Fritz has begun his instructions at our new church and will be confirmed in two years' time.

Threshing grain on the farm of Rike and Joseph Kolb (front) in about 1902. Members of both of their families were helping, including young Fritz Schefus on top of the blower stack and John Kolb (second man from right) with his children Anna beside him and Eddie in front.

A vintage postcard dated 1910 shows the parsonage, original church building and school at St. John's Lutheran in Fairfax.

March 2, 1908

Our son Ernest was wed on February 26th to Theresa Tauer, a Bohemian girl from New Ulm. Unfortunately it was not the happiest of weddings, as it was a forced marriage and a mixed marriage. When she told him she was expecting a child, he said that he would do the right thing and marry her. However, knowing the pain he would cause Georg if yet another of his children would convert to the Catholic faith, Ernest proposed that Theresa join the Lutheran church. But Bohemians are strong Catholics and her parents would not allow that to happen. An accord finally had to be reached, and so Ernest and Theresa were married in the Catholic Church. She will raise their children as Catholics, but Ernest will remain with our Lutheran Church.

As Ernest was still living with us, Theresa chose to remain with her own parents during her confinement. Sadly the babe arrived early, a boy named Ernest for his father. He was born two days ago, died yesterday and was buried today. Ernest and Theresa are married now for better or for worse, and we pray that they will have a good marriage and more children to come. Ernest has rented a small farm in Camp Township, Renville County, and they will now begin their life together. I did not have enough notice to make them a wedding quilt, so I gave them one that the girls and I had made a few years ago. Theresa was quite pleased with the gift.

August 21, 1908

We are having a busy year with three weddings! As noted, Ernest was wed in February. On June 2nd our daughter Emma married Herman Bakeberg, and our son August has announced that he will be marrying Emma Bakeberg on October 6th. Herman Bakeberg and Emma Bakeberg are brother and sister, and Adam Wenigar who is married to our Anna is a half-brother to them. Of course this means that three members of our family will have married three members of the Bakeberg family. We only wonder why these two young couples did not decide to have a double wedding and save us much trouble and expense.

As it has become a custom to give my children wedding quilts, Emma chose her favorite quilt from among the ones that she helped piece and quilt over the past few years. We also gave a quilt to August and his bride, and they were well pleased with the gift. When we make a quilt, we put our hearts and souls into it. They are truly a labor of love and are much prized by those who receive them.

Several weeks ago a traveling photographer stopped by and offered to make an image of our farm. I feared the price was too dear, but Georg is very proud to be a landowning farmer (a high status in Germany) and he thought it a splendid idea. The photographer set up his camera equipment at some distance and had Georg stand near the barns and myself near the house while he made the photograph. Today the man returned with a large hand-tinted portrait of our farm, presented in a

This hand-tinted photograph of the farm of Georg and Carolina Schefus near Fairfax, Minnesota, is dated 1908. The buildings from left to right are the granary, house, summer kitchen (in front of house), machinery shed, corncrib (in back) and the barn.

lovely oval-shaped wooden frame with beveled glass. We are delighted with the portrait and have hung it in a place of honor in our sitting room. It reminds us of how much we have accomplished since we stepped off the boat nearly penniless into the unknown new world.

October 30, 1910

Our family has had both happiness and heartbreak. First the happiness: Our oldest son William was finally married in September at thirty years to Ida Schewe. Fortunately, Gustie and I had finished a fine quilt last winter and so we had a wedding gift at hand. The couple has settled onto the adjoining farm that Georg purchased five years ago. In return for all the years that William labored on our farm, Georg gifted him with half the current value of the farm and took a mortgage from him for the other half. Now Georg and I have only Augusta and Fritz left at home. Gustie is twenty years and Fritz will soon be eighteen, so my children are all but grown.

Next the terrible heartbreak: Our twenty-eight-year-old son August died on October 1st in a tragic accident. He had taken a wagonload of grain to Fairfax to sell late in the day. After transacting his business and stopping for a drink with friends, he was returning to his rented farm in Wellington Township. His team of horses was rather spirited, and it is presumed that they bolted and ran away, most likely spooked by lightning storms in the area. As they turned a corner too sharply, the wagon tongue dropped and caught in the ground, overturning the wagon. August was thrown about sixty feet and landed on his head, breaking his neck and killing him instantly. When the horses arrived home without him about ten o'clock that night, wild-eyed and sweating and dragging the remains of the wagon, his poor wife Emma became exceedingly alarmed. Leaving her year-old son Herman sleeping, she mounted a horse and hastily rode to the neighboring home of the Schmechel brothers. Paul returned with her horse to stay with the babe, while his brother Ewald quickly hitched up a team and took Emma to search for August. They soon found him lying dead in the road amidst the wreckage of the wagon.

A great many people attended his funeral, as August was an upright young man and well-liked in our community. Poor Emma is heart-sick, being widowed after less than two years of marriage and left with a babe to raise on her own. It has been a terrible shock to our whole family. I had always counted myself blessed to have not lost any of my babes, but now I have lost a grown son and the pain feels near to suffocating.

November 2, 1913

Today Georg and I have been married for forty years. Our children surprised us with a small celebration party, and they gifted us with a beautiful set of china with wine-colored roses and gold decoration. I will treasure it always and use it for special occasions. With our nine children, their seven spouses and fourteen grandchildren our house was quite crowded. Everyone brought food and we feasted well. I felt very blessed to be surrounded by my loving family and for forty years of marriage to a kind and hardworking Christian man who has provided well for me and our children.

July 12, 1915

The farm work was becoming difficult for Georg as he is getting on in years and has some health problems, and so we retired from farming after the harvest last fall. We moved into a small house in Fairfax, leaving our twenty-two-year-old son Fritz to work the farm, although Georg still goes out to lend a hand when he is needed. Our youngest daughter Gustie moved to town with us and works as a waitress at Sell's

Cafe. She has a sunny disposition and is a favorite with the customers and employees. She enjoys having money of her own for clothing and small luxuries. Gustie has never wanted for suitors, but is in no hurry to marry although she is already twenty-five years of age.

Augusta (Gustie) Schefus had her photograph taken at a studio in Fairfax, Minnesota, in about 1910.

St. John's Lutheran in Fairfax is constructing a new brick church building with beautiful stained-glass windows. All the able-bodied men are helping however they can. Our son Ernest is using his horses and wagon to haul building materials to the site. Georg often walks over to help or at least instruct the younger men in how things should be done.

Ernest and his wife Theresa had a third son named Elmer born on February 28th. Their other two sons, George and Mike, being six and three years old, are quite a rambunctious pair. It was difficult enough for Theresa to take them to the Catholic Church by herself, and she knew it would be even more challenging as their family grew. She decided prior to Elmer's birth to convert to the Lutheran faith, so that the family could worship together. As a result little Elmer was baptized in our church, and Georg and I were most pleased about that.

I finally have time to devote to my quilting. I enjoy walking uptown to the dry goods store and choosing just the right colors or prints and not having to make do with what is at hand. What a luxury that is! Gustie enjoys quilting with me in the evenings too, and I tell her that if she does not marry soon, she will have more quilts than she can ever use.

A wonderful star quilt most likely made by this little girl's mother or grandmother is featured prominently in this photo postcard from about 1920.

January 31, 1917

I am in this New Year overcome by death. First it snatched my daughter Anna and now my husband Georg. I am overwhelmed with grief, but feel obligated to record these events.

Anna was diagnosed with acute kidney disease in December. After only a few weeks she took a turn for the worse, fell unconscious and was claimed by the angel of death at her home on January 7th. Georg was much anguished that he was by then quite ill and confined to bed and was unable to bid his child farewell or attend her funeral. I was distressed not to be able to properly attend to Anna in her last days, but I quite had my hands full in caring for Georg. Anna was only thirty-three years old and leaves bereft her husband Adam Wenigar and two young children, Harry ten and Evelyn four years. Because Adam is unable to care for the children on his own, they have been farmed out to various relatives for the present time.

I had not yet recovered from the blow of losing my daughter, when only four days later Georg Schefus, my dear husband of over forty-three years, gave up his struggle. On January 11th he departed this life for a better world. Family and friends gathered at our home that day to pay their last respects. He had suffered a lingering illness from heart and kidney problems and passed on at the age of sixty-six years. I know it must be a sin, but a part of me was relieved that he was no longer in the torment of pain which he had endured. The exceptionally large number of attendants at his funeral filled our spacious new church and bore evidence that he was held in esteem. There are those who try to comfort me by saying that life goes on. But having lost two loved ones in a short time, it seems to me that it is more like death that goes on. I find myself staring out the window numb-like and do not even have any interest in doing my quilting.

Georg left the north half of the farm to me in his will and then upon my death to our youngest son Fritz. Title to the south half of the farm passes directly to Fritz, along with four horses, four cows and the farm machinery. Under the terms of the will, our children Ernest,

Anna and Augusta each receive $1,000. However, Rike, Minnie and Hannah inherit only $250 each, as Georg had never completely forgiven them for leaving our church to marry into the Catholic religion. William and Emma had already each received their portion, William the adjoining farm and Emma money towards a down payment on their farm. As August was deceased at the time the will was signed, his son Herman was left $250 in his stead. Since Anna died after the execution of the will, her share will be held in trust for her children.

Georg had his will drawn up in 1915 when we were still living on the farm. He left the half of the farm with the house and buildings to me so that I would have a home as long as I live. Some of our other children think it unfair that Fritz alone should inherit the home farm. However, Georg told me that in return Fritz is obligated to provide for my care and support until my death. This could in possibility be several decades if I were to live to a great old age. I am still too overcome with grief to decide whether to remain in town or return to the farm. I will put that off until I can think more clearly.

July 3, 1917

This spring I sold the house in Fairfax, and Gustie and I moved back to the farm. Fritz was having a hard time managing on his own and needed someone to keep house for him. Men are really quite useless when it comes to doing laundry, cooking or keeping some cleanliness in a home. I never did take much to town life, and I am happy to be back on the farm in which I invested so many years of my life and which was our family's greatest dream.

Today is Gustie's twenty-seventh birthday. While she enjoyed living in town, she says her place is here with Fritz and me. She is such a devoted daughter and sister, and she knows how much we depend on her. Adolph Schumacher, a neighbor man who has been courting Gustie for some time, came to our farm yesterday and took photographs of

Gustie and me outside by the apple trees. He is quite enamored with his fancy new camera and even develops his own pictures. I am eager to see how these photographs turn out, and he has promised to bring us copies.

These photos of Carolina Schefus and her youngest daughter Augusta were taken on their farm by a neighbor in about 1917.

Gustie has confided in me that she and Adolph have discussed marriage. He and his unmarried brother Albert jointly own their family farm, but their older spinster sister Emma inherited a small parcel where the buildings are situated. Because she was not married, her parents ensured that she would always have a roof over her head. Emma is a sour woman, having been disappointed in love and in life. She is also a bossy woman, and Gustie would never tolerate living with her and taking orders from her as the mistress of the house. Likewise, it would be impossible for Gustie and Adolph to marry and live here, as half of the farm belongs to Fritz and the rest of it will go to him when I am gone. Besides, I expect that he will soon marry and have a family of his own. The only solution would be for Adolph to sell his half of their farm to his brother and buy a farm of his own. However, he has not consented to this and consequently Gustie has not agreed to marry him.

I do want Gustie to marry and have a life of her own, but I am also selfish enough to want her beside me. She tells me that no matter what happens, she promises to care for me for the rest of my life. More than death itself, I fear the inevitable decline that awaits old age, which can trap children in their duty to care for older relatives. I would not want either Gustie or Fritz to feel that they could not marry and must sacrifice their own lives for my sake.

March 21, 1918

My younger sister Wilhelmina is a courageous and enterprising woman. She and her husband Anton Seesz farmed for about thirty years, renting various farms but never able to purchase their own, all the while growing a family of ten children. A few years ago they moved into Fairfax, where Anton worked at various jobs. Because of his fondness for drink and his inability to provide for their large family, Wilhelmina was forced to throw him out of the house and find a way to feed and clothe her children on her own. There are not many job choices open to women, but she has always been a wonderful cook, and she bravely opened her own restaurant and bakery last fall. Wilhelmina hired an experienced baker and also has her six sons still at home to help her, ranging in age from ten to twenty-five years. I am so proud of my sister, and I know she will make a success of her new business!

December 13, 1918

I am deeply bereft and my emotions are quite raw with grief. Every morning when I come awake, my first thought is of what death has stolen from me. My dearest daughter Augusta died on October 19th of that fearful epidemic being called the "Spanish Influenza," at only twenty-eight years of age. The epidemic began last spring among the

This photo of the Seesz Bakery & Restaurant, with Wilhelmina Seesz at the left and her son Edward second from right, was taken in about 1918.

troops fighting in the Great War in Europe and quickly spread all over the world throughout the summer, even though that is not typically the season for influenza. Its preferred victims were not young children and the elderly as is usual, but instead healthy and strong young adults. Many people in our area have been stricken and a number of them have died, suffocating as their lungs filled with blood and fluid.

Gustie first complained of not feeling well on rising that October morning and was soon confined to her bed, running a high fever and soaked in sweat. Fritz and I were much worried that she had contracted the Spanish Flu, but I nursed her as best I could. We did not have the doctor out, as he has made it known that he can do nothing to combat this terrible killer. A person must either recover on their own or die, and there is naught to do but wait it out. By noon poor Gustie was violently coughing up mucus and blood, and by mid-afternoon she was struggling for air, with blood gurgling from her mouth. All the while I was begging God to be merciful and spare her and take me instead. I am old and have lived out my life, but Gustie was still young and had most of her life ahead of her. It was a most heart-wrenching feeling to watch her suffocate and be able to do nothing for her. God did not accept the bargain of my life in exchange for hers, and she died in her bed before suppertime with only myself at her side.

I would not allow Fritz into the bedroom for fear that he might contract the disease, and likewise we did not ask other family members to say their farewells. Most towns in the area have cancelled all church services and public gatherings as a precaution against spreading the infection. We could not even hold a public funeral for Augusta and had only a simple graveside service with our immediate family present. She is buried in the plot next to Georg, where I too will soon rest, and I ordered a large expensive headstone for her grave to commemorate her too-short life. Gustie's sweetheart Adolph Schumacher is sorely grieved and bemoans the fact that he did not marry her when he was able. He swears he will never marry but will grieve for Gustie the rest of his life.

After the funeral I could only lie in bed and cry. I could not rouse myself to dress or cook, and I thought to die from pure grief. Neighbors and family stopped by, bringing meals, cakes and comfort. They told me if I needed anything to let them know. How could I tell them that what I needed was Gustie alive and well again? Or else Georg back with me to share the heavy weight of sorrow? After some days I found myself still breathing and so I got up and started going through the motions of being alive.

Now that I have lost three children after they were grown—August, Anna, and Gustie—I know why it is said that the hardest thing to bear is the loss of a child. Every day I feel around me the empty space where their lives should have been. I had always imagined that the death of a spouse would be the most difficult of all. But Georg had been in ill health for a few years, and so I felt I lost him little by little and his death came as no surprise. I grieved so much for him as he grew sicker and death became inevitable, that I had no tears left in me when he did pass on.

I always felt so blessed that I had never lost any babes or young children as most women do. But what I was really feeling was more prideful and boastful, like it was something of my own doing and not purely of God's grace. I expect I am now being punished for my sin of pride.

November 8, 1919

It has been over a year since Gustie died and I still miss her every day. She was such a loving daughter that I find life difficult without her. At first I shook my fist at God for taking her, as well as Georg and my other two children, but life is just too hard without faith. There are no tears in heaven, and it is only those of us left on this poor earth that weep.

According to the newspapers, the terrible Spanish Flu has run its course. They report that this epidemic killed more people than even the infamous Black Plague of the 1300s and more than died in four years of the recent Great War. When the deaths have been tallied, it may have killed as many as a half million Americans and fifty million worldwide. It is unbelievable that this monstrous killer could search out and find us on our little farm in this rural area of Minnesota.

Fritz is managing well working the farm, but William lives on the neighboring farm and the brothers sometimes help each other with the bigger jobs like planting and harvesting. I cook meals, wash clothes and keep house, and Fritz is happy to have me here with him. There was a girl that he was sweet on for several years, but he was too slow to propose marriage and she wed someone else last year. Fritz has now turned twenty-seven and I would like to see him marry before I die. Of course, any woman he married would have to move into my house and provide care for me in my old age. I pray this is not hurting his chances of marriage.

July 25, 1922

I am growing frail at sixty-seven years and have had pains in my stomach for some time. I was to the doctor last spring and he gave me some medicine, but it has not helped. He now says there is a cancer growing in my stomach and, as everyone knows, there is no cure for that. I am finding as I get older that life quite often ends up with declining health and faculties, death of family and friends, and just plain lonesomeness. I do not think it is a blessing to be given long life. If I must endure the loss of more family or if I must suffer sickness and pain, I pray that death will be kind enough to intervene and quickly take me away.

When Georg and I left Germany those long years ago, we could not have imagined what lay ahead of us. Although we suffered hardships, we endured by our hard work and a faith that could not be shaken. How very blessed we were to succeed in our new homeland and to be able to obtain our own farm and raise ten good children. It seems as though those years have passed as in the twinkling of an eye as the Bible says. Even though later in my life I suffered the loss of loved ones, I know that I will not be long for this poor earth and will soon be reunited with them in heaven. I look forward to that time promised in the Book of Revelation when, "God shall wipe away all tears from their eyes and death shall be no more."

Author's Note:

Carolina Schroeder Schefus died of cancer of the liver and spleen at the family farm on December 22, 1922, at the age of sixty-seven years and her funeral was held on Christmas Day. Her son Fritz never did marry and later in life he sold the family farm to his nephew Elmer Schefus. Elmer and his wife Elda raised six daughters on this farm and rebuilt most of the buildings, including the house. The farm remained in the Schefus family for over one hundred years.

7

ELIZA'S STORY: MY GRAND ADVENTURE

This story is based on the life of my great-grandmother Eliza Peters Meyer (my mother's paternal grandmother), who was born in 1861 in Hanover Province, Prussia, Germany. She immigrated to America with her husband and son in 1884. We do know that Eliza actually was a quilter, as she gifted my mother with a beautiful "Grandmother's Flower Garden" quilt.

A vintage photograph from Germany, circa 1880, depicts a lovely young woman in traditional dress.

REFLECTIONS ON MY LIFE BY ELIZA PETERS MEYER
DATED JANUARY 1939

My granddaughter Elda Meyer is in her second year of college and was assigned to write about someone who has been an inspiration in her life. She has chosen me as her subject, as she thinks I am very courageous because I once left behind the life I knew and took up the challenge of a new world. Elda is a quiet and shy girl and cannot imagine leaving the safety and security of home and family for an alien country. I was just a brash young woman when I came to America and what did I know of hardship and adversity? I thought my life would be one great adventure. I am not the kind of woman about whom stories are normally written, but Elda has asked me to set down the details of my life, and so this is my story.

Childhood

My name is Catherine Dorothea Elizabeth Peters, but like many Germans, I am not called by my first given name but rather known as Elizabeth or more often Eliza. I was born on June 18, 1861, in the village of Gross Ellenberg, Hanover, Prussia, Germany. My mother, Catherine Elizabeth Schulze, was a twenty-seven-year-old unmarried farmhand when I was born, and so I was recorded in the church's baptismal records as illegitimate. Juergen Heinrich Wilhelm Peters, nineteen years old at the time of my birth, later declared himself to be my father. My mother and father were married in 1863, when she was twenty-nine, he was twenty-one, and I was almost two years. I was then legitimized and my surname was changed in the church records to Peters. My parents had another daughter, Wilhelmina, born ten years after they married.

My father, usually called Wilhelm Peters, was also an illegitimate child, born to Margaretha Dorothea Peters in 1841. His father was named as Juergen Heinrich Clasen III, but the two were never wed. My grandmother, Margaretha Peters, never did marry or have other children. I do believe her experience as an unmarried woman with an illegitimate child turned her bitter, as she was not a happy woman.

I suppose I was an ornery child, full of spunk and vinegar, but I knew from an early age what I wanted and that one did not get ahead by being meek and mild. My mother raised me to be independent and to grow a backbone, so I have always been considered to be feisty, strong-willed and hardheaded. I remember one of my teachers telling my parents that I was bright and clever. Later I overheard Father complaining that she should not have said that in my hearing, as I could get conceited and "uppity." Mother only laughed, "She takes after the two of us, so of course she is bright and clever and probably conceited and uppity too!"

I expect I was considered a show-off, but I never pretended to be stupid or deferential as did some of the girls. I was not popular with the boys either, but I never let them get ahead of me nor best me in anything. Everyone warned me that I would never find a husband if I did not learn to curb my tongue, but I could not change my nature. From what I have noticed, the type of man who chooses a meek wife is likely to become a tyrant towards her and trample her underfoot. Fortunately, there are some men who like independent and feisty women who can speak their mind and be their equal, and I was fortunate to find just such a man to marry.

Married Life

I was wed to Johann Heinrich Friedrich Meyer, known as Fritz Meyer, on December 18, 1882, at the Lutheran Church in Lehmke, Hanover, Prussia, Germany, when I was twenty-one and he was twenty-three years of age. Fritz had been born in 1859 in the nearby village of Emern. Prior to our marriage he served in the German Army, which at that time was compulsory service of three years' duration. He gifted me with a photograph of him wearing his army uniform, and I still have and treasure it to this very day.

This photograph of Fritz Meyer in his German Army uniform was taken about 1880 in Hanover, Germany.

Following our marriage we lived in the village of Gross Pretzier, where Fritz worked for others as a butcher in the winter and as a mason or bricklayer in the summer. His father was employed as a farmhand, but did not own land. Fritz occasionally also worked as a farmhand, especially during the planting and harvesting seasons when extra hands were needed on farms.

Our first child was born May 6, 1883, a healthy and robust son whom we named Friedrich, but we called him Fred to distinguish him from his father. Of course everyone was counting the months on their fingers since we had been married for less than five months at the time of his birth. But I was a strong and independent young woman, and I just ignored those who would snub me and held my head high. I had the husband I had chosen, who loved me and gave me the child I wanted. Why would I care what those busybodies thought or said about me?

Emigration to America

Beginning in the 1870s there was a large wave of emigration from Germany to America, caused by unemployment, crop failures, military conscription, constant wars and high taxation. My mother's brother Fritz Schulze had emigrated in 1868 and sent letters home to Germany describing the bounty of the land and the ease with which farmland could be acquired.

As with many men, Fritz loved farming. Land is of the utmost importance in an agrarian society such as ours. I imagine it goes back to when God created Adam and put him in the Garden of Eden to dress it and keep it. He told him to be fruitful and multiply and replenish the earth and subdue it. Ever since then, men have had within them this primary purpose and goal.

Even though Fritz was skilled in two trades, he dreamed of owning his own farm and being his own master. Because of the inheritance system and overcrowded conditions in Germany, there was no land available for purchase in our area, even if one did have money. German families generally were large and poor, and as they divided their farms between their children, they slivered it up into parcels that were incapable of supporting their families. To cope with this land shortage, most farmers had to supplement their income by hiring out as laborers or working at a trade.

In addition, our German state of Prussia was always waging wars with its neighbors that we were forced to support with heavy taxation. It was very difficult to get ahead in life if everything one owned or earned was subject to taxes. Fritz did not want to be a soldier but was conscripted into the army anyway. He endured his three-year service, but could have been called back as a reserve soldier at any time on the whim of the government.

One of the major lures of emigration to America was the promise of abundant and cheap farmland. In addition, it was said that America was a land of freedom, where the government did not demand a good part of your income in taxes and control so much of your life. Fritz very much wanted to farm, and he was independent and ambitious and wanted to make something of himself. Thus he determined that we should emigrate to America, where there was opportunity and freedom. I was brash and bold and in love with my husband, and I believed we could be happy anywhere. Our young selves thought it would be a grand adventure to travel across the ocean to the New World for land and lives that would be ours alone.

But what a long and involved process it was to get permission to leave the country. First, Fritz had to ask permission of the county government for us to leave Prussia. Secondly, the county government had to ask the military office if he was allowed to emigrate since he was still a reserve soldier. Next, the county government asked the district government for permission for emigration. Fritz then had to return to the county government to receive our passports. He had to return a final time to receive travel documents, a military passport, and our three birth records. After months of waiting, we were at long last able to say our farewells.

Our Long Sea Voyage

My husband Fritz and I, at the ages of twenty-four and twenty-two, together with our one-year-old son Fred, embarked on this daring passage across the wide ocean, knowing that in all probability we would never see our families in Germany again. I was so caught up in the excitement, it was not until we were packing that I actually took in the finality of our decision. How very difficult were the good-byes to our parents, siblings, relatives and friends! As there was by then no other course imaginable for Fritz, we started off on our new life with plenty of courage and high hopes for the future.

We sailed from the port of Hamburg, Germany, on May 7, 1884, in steerage class on the steamship *Frisia* of the Hamburg-American Line, which still used two masts of sails to supplement its steam power. The *Frisia* was 350 feet in length and 40 feet broad, and it carried 24 cabin passengers and 917 steerage passengers on this voyage. As the ship left the port in Hamburg, everyone crowded onto the deck to watch our motherland fade into the distance. Some had tears in their eyes or were openly weeping, knowing that they would never return.

Although conditions for steerage passengers had improved over time, we were still considered to be cargo. On our ship the space for steerage passengers was divided into three rooms, with the front one for single men, the large middle room for families, and a smaller rear room for single women. Each room had beds along both sides about six feet wide, arranged in two stories, and considered wide enough for three or four people. Meals were served in shifts in a dining hall, and the food was adequate but not very tasty.

As other immigrants, we were unaccustomed to the sea, and seasickness became an expected and dreaded part of the voyage when the seas were rough. The constant rising and plunging of the boat on the mighty waves felt like we were crossing mountains. During storms the trunks and barrels and everything not nailed down flew from side to side, and we held on to our berths and young Fred to avoid flying too. The ship had limited toilet and bathing facilities with little privacy and only salt water available for washing. Most people did not wash often as the salt water made one's skin itch. As a result, the steerage compartments were dark, smelly and unsanitary, and it was a most unpleasant journey!

We German women are well known to be fastidious about keeping our homes clean, even scrubbing our doorsteps and sweeping our front yards. But on the ship it was near impossible to keep our surroundings and persons (especially little Fred) in some state of cleanliness due to the seasickness and congestion and rough provisions. A perpetual stench permeated the ship. When the weather was good, we climbed the steep stairs and walked the deck of the ship often to breathe fresh air and bask in the sunshine.

Besides the clothing, personal possessions, and bedding that we needed for the voyage and carried with us, we were allowed to stow one piece of baggage. This was a large wooden trunk that Fritz had made when he was sixteen years old to take with him to hold his belongings when he joined the military. On the front of the trunk were his initials "HFM" and the date "1875." "HFM" stands for Heinrich Friedrich Meyer, as Fritz's first given name of Johann is so common that it is usually dropped from usage, and 1875 is the date when he made the chest. This large trunk contained all of our extra clothing, linens and household goods, as well as a mantel clock in a wooden case that Fritz was very proud of.

The original wooden trunk and mantel clock brought to America by Fritz and Eliza Meyer in 1884 remain in the family's possession.

It also held my most prized possession, a sewing machine. Fritz had bought it for me as a wedding gift with his military pay. It was an amazing thing! I was the first woman in my village to own one, and everyone was envious of how fast I could stitch seams with it, although I had to operate it with a hand crank. This sewing machine was replaced some years later when Fritz bought me a new Singer model in a handsome wooden cabinet with a foot treadle. The wooden mantel clock still runs well and sits in a place of honor in our parlor. Fritz's old wooden chest remains in our possession, and I use it to store the heavy winter quilts over the summer months. I keep it as a reminder of how little we owned when we first stepped off the boat into this New World.

In talking with others on the journey, we found that immigrants from northern Germany were usually traveling to Wisconsin, Minnesota, Illinois or other Midwestern states, where the cool climate, landscape and farming conditions were similar to our homeland. As was typical, we had chosen to settle in Minnesota because we already had relatives living there. My mother's brother Fritz Schulze had emigrated to America in 1868, had purchased a farm in Minnesota, and was living there with his wife and children.

A vintage photo from the early 1900s shows a toddler beside a hand-operated sewing machine.

Arrival in America

Our little Meyer family arrived at the port of New York on May 20, 1884, after a voyage of thirteen days that seemed interminable. What a welcome sight the city was after so long of seeing nothing but endless water! As we arrived in New York Harbor we sailed past Bedloe's Island, where we were told a very large statue was to be erected, a gift from the people of France representing liberty. Construction was underway on the pedestal for it inside the walls of Fort Wood, an old Army base in the shape of an eleven-pointed star. When we later saw pictures of the Statue of Liberty, we wished it had been there to welcome us.

We were processed through Castle Garden Immigration Center, which we were told had originally been a fort and later an amusement hall. Since thousands of immigrants passed through the center each day, the procedure was fairly efficient but still took us about five hours to complete. With everyone lugging their heavy baggage and bundles with them and with such throngs of people, the lines progressed very slowly. We read in the newspapers some eight years later that a new immigration station was opened on Ellis Island and wondered if the process went any smoother there.

The medical inspection began as we ascended the stairs, with doctors watching closely for signs of health problems such as weakness or breathing difficulties. Another doctor examined the face, hair and hands of every person in what was known as a "six-second inspection." If he found any indication of disease, he marked a letter on the person's coat lapel with chalk to indicate that further examination was needed. Those immigrants with the mystifying letters were pulled out of the inspection line and taken to special examination rooms, where other doctors with the help of interpreters would give them a quick check-up and further inspection for the ailment indicated by the chalk marks. The final and most feared part of the medical examination was the check for trachoma, a highly contagious eye infection that can cause blindness and was common in Europe. Doctors checked for this disease by using a buttonhook to turn back a person's eyelid, which was a painful but thankfully quick procedure.

The medical examination was intimidating and many were frightened of being rejected and sent back to their port of origin. Since most women have never been touched or seen partially unclothed by a man other than their husbands, some were terrified by the prospect of being examined by a male doctor. Sick children from twelve years or older could be sent back alone, but for those under twelve years one parent was forced to accompany them. Those persons who were considered to be too weak or too sick to work were rejected, so they would not become a burden on society. Fortunately, we were young and healthy and had no such fears.

Next we had to line up at an inspector's desk for a legal examination. This was jokingly referred to by a man standing in line as "waiting at St. Peter's gate for the Day of Judgment." The inspector interrogated us very rapidly regarding our names, ages, nationality, destination, occupation and other information to see if it matched what was written in the ship's manifest. We also had to show the amount of money we carried, as it was important that new arrivals should have enough money to support themselves and start their new lives. After finally clearing inspections and receiving permission to leave, we were provided with information on food and shelter, had our money exchanged for American dollars and were sold railway tickets to our final destination.

Life in America

We traveled west on the railroads, and after some days finally arrived in the town of New Ulm, Minnesota, near the farm where my Uncle Fritz Schulze lived with his family. How happy we were to have him there ahead of us to lead the way! We stayed with Uncle for a few weeks until Fritz was able to locate and purchase an eighty-acre farm nearby in Ridgely Township, Nicollet County, for $1,200 payable over five years. We were most pleased to find adjacent to our land a small country church called St. John's Lutheran of Ridgely Township, knowing that we would not have far to go to attend services. Even better was the fact that this area was settled primarily by Germans and the church services were held in German.

There was a small house on our new farm, along with other farm buildings, but it took all the money we had left to buy horses, livestock, equipment and seed to get the farm started. The first year was quite a challenge, having to make do without many comforts. Fritz proved to be a good farmer and the soil was rich and the crops abundant. He also continued to use his masonry skills to build foundations for houses and barns for others and to put in cisterns to store water, which brought us additional income. Oh, the blessedness of independence and the security of owning land and the satisfaction of providing for our family!

Fritz was pleased to be living in such close communion to nature and the cycles of the seasons. He wrote letters back to his family in Germany, singing the praises of our new country and the joys of farming and the abundance of the land. I also wrote to my family of how well we were established in our new home and how much I missed them. In the fall of 1885, after our second good harvest, I wrote to tell my mother that I was once again with child. My father Wilhelm Peters was a farmer but had only rented land and was never able to purchase a farm in Germany. When he heard how we were prospering on our own farm, he began to think that they should come to America as well. Mother was sorely missing us, especially her little grandson Fred, and would be sad not to ever lay eyes on the grandchild that I was carrying. So it was agreed that my parents, younger sister and grandmother would make their own journey to America the following spring.

Our Growing Family

After a difficult confinement, I was delivered of our daughter Elise on March 27, 1886, at our home. I had a midwife to help me, but I so wished that my own mother could be in attendance as she had been when our Fred was born. We mostly called our daughter Lizzie instead of Elise, as that seemed to suit her fiery temperament better. She was a demanding baby right from the start, always fussing and screaming and wanting attention. Fritz used to tease me, "She is such an ornery and feisty little thing! I wonder where she gets it?" That made me recall when I was young and my own mother was upset with me, she would exclaim, "I hope someday you have a daughter just like yourself!" And I would think, "Now I know what she meant!"

Later that spring of 1886 my parents Wilhelm and Catherine Peters (ages forty-five and fifty-two) arrived from Germany with my sister Wilhelmina (age thirteen) and my father's mother Margaretha Peters (age seventy-one). My grandmother was a rather crusty old woman and apparently put up a fuss about coming. But as my father is her only child, she had no one else to care for her in her old age and so she was forced to accompany them. How happy I was to be reunited with my family, as I had thought when we left Germany that I would never see them again in this lifetime. Of course they were delighted to meet our newborn Lizzie and see little Fred again, by then a lively bouncing three-year-old.

Prior to their arrival my parents had asked Fritz to find a small farm for them to buy, as they would still have some savings left after their journey. Upon seeing what was available in the area, Fritz decided instead to purchase a larger 160-acre farm for our family that was just over the county line in Cairo Township, Renville County. This new farm was on land owned by the railroad and deeded to it by the state in return for the building of a railroad line, and at that time had a log cabin and another small house on it. He then asked my parents to buy out his interest in the eighty-acre farm that we had been making payments on for two years. So we settled onto our new larger farm, and my parents, sister and grandmother settled onto our previous smaller farm.

My father Wilhelm Peters was also a good farmer and had good harvests. Three years later, on July 18, 1889, after making the final payment he received title to his farm. He was forever amazed at how quickly he was able to become a landowning farmer in this new country of ours. Fritz and I also continued to prosper on our new farm in the following years. Some years were better and some were worse, but overall we were greatly blessed with good weather and abundant crops.

A studio portrait of Fritz and Eliza Meyer and their children Fred and Lizzie was taken in about 1887.

During this time, I became intrigued by the photographs that were becoming so popular and how accurately they portrayed images. I wanted such a portrait made of my children while they were young, but Fritz thought we should have a family portrait made instead. One day when we needed to go into New Ulm for our marketing, we dressed in our best clothes and sat for a photograph at the Anton Gag studio. I was thrilled with it and had copies made for family and friends.

Our third and last child, Wilhelm Friedrich Heinrich Meyer (known also as William, Willy, or Bill), was born on June 30, 1891, at our farm in Cairo Township. He was a quiet placid child, content to watch his older siblings. Fred was already eight years old and Lizzie was five years old, and we had begun to fear that we would not have any more children. So little Willy was a welcome addition to our family and much spoiled by everyone. I had to warn them that children need a firm hand, some discipline and an occasional spanking, or else they will grow up thinking their whole life will be gay and happy, with no disappointments or hardships. A bit of suffering while one is young is good preparation for adulthood. I know that some people consider me to be a hard woman, but I consider myself to be strong and realistic about life. I speak my mind and I never apologize for who I am. I dearly love my children, and I only want to give them happiness and what is best for them.

Farm Life in Minnesota

In the late1800s the usual crops raised were wheat, oats, rye, barley and corn. Plowing was done with a walking plow pulled by horses, seeds were dropped into the furrows by hand, and weeding was done with a simple hand hoe. Wild grass was cut for hay to feed the live-stock over the winter and was stored in the loft of the barn. Corn was harvested by walking through the rows and cutting off the corncobs with sharp knives. The corn would be husked by hand and put through a hand-cranked machine to remove the kernels from the cobs.

By the time we came to Minnesota, wheat was the dominant crop being grown. As farmers began raising more wheat for market, flour mills sprang up powered by water, wind and steam. Railroads expanded to carry the flour to other parts of the country, and towns were established at about ten-mile intervals along the railroad lines to provide water for the steam engines. Nearby Brown County alone had twenty-two different mills, with one of its towns, Sleepy Eye, having the largest inland mill in the world. For several decades Brown County was the third highest in flour milling volume in the country, trailing only Buffalo in New York and Minneapolis in Minnesota. We raised wheat to be ground into flour for ourselves and also as a cash crop to buy such items as sugar, salt, coffee, cloth, shoes and household goods that could not be produced on the farm.

A vintage postcard picturing the Eagle Roller Mill in New Ulm, Minnesota, bears a postmark of 1912.

Thankfully by the time we started farming, harvesting grain was no longer done by hand but was accomplished with the use of mechanical binders to cut and bind the stalks of grain into bundles. Steam-operated threshing machines then moved from farm to farm. Each farmer provided labor from family and neighbors to load and haul the bundles of grain from the fields, pitch the grain bundles into the thresher, then to stack the straw and haul away and unload the grain. The farm women cooked a huge noontime dinner to feed the hungry threshing crews, as well as two large lunches served mid-morning and mid-afternoon. We women did nothing from sunup to sundown for days but cook and bake and wash dishes!

Farmers kept a variety of animals for family use. Horses were used for fieldwork and pulling wagons. Pigs and cattle were butchered for meat. Chickens, ducks, geese and turkeys were raised for eggs and meat, and their feathers were used to stuff pillows and comforters. The responsibility of caring for the poultry typically fell to the farm wife. Surplus eggs were sold in town for "egg money," which went to buy groceries and household items. Each farm kept a few cows to provide milk for drinking, with the excess separated into cream and skim milk. The cream was either used by itself or made into butter, with the excess sold to a creamery in town. The skim milk was fed to the pigs, and the barn cats got a bowl of it too.

Every family kept a large garden and orchard, and women canned the surplus fruits and vegetables for winter. Cooking, baking and canning was done on a wood-burning cook stove even in the heat of summer. Laundry was done by scrubbing clothes on a washboard, cranking them through a wringer clamped to a table, and then pinning them on clotheslines to dry. Most clothing was made of cotton or linen and needed to be ironed using flatirons heated on the wood-burning stove. Water for drinking, cooking, laundry and bathing was pumped into buckets and carried from a well or cistern, and light was provided by candles or kerosene lamps. An outdoor toilet was used, and bathing was done in a laundry tub in the kitchen, usually only on Saturday nights.

Land and More Land!

By 1892 we were prospering so well with farming that Fritz bought forty acres of land across the road from my cousins, the Schulzes. He had earlier purchased a woods lot along the Minnesota River for cutting firewood for cooking and heating our home. How satisfying it is to plow, plant, tend and finally harvest the fruits of one's own labor!

Even as our plants took root in the rich soil of our farm, so too we sank our roots into our homestead and our new homeland.

On April 1, 1895, Fritz made the final payment and received title to the 160-acre farm in Cairo Township that we had been purchasing since we moved there in 1886. Two years later, on August 24, 1897, Fritz also bought a 160-acre farm in nearby Ridgely Township, Nicollet County, next to the one that my parents owned. It had come up for sale and Fritz just could not resist the lure of owning more land! Our oldest son Fred was twelve years old and already a big help around the farm, and Fritz reasoned that we had two sons who would someday each need a farm of his own. Our family subsequently moved to this Ridgely farm, which had a newer and larger house and better farm buildings, and the Cairo farm was then rented out. We continued to marvel at the riches and bounty of this land, and how with some hard work and perseverance, almost anyone could be a landowner.

Lives Ending and Lives Beginning

My grandmother Margaretha Peters died on August 5, 1898, at the advanced age of eighty-three years. I don't wish to speak ill of the dead, but she was a difficult woman. She lived with my parents from the time they were married and often ordered my mother around. As a result, my mother cautioned me, "It is one thing to live with or care for your own mother, but quite another to live with your husband's mother." My Schulze cousins were known to remark about my grandmother, "They should have left her in the Old Country!"

As our two sons grew, they favored their father much in looks and temperament, both of them being of a quiet, patient and hardworking nature. Our daughter Lizzie on the other hand was cut from the same cloth as myself—independent, plucky and bold. As she grew older, I sometimes felt I was looking into a mirror at a younger reflection of myself. Fritz liked to tease me, "How did we manage to make such a child? Soon I will need to beat the boys off with a stick!"

This studio portrait of Lizzie Meyer was taken about 1906 in Fairfax, Minnesota.

My parents Wilhelm and Catherine Peters were finding the farm work difficult as they were growing older, and in 1906 they retired and sold their farm to us for the sum of $4,000. We then moved them onto the farm that we owned in Cairo Township, where they lived out their lives. Fritz was amazed and elated to find himself the proud owner of three farms. That would never have happened had we remained in Germany!

In 1907 our son Fred married Frieda Franz, who was our pastor's daughter. The Franz family had first emigrated from Germany to Texas, where Frieda was born and where her father was a Methodist minister. After Frieda's mother died her father took his young children back to Germany, married his deceased wife's sister and returned with them to Texas. However, the second wife could not tolerate the extreme heat there, and they moved to Minnesota where Rev. Franz obtained a position as a Lutheran minister in our little church. It was rumored that the Synod required Rev. Franz's sermons to be approved by Rev. Albrecht at St. John's in Fairfax before he could preach them. As far as we could tell, this was either because he was trained as a Methodist minister or because he was known to be a drinking man or perhaps both.

There were not many unmarried young women in the area, and Fred had been keeping company with Frieda Franz for several years. She was rather plain-featured but was hardworking and a good Christian woman. When Rev. Franz passed away in January 1907 he left his wife and daughter practically destitute, and they knew they would need to vacate the parsonage soon to make room for a new pastor. When Fred realized their predicament he asked Frieda to marry him, and they were wed on June 12, 1907. I had hoped my handsome son could do better than plain Frieda, but it was his decision to make.

Fred Meyer and Frieda Franz, shown in their wedding photograph, were married on June 12, 1907.

The young couple made their home on the former Peters farm, now owned by us, and Frieda's stepmother lived with them. She was a demanding and irritable woman, and I felt sorry for Fred for having to live with her. I was glad a few years later when she went to live with another of her married daughters. My daughter-in-law Frieda and I did not always get on so well together either. She was not open to suggestions on how Fred liked his food prepared, how to properly run her household, or help with raising her children. Perhaps we were both too strong-willed and hard-headed.

Within the next six years' time Fred and Frieda were blessed with four healthy children: Arnold, twins Elsie and Esther, and Wanda, although sadly another infant daughter died at birth.

Our daughter Lizzie married Edward Bleick on April 26, 1910, and they farmed nearby in Cairo Township, Renville County. They subsequently had two daughters, Ruth in 1914 and Delores much later in 1925. Whenever Lizzie complained to me that her daughters were too spirited and had very strong minds of their own, I told her, "Just look at the children's mother and grandmother! As it is said, the apple never falls far from the tree!"

In the winter of 1916 an epidemic of influenza claimed the lives of my parents just days apart. Even though they were elderly and in declining health, their illness and deaths quite overwhelmed me. Somehow we feel our parents will always be there for us. It was quite a blow to lose both at once.

My mother Catherine Schulze Peters died on January 21 at the age of nearly eighty-two years. My father Wilhelm Peters was so devoted to her that upon her death he lost his will to live and succumbed to the influenza four days later at the age of seventy-four years. We had not yet buried my mother because my father was so seriously ill and we needed to care for him. Because it was very cold at the time, we stored my mother's coffin in the granary until after my father passed and then held a double funeral for them. I took some comfort in knowing that they made their final journey together, as they would have wished.

Catherine and Wilhelm Peters, the parents of Eliza Meyer, are shown in this studio photograph from about 1910.

Our son Fred then purchased from us the Cairo farm where my parents had been living for the token sum of $1,000. Frieda had recently come into a large inheritance of $3,000 from a cousin in Germany. As the house on this farm was quite old and small, Fred and Frieda used her inheritance to build a large new house.

I did not like the way they designed the house, and I convinced Fred to change the plan and build the kitchen to the back with a flat roof. Frieda was not happy with this arrangement and was rather cool in her treatment of me after that time. Recently there were problems with the roof leaking, and of course everyone blamed me! I know that my cousins, the Schulzes, consider me to be bossy and did not think I should have interfered with Fred and Frieda's house plan. I do honestly believe that they were ever jealous of me and my independent spirit!

After living in this country for thirty-four years, Fritz filed a declaration of intention to become a naturalized citizen of the United States at the Nicollet County Courthouse on June 27, 1918. Our son Fred also applied for citizenship at the same time in Renville County. They were both very proud to be citizens of this great country, and Fritz expressed his feelings well on that subject: "I have worked hard and sweated to make something of myself in this country. I stand with my own two feet on my own ground and I am a free man! To be free is worth buckets of sweat!"

Retirement

By 1918 our younger son William was ready to marry, and we had always intended that he should take over our farm from us when we retired. However, Fritz wanted to keep farming until he was sixty and so a compromise was reached. In April of 1918 we sold our Ridgely Township farm to William. He was wed to Emma Mattke on September 10, 1918, at St. Paul's Lutheran Church in New Ulm, at the respective

This photograph of William Meyer and Emma Mattke was taken for their wedding on September 10, 1918.

ages of twenty-seven and twenty-four years. They lived together with us on the farm for one year. Remembering the difficult relationship between my mother and my grandmother, I tried to be kind to Emma, and with her sweet personality we got on quite well together.

William and Emma's first child, Elda, was born on July 21, 1919, and Fritz and I were happy to spoil her in the first months of her life. When the harvest was completed in the fall, we retired from farming and bought a home in New Ulm. After the hard work of a farm, it was a luxury to get up when I pleased, to go shopping whenever I liked, and to take life a bit easier.

In 1920 our children decided that we should have a family portrait made. What a wonderful idea that was, and how I love looking at it and seeing all my loved ones!

I am not a vain woman and have never kept count of my wrinkles. Even though I have not yet reached the age of sixty years, I am surprised at how old I appear in this picture. I have not so much minded the grey hair and wrinkles that come with old age, but I have minded losing most of my teeth and the sunken look it gives my face. When children are in the womb, they take what they need from their mothers to grow their own bones, and as a result most women my age have lost their teeth. Then after we go through the change, our bones grow weak and our bodies fold in on themselves leaving our backs bent and humped.

After this picture was taken, our son William and his wife had three more children, LaNeta born in 1921, Delores in 1923, and Ralph in 1925, and our daughter Lizzie and her husband had another child, Delores, born in 1925.

Fred and Frieda's daughter Esther died tragically at age twenty of septicemia or blood poisoning. In August of 1930 she and the other children helped Fred pull weeds in the fields. When Esther developed a rash on her arms and legs, she was embarrassed, covered it up and swore her twin sister Elsie to secrecy. When the rash turned into cysts and the poisons spread to her bloodstream, Esther became severely ill and was admitted to the hospital in New Ulm. Her condition was so painful that she could not bear to have anything touch her skin and a tent of sheets was erected over her body. The sores spread to her mouth

The family of Fritz and Eliza Meyer (seated, ages 60 and 59) had this studio portrait taken in 1920. Left: daughter Lizzie, her husband Edward Bleick and their daughter Ruth. Back center: son William, his wife Emma, and their daughter Elda. Right: son Fred, his wife Frieda, their daughters Esther, Elsie and Wanda, with their son Arnold in the center of photo.

and throat and internally, causing her even greater pain. She passed away in November 1930. In those days we laid out the dead at home right in the living room until the funeral. Friends and relatives came by to pay their respects and give their condolences. Esther's death was especially hard on her twin sister Elsie, as the two girls had always done everything together and had even been dating brothers.

This studio photograph of Elda, Delores, and LaNeta, daughters of William and Emma Meyer, was taken in 1924.

The Great Depression

We are still in what is being called the "Great Depression," which began with the Stock Market Crash of 1929 and has continued these ten years. Many farmers lost money when the banks went bust and closed in the early 1930s, and then as the economy worsened others were not able to meet their mortgage payments and lost their farms to foreclosure.

An even worse blow to farmers was a severe drought across the Great Plains during the mid-1930s. It caused the topsoil to be carried away by strong winds and resulted in dust storms and soil erosion. Wheat farming had expanded in the early 1900s to the south and west, in such states as Oklahoma, Kansas, Nebraska and the Dakotas. Those open grass-covered prairies were never meant to be put to the plow with nothing left to hold down the topsoil. For a string of years the temperatures soared, the rains failed to come, crops withered in the fields, wells went dry, and soil turned to dust. Then the winds blew and took the topsoil along with it. Many developed breathing problems from inhaling this fine dust into their lungs and some contracted "dust pneumonia" which was often fatal.

Thankfully Minnesota was not as hard-hit as the "Dust Bowl" states, but we also had droughts and some frightening dust storms in the mid-1930s. At times the dust blew so hard we could scarcely see the barn from the house, and we had to wear wet bandanas tied over our noses and mouths to be able to breathe outside. If the dust cloud was thick enough, the chickens would go to roost in the middle of the day, thinking it was evening. The dirt would pile up along the fences and buildings like snowdrifts, and the dust would blow through the cracks around the windows and doors and just get everywhere and into everything. These times are already being called the "Dirty Thirties" with good reason!

Our family has been fortunate. Our three children and their spouses own their farms, and they have been able to survive better than most during this Depression. Unlike those in the Dust Bowl or urban areas where people are quite literally starving, at least farm families have enough to eat. A common but true saying among farmers is, "We have everything but money!" Our families have large gardens and orchards to provide vegetables and fruit and have livestock and chickens to provide meat, milk and eggs. However, such goods as coffee, sugar and shoes are rationed. It is difficult to obtain enough sugar for baking and canning, and each person is allotted only one pair of shoes a year. Fritz and I have a large garden in back of our house in town, and our children bring eggs, milk and meat to us. We are far luckier than many others.

We read in the newspapers that up to one-third of the men in this country are out of work and searching for any job possible. Some load their families and few possessions into a car or truck and go where they have family to take them in or where they think there might be work. Some men are so ashamed of not being able to feed their families that they actually abandon them to the pity of their kin or neighbors. Men that we call "hobos" ride boxcars from town to town seeking work, and it is not unusual to find a man knocking at the back door. I always find something, even if it is only bread with butter or leftover food from a previous meal. If these were my sons and they were hungry, I would be grateful to another woman for feeding them.

Our sons tell us that hobos also pass through the countryside looking for work on farms. Most are honorable men down on their luck and too proud to ask for a handout, and they ask to chop wood or do some chore to earn their food. They are so grateful to eat a home-cooked meal or wash up by the pump with a rag and soap or bed down on some fresh straw in the barn. If a man mentions a wife and children "back home," Fred or William try to find work so that they can earn a dollar or two to send to their family.

No one has much money these days and so bartering often takes the place of cash. A popular saying is that we "use it up, wear it out, make do, or go without." Visiting with family, neighbors, and friends is our usual form of entertainment and costs nothing. We truly appreciate that there is nothing in this world more important than family and friends.

Quilting

Quilting has long been popular in this country, but there has been renewed interest in recent times. I had always admired the beautiful patchwork quilts made by others, but there was so much work to be done on the farm that I felt I had to wait until we retired before I could take up such a hobby.

After we moved to New Ulm, I found I had extra time on my hands. I was used to being busy and did not want to sit in my rocking chair waiting until death came to find me. Fortunately, a group of neighborhood women formed a "quilting bee," and we met at each other's homes one afternoon a week to do our hand-piecing. We learned different aspects of quilting from each other, shared quilt patterns, ideas and fabrics, exchanged recipes and stories of our lives, and laughed and sometimes cried together.

During the 1920s the lighter pastel color schemes became popular, and interest in quilting saw a revival. Magazines and newspapers printed quilt patterns. Quilt blocks stamped with designs for embroidery were sold quite inexpensively. Appliqué quilts were designed by professional artists and sold in kits. They were especially beautiful, usually done in floral designs in a central medallion style and are favored to this day by those who can afford them.

When the Great Depression came upon us, not many had money to buy new fabrics for quilts, and so we used the scraps left over from a lifetime of sewing dresses, aprons, shirts and other clothing. We often swapped fabrics to get a certain color or a bigger variety in a scrap quilt. If we didn't have money for batting, we would use an old quilt or blanket or a piece of flannel between the top and bottom layers. Unbleached muslin was very often used for background fabric and quilt backing, as that could be purchased economically. Fritz set up my quilting frame in the extra bedroom so I could do hand quilting whenever I had spare time.

I had always made serviceable quilts tied with yarn, but this new form of quilting was something creative and required practice and skill. The first quilts that I made had fairly simple designs, but I was pleased with them and used them on our beds. I next made quilts for my daughter and my two daughters-in-law, using more complicated patterns and getting better at my stitching. It was heartening to find that my imagination was still alive and well. I believe our souls yearn for color and creativity, and quilting was a way we could create something of beauty to brighten our sparse and drab lives, without spending much money.

Since we moved to this country we have been buying most of our staples such as flour, sugar and salt in white or brown cloth sacks. I pulled out the stitching, bleached the bags to remove the printing, and then used these sacks to make clothing, dishtowels or quilt backing. A few years ago some of the bag manufacturers began using colorful printed fabrics for their bags and put their logos on removable paper labels. Because chicken feed is also sold in these printed sacks, they have become known as "feedsacks" or even "chicken linen." The quality of the fabric often depends on the sack's contents; for instance, flour sacks need a finer weave than a bag of wheat seed. Much of the feedsack fabric is indistinguishable from yard goods purchased off the bolt, and the best part is that it is free.

Naturally we all use the feedsack fabric for making clothing, as well as aprons, curtains, tablecloths and quilts. This source of free fabric has been a godsend for many during these hard times of the Great Depression. Because most housewives will choose the brands with the prettiest bags, the manufacturers try to outdo each other in prints and designs, and as a result the feedsacks come in a dizzying selection. There is everything from pastel small scale prints to vivid large scale prints to solid colors from which to choose. I often buy three or four bags at once of the same design so I have enough fabric to sew a dress or back a quilt. If Fritz is going to the store without me, I will give him a swatch and ask him to find more bags with the same print. Otherwise, who knows what ugly color or odd design he would come home with? He always complains that he had to spend time searching through the whole stack of bags, only to find the one I wanted was at the very bottom!

The "Grandmother's Flower Garden" quilt made with hexagons became very popular during the 1930s, and this was my favorite pattern. It uses an English paper piecing method, with hexagons traced onto paper and the fabric folded around the papers and basted. The hexagons are then hand-sewn together to make flowers and the papers removed. I loved coordinating my scraps of solids and prints to create pleasing color combinations to make each flower different.

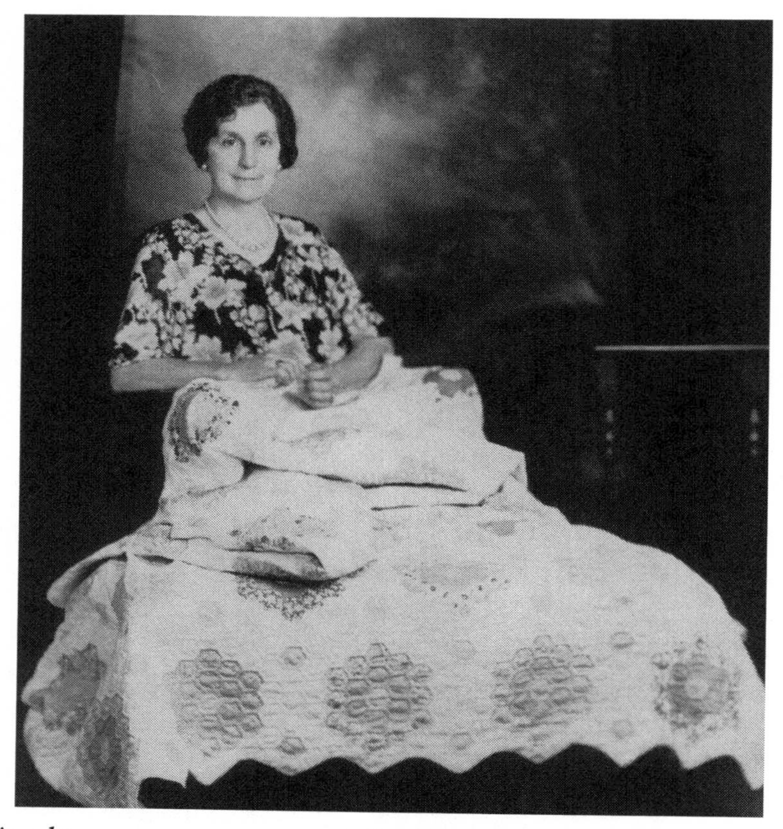

This unknown woman was so proud of her "Grandmother's Flower Garden" quilt that she had a formal portrait taken with it during the 1930s.

My friends and I also made quilts we called "Friendship Daisy," composed of blocks with a large flower appliquéd in each. It was so named because we traded fabric pieces with friends in order to have a greater variety for the petals. It was also considered to be a "charm quilt" when we used a different fabric for each petal in the quilt. The usual setting was to place the blocks in rows with the stems all pointing in the same direction and with sashing between the rows. I liked to set mine with four stems coming together to form a larger block, and I also liked to use a single color for the petals of each flower instead of mixing them for a scrappy look. Sashings and borders in a soft aloe green finished it off nicely.

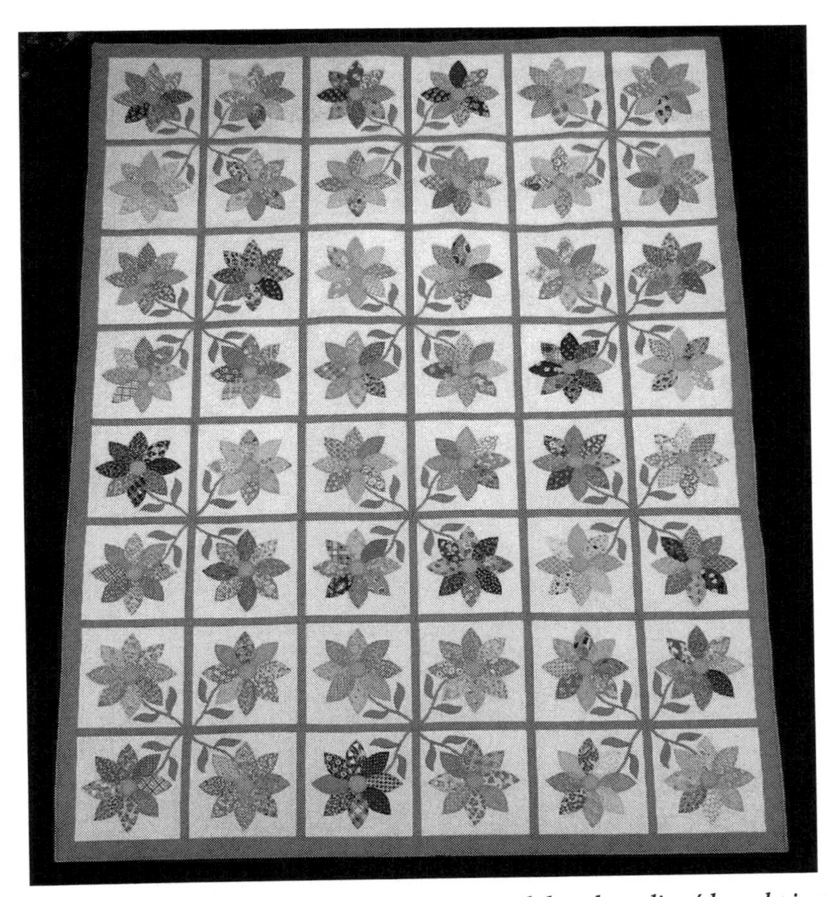

***FRIENDSHIP DAISY CHARM QUILT:** Designed, hand-appliquéd, and pieced by Lanie Tiffenbach using 1930s reproduction fabrics, with each petal being made from a different fabric. Long-arm machine quilted by Holly Younger.*

I loved using my creative abilities to make something that I would be remembered by and that would be treasured after I was gone. Once I had finished making quilts for myself, my daughter and my daughters-in-law, I wondered what to do next. I did not know if I could complete a quilt for each of my nine grandchildren in the time I had left to me on this earth, and so I decided to make a quilt for the oldest daughter of each of my three children. It generally took me about a year to cut, piece and quilt one, and I struggled to finish the third one as my eyesight was getting worse each year. I could no longer thread my own needles, but I had to ask anyone that came by with "younger eyes" to thread up a dozen needles so I could continue to quilt. Fred's daughter Elsie, Lizzie's daughter Ruth, and William's daughter Elda each received one of my Grandmother's Flower Garden quilts. Elsie was married and immediately put hers on their bed, but Ruth and Elda put their quilts in their "hope chests" for when they later married. My three granddaughters were delighted with their quilts, but of course, the younger girls were envious. I wished then that I had started quilting earlier in life or could continue on quilting.

Reflections on My Life

Although it is fifty-five years since we arrived on the shores of this New World, Fritz and I continue to speak German as our mother tongue, and we have not needed to learn much of the English language. Our children have one foot in each country, as they can speak enough English to get by but still mostly speak and think and dream in German. Our grandchildren first learned to speak German at home and only learned English when they started school, but now they speak mostly English and little German. So we are gradually becoming less German and more American, and I believe that is a good thing.

Our grandchildren did all attend "German school" at our church in the summer where they learned to read and write German, and they even had to memorize their catechism in German. Their little country church still holds its services in German, but this coming year some of the services will be in English. After Fritz and I moved to New Ulm, we transferred our membership to St. Paul's Lutheran Church.

On December 18, 1932, Fritz and I celebrated our fiftieth wedding anniversary, a great milestone that very few couples reach. How blest we were to have our family and friends around us for a celebration! Even though we were well into the Depression, I concluded that to be happy all a woman needs in this world is a man who loves her and the family they have made together.

I sometimes imagine my life as a patchwork quilt that has been pieced together from all my experiences, knowledge, joys and sorrows.

I envision that it would look much like a "crazy quilt." There are bits and pieces and scraps of every color and shape and size representing the many stages and events in my life, large and small. There is sunny yellow for my happy childhood, deep purple for the joy of my marriage, bright blue for the endless ocean we crossed, red for the births of my children, black for the loss of loved ones, green for the farms we owned, drab colors for the endless chores to be done, and so on through the rainbow. The good times are represented by fine even stitches and the difficult times are the uneven stitches or poor seams that sometimes had to be picked out and sewn over again. Some of the individual pieces are not so pretty on their own, but taken all together they make up a thing of great beauty.

A photo postcard from about 1920 shows two adorable children who are their mother's pride and joy, along with her patchwork "crazy quilt."

When I was a young woman making plans with my husband for our brave journey from the Old World to the New World, I thought that my life would be filled with grand adventures. However, when I look back over my life, it seems that so much of my time was spent in doing the needful things that had to be done each day to care for my family and home. But I am not disappointed in my life. Rather, I am grateful that we prospered in our new home and raised a good family, which after all is the greatest blessing any woman could ask for.

Fritz and I now consider this country to be our homeland. We built and planted and harvested here season upon season. Just as the land belonged to us, so we also belonged to the land. Our sweat lies all over those acres, now being planted and harvested by our sons in their turn. We have made something of ourselves through our daring journey and our toil. Our children and their children for many generations yet to come will reap the rewards.

Written this tenth day of January in the year of our Lord one thousand nine hundred thirty-nine.

Signed: Eliza Peters Meyer

A note at the bottom of the paper was added at a later time:

My grandmother, Eliza Peters Meyer, died on June 7, 1940, of a stroke just short of her 79th birthday. My grandfather Fritz Meyer then moved back to the family farm, where he lived with our family until his death on November 29, 1943, from kidney failure at the age of 84 years.

The two Meyer family farms, one in Renville County and one in Nicollet County, have both remained in the Meyer family for well over 100 years until the present time, having been passed down from father to son for five generations.

I treasure this story of my grandmother's life, and I marvel at her courage and resilience. I think of her whenever I look at the beautiful quilt that she made, which my children later slept under. I love to picture my grandmother as an adventurous young woman standing on the deck of the ship. She is holding her infant son with her young husband's arm around her, looking out towards America and towards her future.

Signed: Elda Meyer Schefus

ABOUT THE AUTHOR

Lanie Tiffenbach is a native of Minnesota and grew up in the area where her immigrant ancestors had settled some generations earlier and where many of the events mentioned in this book occurred. Interesting facts and rich family lore uncovered in her meticulous and intensive genealogical and historical research inspired her to tell the stories of her women ancestors.

Lanie is also an avid quilter, and for this book she used quilts from her own collection of antique quilts, as well as quilts she has made with vintage or reproduction fabrics and patterns from earlier times. To further illustrate her book she used family photos, wonderful antique and vintage photos, and paper ephemera from her personal collection.

Lanie Tiffenbach currently lives in Denver, Colorado, with her husband and has two adult sons and one precious granddaughter. She can be contacted at tiffenbach@gmail.com.